PHILIPPA THE HUNTRESS

The aristocratic gentlemen of Leicestershire were agreed on two things.

Lady Philippa was without doubt the most tempting and elusive quarry in the county for any gentleman on the hunt for both beauty and fortune.

And the annual fox hunt was definitely too demanding and debauched for any proper lady to take part in.

Philippa had her own ideas on both subjects, however.

No male would ever run her to ground while she had her wits and wiles about her.

And none would dare stop her from mounting her campaign to leap the barriers of ladylike propriety in order to prove herself a match for the haughty Viscount Rochford . . . even though she risked a fall that might break not only her neck but her heart. . . .

(*For a list of other Signet Regency Romances by Amanda Scott, please turn page. . . .*)

Mistress of the Hunt

Amanda Scott

A SIGNET BOOK

NEW AMERICAN LIBRARY

For Terry

NAL BOOKS ARE AVAILABLE AT QUANTITY DISCOUNTS WHEN USED TO PROMOTE PRODUCTS OR SERVICES. FOR INFORMATION PLEASE WRITE TO PREMIUM MARKETING DIVISION, NEW AMERICAN LIBRARY, 1633 BROADWAY, NEW YORK, NEW YORK 10019.

SIGNET TRADEMARK REG. U.S. PAT. OFF. AND FOREIGN COUNTRIES
REGISTERED TRADEMARK—MARCA REGISTRADA
HECHO EN CHICAGO, U.S.A.

SIGNET, SIGNET CLASSIC, MENTOR, ONYX, PLUME, MERIDIAN and NAL BOOKS are published by New American Library, 1633 Broadway, New York, New York 10019

First Printing, February, 1987

1 2 3 4 5 6 7 8 9

PRINTED IN THE UNITED STATES OF AMERICA

—1—

WARMTH WAS CLEARLY not of prime consideration in the great stone hall at Chase Charley, for although a fire burned determinedly in one of the twin marble fireplaces, the dancing flames accomplished little by way of taking the chill from the dreary mid-November afternoon. The chamber's two occupants, however, were neither of them in a mood to consider the temperature or the splendid surroundings, for they had not so much as taken seats upon any of the green-velvet-covered walnut furniture but stood facing each other, the gentleman earnest, the lady resigned.

To be sure, the gentleman's natty attire argued a taste for the magnificent, so having been left for some moments to his own devices while the lady's dignified butler excused himself to discover her pleasure, he might well have taken a moment to appreciate the restrained masculine splendor of the forty-foot-high perfect double-cube hall. He no doubt had had sufficient time to admire the stone bas-reliefs above the twin marble chimneypieces, carved more than a hundred years before by famous designer Michael Rysbrack, and the enormous chandelier suspended on a great long chain from the center of the high ceiling's circular motif, which incorporated the Raynard coat of arms on a pale blue background surrounded by decorated side panels. While pacing the black-and-white diamonds of the parquet floor, he must certainly have noted, above, the stone-balustered balcony supported on ornamented masonry brackets, which formed a projecting gallery at first-floor level around all four walls of the great chamber. In fact, had his thoughts strayed so far from the purpose of his visit, he might well have marveled at having discovered such splendor in the twelfth Baron Wakefield's so-called hunting box.

On the other hand, it would never have occurred to the slender, dark-blond Lady Philippa Raynard-Wakefield to wonder at such a thing, for she considered Chase Charley to be just one among many of her late husband's holdings and, for that matter, one that was smaller and a good deal more comfortable than his principal seat, Wakefield Priory, in Sussex. If she had given any particular thought to the setting of the present discussion, that thought had been merely one of gratitude for the fact that her butler, the estimable Bickerstaff, had had the good sense to leave Mr. Arnold Quinlan to kick his heels in the hall rather than permit him to invade the privacy of any more favored chamber.

Though she was herself feeling the chill and knew that Mr. Quinlan, attired as he was in little more than the buff breeches, brilliant waistcoat, and equally bright blue coat of a gentleman of fashion, must be feeling it too, she had no wish to encourage him to repeat his visit by desiring him to remove with her to some other, warmer room. She wished, in fact, that he would take his departure, for he had begun to bore her. Idly she picked a fluff of lint off one long sleeve of her tawny cashmere afternoon dress and rolled it between one slim finger and her thumb.

Mr. Quinlan had been waxing eloquent for some moments by then, but her movement brought him to recognize at last that his hostess was inattentive. Drawing himself up so that he might very nearly enjoy the advantage of looking down at her, he squared his padded shoulders, firmed his jaw, took two steps toward her, and grasped one softly rounded cashmere-clad arm. Then, his earnest, youthful dignity quite unimpaired, he looked searchingly into her ladyship's dark brown eyes. Those dark eyes, which were set becomingly well apart in her attractive oval face, were open wide now, regarding him calmly, albeit with a flicker of indignation.

"Philippa, you must marry me," he said, adding as he gave her arm a little shake, "Dash it all, I insist upon it."

"Pray, unhand me, Mr. Quinlan." There was quiet emphasis upon the formal use of his name, and Lady Philippa's pleasant voice carried a chill distinct enough so that no one of the slightest sensitivity could fail to notice it. Her gaze shifted pointedly to the hand clutching her arm.

"Oh, very well," Mr. Quinlan said, releasing her with sullen abruptness, "though I must say you might be a dashed sight more civil to a fellow who's taken the trouble to pursue you from London clean into the wilds of Leicestershire."

"Please, sir," Philippa said, stepping away from him, "disabuse yourself of the notion that I must regard such pursuit as either romantic or desirable."

"Dash it, Philippa—"

"No," she said more sharply, moving at the same time to elude him as he sought to grasp her arm again. In a vague hope of making her movement seem a natural one, she continued casually toward the nearer of the two tall green velvet-draped windows that flanked the impressive double-doored entry. The window overlooked a parapeted porch and lateral stairs leading down to the circular front drive and smooth, still-green, gently sloping lawn. As far as her eye could see, the landscape continued in an orderly progression of hedgerows and wide green fields, sloping steeply at first, then more gently down to the valley floor and the River Eye. Beyond, she could see more flat fields and knew they stretched as far as the hills of Belvoir, some fifteen miles to the north.

The river flowed as a mere brook at first from the low, undulating hills behind Chase Charley, widening significantly as it tumbled merrily down the slope to the village of Whissendine at its foot and beyond for nearly five miles, sweeping and swirling over stones and around boulders to Wyvern Towers, the seat of the Drake family, Earls of Wyvern for nearly as long as there had been Barons Wakefield. Today, in the gloom, the twin dark gray towers, looming as they did out of the trees around them, seemed almost menacing, like a setting for some lurid gothic romance, but on sunny days Philippa had often allowed her whimsy to drift to fairy tales when she looked down upon the scene. The brook, becoming deeper as it continued to widen, curved sharply a short distance beyond the towers, much, Philippa had often thought, as though having decided to become a river, it had changed its mind about its destination and resolved to join the River Wreak at Melton Mowbray just to see what all the fuss was about. Certainly, Melton had become amazingly popular among sporting gentlemen as the new century had progressed. On a clear day one could see the little town from Chase Charley. One could not do so today, however.

Mr. Quinlan had continued silent behind her, and much as she would have liked to prolong her examination of the view, she knew she must not. Turning, she said quietly, "You must believe, sir, that I am fully conscious of the honor you do me by offering me your name, but I have determined not to marry again."

"You can't mean that," he said. "No female wishes to remain unwed." When she said nothing, he continued to regard her in disbelief for some moments. Then his brow cleared, and he snapped his fingers. "I have it. You want courting. Crashed my fence and nearly came a cropper. Not to worry, begin a new cast, that's what."

She shook her head, amused in spite of herself that he had fallen so easily into the vocabulary of the hunt. "Do not think to change my mind, sir. I am entirely resolute."

"But, dash it, Phil . . . Oh, very well," he amended quickly when her eyes narrowed, "though why a fellow mustn't call you by name when he's offering his hand in marriage is more than I can see."

"The point, Mr. Quinlan, is that I have not accepted your generous offer. Indeed, I cannot think how you managed to persuade yourself that I would, for we are not by any means well-acquainted. We cannot have met in Town above three or four times."

"Saw your magnificent blue eyes and—"

"My eyes are brown, sir."

"So they are," he agreed, peering at them and then continuing unabashed, "Saw how beautiful they are and tumbled straight into love."

"Do not take me for a mooncalf," she said tartly. "You, like so many others, became enamored of my fortune. I cannot think why gentlemen must look upon a wealthy widow as a quarry to be hunted. No, no," she added, when he seemed about to issue a wide-eyed protest, "grant me my intelligence, sir, and be grateful that your trip will not be entirely wasted. The George Inn in Melton Mowbray is an outstanding hostelry, and I am persuaded that if you send word to Mr. Assheton-Smith at Quorndon Hall, he will be happy to include you in tomorrow's hunt if there is one."

"Much you know," was the near-sulky rejoinder. "The only reason I might be able to engage a room at the George without having made arrangements to do so months ago is that everyone knows the scent in Leicestershire is devilish low in November."

'No, is it?" Philippa regarded him with curiosity. "I didn't know, though I expect that is why his lordship—my late husband, you know—always chose to spend November in Scotland. Why is the scent low?"

He seemed taken aback by the question. "Why? Lord, I don't know. The damp weather, perhaps, though it's just as damp in December and January, I should expect. I cannot think why you—a gently nurtured female, after all—should care about such things, or why you should wish to come into Leicestershire, for all that. To my way of thinking, it was a crack-brained thing to do."

"Well, you see," she said gently, "I was seeking privacy. I had hoped to find it in Town when so many people seemed fixed in Brighton with the Regent, but it was not to be."

"I do see," he said stiffly, turning to retrieve his curly-brimmed beaver hat from the green velvet chair where he had deposited it earlier. "I suppose I should thank you for condescending to receive me at all."

"Don't be absurd, sir, you had traveled a good distance. I could not deny you." Not, she added silently as she moved to pull the bell rope, when she had never expected to be pursued so tenaciously. She must remember to instruct Bickerstaff more carefully in the future.

Mr. Quinlan, having accepted his congé at last, made no further attempt to delay his departure but allowed the stately white-haired Bickerstaff to show him out the way he had come in. Philippa did not wait to see him go but made her escape through the great stair hall before he had disappeared through the front doors and down the steps to call for his horse.

The present house at Chase Charley, designed by Colen Campbell and built under the direction of a local architect on the site of a much older, much less convenient domicile, had been completed in 1735 and was pure Palladian in structure. Seen from the outside, the rectangular pale-yellow-brick central block was perfectly proportioned with a white marble pediment and pilasters in the middle and Venetian windows in the shallow corner projections. Colonnades connected it to small pavilions on either side, one housing the stables and estate offices, the other the laundry, stillroom, and dairy. Inside, the chief rooms were arranged symmetrically on either side of the central two-story great stone hall and equally magnificent baroque saloon. Thus did the dining room and billiards room off the west side of the stone hall agree in their dimensions with the common parlor and the library off the east side. So, too, did the sizes of the yellow drawing room and blue damask bedchamber to the east of the baroque saloon agree with those of the green drawing room and green velvet bedchamber to the west of it. Even the small bedchamber off the library, used by the late baron upon those occasions when he had been too weary to climb another flight of stairs to the family apartments, had its mate in an equally small bedchamber off the billiards room, which was used when the house overflowed with sporting men. The great stair hall was matched in convenience if not in magnificence by the west stair hall, and there were likewise service stairs at each end of the house.

Upstairs, while the family apartments in the east wing remained symmetrical in arrangement to each other and to the rooms below, the rooms in the west wing had been arranged for convenience rather than symmetry and, except for the breakfast parlor and a small sitting room, consisted mainly of guest bedchambers. The stone hall gallery provided access from the east to the west wing of the house.

As Philippa entered the stair hall, the great mahogany flying staircase with its carved balusters, their newels formed as Tuscan columns and surmounted by round glass candleholders, seemed to swoop around and above her. The walls of the staircase, as well as those of the passageway leading from its upper landing, were hung with portraits of Elizabethan statesmen, of the royal Stuarts, and of the Raynard and Wakefield families, but Philippa, having seen them all before, hurried up the stair and along the passageway to the morning room, where she had been helping to search for a recent inventory of the house's contents when Bickerstaff had come to inform her of Mr. Quinlan's arrival.

When she entered the cheerful yellow-and-white room, a lady of late middle years and comfortable figure, who was attired in lavender silk and seated at a deal table strewn with papers, looked up from her intent perusal of one of these, her severe expression softening noticeably. By the time she had removed the silver-rimmed pince-nez from the bridge of her button nose, her pale blue eyes were twinkling.

"Another one, my dear—this Mr. Quinlan?"

"Indeed, ma'am, and most insistent."

Miss Adeliza Pellerin clicked her tongue in annoyance. "Mercy me, I knew I ought to have accompanied you. 'Tis not seemly for you to meet with young men without a chaperon, my dear, and that's the nut with no bark on it."

"Nonsense, Cousin, it is quite customary for a lady to receive a proposal of marriage privately."

'Not without the young man applies first to her papa, it isn't," countered Miss Pellerin.

"Well, for him to ride into Yorkshire to seek Papa's permission to pay his addresses to me and then back here to find me afterward would be absurd. Not only have I had more than my share of experience dealing with would-be suitors, but having been a widow these two years and more, I am scarcely a green girl who wants careful watching."

"I collect that you were able to speed Mr. Quinlan on his way, then?"

"Easily, for despite his insistence, he was not nearly so determined or so arrogant as some I have encountered since poor Wakefield was so obliging as to leave me a wealthy widow. Beyond pointing out that he had pursued me into the wilds of Leicestershire—"

"Wilds?"

"Indeed, his very word. But aside from that, he was rather docile."

"Disappointingly so, perhaps?"

"No, of course not. I was grateful that he was no worse." Philippa sighed, taking a seat opposite Miss Pellerin. "I truly believed I should escape all this attention by coming here. I never thought any of them would follow me."

"Well, they say Leicestershire is a man's county, after all. You won't escape the company of gentlemen altogether by coming here."

"Oh, but they never paid any heed to me here before. They thought of nothing but their hunting and shooting. Even when I hunted with the Belvoir, the men ignored me and the other ladies entirely, fixing their concentration upon the hounds and the fox."

"Your husband was nearby," Miss Pellerin pointed out gently.

"True, but he was amused rather than angry whenever men flirted with me. He always said it was no more than he would expect of any intelligent young man, and he always made it clear that he knew I had too much sense to be impressed by such stuff. Schoolboys, he thought most of them." Philippa was silent for a moment, collecting her thoughts, but when she looked at Miss Pellerin and realized from her sympathetic expression that the older lady was misinterpreting her silence, she smiled to reassure her. "Truly, ma'am, I held Wakefield in the greatest esteem and affection, but he was many years my senior, and it was in the nature of things that he should predecease me. Indeed, he prepared me for widowhood much more carefully than my parents had prepared me for marriage, and after his long illness, I am sure that no one of compassion could have wished for him to linger. I confess, I felt little more than sad relief at his passing."

"But you scarcely saw anyone after his death, my dear. Except for your servants—excellent folk, I am sure—you were alone at Wakefield Priory for an entire year and more."

"At first I was exhausted," Philippa explained. "Despite the servants, I did much of the nursing myself, you know, because he fretted at having others attend to him and he liked to talk with me, to instruct me with regard to such matters as I should have to attend to after his passing. The last months were particularly difficult. For a long time afterward I wanted only to rest." Her quick grin flashed, showing even white teeth. "I look dreadful in black, if you must have the truth, and there was no one I particularly wished to see and nothing

I particularly wished to do, beyond setting our affairs in order. And that, I daresay, I managed to accomplish only because of Wakefield's careful teaching, for when Edward and Jessalyn were down for the long vacation that first summer, I attended to them more as though they were characters in a dream than as a proper stepmother ought to have done. But somehow the months just disappeared until one day I realized that the year was well behind me and a new London Season lay before me. It was the most astonishing thing, as though I had wakened from a long, refreshing sleep."

"That was when you wrote to me," said Miss Pellerin with a reminiscent smile.

"Indeed, it was," Philippa replied, reaching across the table to squeeze the older woman's plump beringed hand affectionately. "My friends and the family had been urging me for some time to pick up the threads of my old social life, but I wanted to do nothing that would reflect dishonorably upon Wakefield's memory. Since you go everywhere and know everyone while maintaining a reputation of the highest respectability, I knew you could only add to my consequence." The saucy grin peeked out again and was reflected by amusement in the older lady's eyes.

"I must say, my dear, that considering the size of your fortune, there is little else needed to add to your consequence. I do think your husband was a mite peculiar, however, to have put you so completely in charge of your own affairs as he did—and the children's affairs as well."

Philippa's eyes continued to twinkle. "After teaching me everything he knew, he could scarcely say I was unfit, ma'am. Moreover, he would have thought himself bound to name his brother principal trustee otherwise, and that he could not bring himself to do. He had no wish to offend Mr. Raynard-Wakefield, so he did name him as adviser to me, but he did so knowing I should have no need for such advice as he might give me. And, I must tell you, ma'am, I certainly prefer being my own mistress to having to answer to a trustee. Imagine how annoying, always to have had to have my expenditures authorized. We should never have had such a good time in London as we did."

"You did enjoy the gaiety and all the attention at the outset, did you not?" Miss Pellerin said.

"Indeed, I found it quite stimulating," Philippa admitted. "But then the pressures increased, with everyone encouraging me to marry again, and it began to feel as though several of the more obdurate of my suitors were beginning to claw at my skirts. I remembered Wakefield's hunting box as a place of marvelous privacy, and since he left it to my use for my lifetime, it seemed the perfect haven."

"Hunting box," repeated Miss Pellerin with a chuckle. "I certainly envisioned something quite different from this when you told me where you wished to go, my dear. Like Mr. Quinlan, I quite thought we should find ourselves in the wilds, but this place is scarcely that. Why, this house is wanting in none of those accessories which would be considered indispensable in a house in London."

"No," Philippa agreed, "although in London the paintings on the walls would be by Constable or Gainsborough rather than by John Ferneley or Ben Marshall. But in Leicestershire, no house can be complete without at least several hunting portraits. I particularly like the Ferneley over there by the chimneypiece—the short-tailed horse falling neck and crop over a flight of rails, whilst the thoroughbred, who ought to be advancing, viciously kicks at the leap his rider desires him to face."

Obediently Miss Pellerin glanced at the picture, but her interests did not include hunting or hunting portraits. "I daresay it is very nice," she said. "You mentioned riding with the Belvoir when you were down here with Wakefield. Do you intend to hunt whilst we are here? I cannot think it a seemly activity for a woman of quality."

"Well, I enjoy the sport immensely," Philippa informed her with a smile, "and I should like very much to attempt it here in the shires again, but not," she added, glad of her newfound knowledge, "until the scent is high. Have you discovered the inventory amongst all that litter, ma'am?"

Recalled to her duty, Miss Pellerin sniffed in exasperation. "I declare, Philippa, no one seems to have attended to this business properly since eighteen-aught-four. You may count yourself fortunate if we discover that your servants have not fleeced you prettily in the meantime."

Philippa grinned at her. "I should be well served, should I not, Cousin? You will forgive me, however, if I do not mention your concern to Mrs. Bickerstaff, since it was her sister who looked after the house in our absence." Amused by her companion's grim look but having no wish to hear again her opinion of the way the household had been run, she added quickly, "Is a ten-year-old list truly the most recent one you have discovered?"

"Indeed." Miss Pellerin replaced her pince-nez, scanned the papers before her, then selected and offered several yellowed sheets to Philippa. "See for yourself, my dear. 'Tis a disgrace."

"Well, it is not my disgrace, after all," Philippa said, taking the lists from her. "I was no more than sixteen then and didn't marry Wakefield until three years later. We spent a bare month here the first year of our marriage and less than six weeks altogether during the second and third, which is when he first fell ill. The last two years, as you know, his illness precluded our leaving Wakefield Priory."

"That is still three years you were in residence here, however," Miss Pellerin pointed out in her prim voice.

Philippa chuckled. "Have a heart, ma'am. I was no match for Mrs. Bickerstaff then, not at the Priory and certainly not here, where during the hunting season I was treated like an accessory whose value was placed slightly higher than that of my lord's favorite dogs but far and away below that of the least of his hunters."

"My poor child!" exclaimed Miss Pellerin, instantly sympathetic.

"Not a bit of it, ma'am." Philippa's eyes danced. "I should scarcely have chosen to return to Chase Charley had my memories been unhappy ones."

"Why on earth did the Raynard-Wakefields call this place by such an extraordinary name?" demanded her companion.

"*They* didn't. Until some fifteen years ago, it was Raynard Hall, for you must know that the Raynard-Wakefield connection is little more than a hundred years old, and this estate belonged originally to the Raynard branch. It was Wakefield's son—Edward, you know—who renamed it. When he was small, it seems there was a slight misunderstanding about where his papa was going when he said he was going to 'chase Charley.' Hunters refer to the fox, any fox, as Charley, of course, but Edward did not know that, for he had never been here himself then. His mama did not enjoy the solitude."

"But you did?"

"Indeed, I had my books, my own horses to ride, and my music. To be sure, despite my lord's numerous guests, I was generally the only female in the house who was not a servant; however, we visited Belvoir Castle several times, and the duchess and her mama-in-law are delightful hostesses, I promise you."

"I have known Isabella for years, of course," said Miss Pellerin, referring to the Dowager Duchess of Rutland, "but although I have encountered the young duchess from time to time, I know little about her, except of course that she is Carlisle's fifth daughter. I have heard it said that she prefers to spend most of her time at Belvoir."

"Yes, but despite a near-eight-year difference in our ages, we have more in common than both of us being daughters of earls," Philippa said with a laugh. "Her eldest child—called Elizabeth after herself—is with Jessalyn in Bath at Miss Blandamore's Seminary for Young Gentlewomen. The duchess and I, as a result, enjoy a somewhat haphazard correspondence, exchanging views on the proper rearing of young ladies."

"It is devoutly to be hoped that the Lady Elizabeth Manners is not such a romp as your harum-scarum stepdaughter," said Miss Pellerin with a grimace.

Philippa managed to smile again, but her companion had unwittingly struck a nerve. There had been no word from Miss Jessalyn Raynard-Wakefield for more than a month, despite the fact that Philippa had made a point of keeping that young lady apprised of her frequent movements. That she had likewise received no word during that same period from the thirteenth Baron Wakefield did not weigh so heavily with her. Edward was an indifferent correspondent at the best of times, and being heavily engaged in his first year at Oxford, he would no doubt have found better use for his time than to waste it writing to his stepmother. Jessalyn was another matter. If a letter did not arrive from her within the week, Philippa knew she would no longer be able to put off sending a letter of inquiry to Miss Blandamore, and she was quite certain that Jessalyn would prefer that she do nothing of the sort.

She did not speak of these concerns to her companion, however, and the conversation drifted to household matters. There was, despite the fact that the pair of them had now been at Chase Charley for nearly a week, still a good deal to be done. The skeleton staff had done an adequate job of keeping the place habitable during their mistress's long absence, but there were still many chores that must be attended to before the beautiful house would meet the high standards of such a stickler as Miss Pellerin. Philippa had no qualms about turning most of the household management over to her companion and the excellent Mrs. Bickerstaff while she dealt with matters of business with her late husband's bailiff, Mr. Weems, and it was to his office in the stable pavilion that she repaired an hour later.

Lord Wakefield had chosen his servants well, and she had quickly discovered that everything about the Leicestershire estate was in good trim. The rents were up again, and her tenants were a contented lot. Mr. Weems's only concern seemed to be that the hunting season reach its peak as quickly as possible, giving Philippa to assume that he wanted the sport over and done so that spring planting might begin as early as the weather would allow. She submitted today to an explanation of his system of bookkeeping, knowing full well that while he was flattered to have her attention, he would firmly resist any suggestion she might be foolhardy enough to make to him. At the moment she had no reason to question his methods, however, so she was able to compliment his skills with sincerity.

She and Miss Pellerin enjoyed a light repast at four o'clock, after which they spent the evening sorting through the desk and writing-table drawers in the library, where a crackling fire kept them cozy and where the glow from a dozen candleholders glinted off the gilt lettering of the books that lined the walls. After several hours of industrious occupation, the two ladies retired early to their separate bedchambers, Philippa's in the southeast corner of the upper floor, adjacent to the morning room, and Miss Pellerin's in the southwest corner, beyond the breakfast parlor.

Like other such houses of its period, Chase Charley had originally been built upon a low ground floor known as a rustic, which had contained several informal family rooms, including a breakfast room, a coffee room, a supping parlor, and a hunting hall, but over the past thirty years or so the family had moved its informal living upward and the kitchens had been moved from what was now the laundry pavilion into the rustic. Thus, as the baron had explained enthusiastically to Philippa upon her first visit to the house, although the servants must now carry breakfast up two flights of stairs to the "new" breakfast parlor, the food actually came warmer to the table than it had in the days when it had been necessary to carry it along the open colonnade from the kitchen pavilion to the rustic. As she surveyed the dishes lined up on the buffet for her examination the following morning, however, Philippa could not see that their warmth or lack of it was of much concern.

"Really, Cousin Adeliza, we must find a better cook. These eggs are green."

"Used a tin pot instead of an iron one, saving her strength," opined that lady as she accepted a silver tray containing the morning post from a straight-faced young footman. " 'Tis a pity your Mrs. Lacy refused to accompany us from London."

Philippa smiled, remembering her cook's outrage at the suggestion that she might be induced to leave the city to take charge of a hunting-box kitchen, but her expression turned to one of scarcely veiled anxiety as she watched her companion begin to sort through the post. When Miss Pellerin paused to look at one letter more carefully, Philippa asked quickly, "Is that from Jessalyn?"

The older lady shook her head. "It carries the Rutland crest, I believe—two unicorns and the famous peacock." She held it out. "I daresay the duchess has heard of your arrival and is very kindly observing the amenities."

Setting her plate down on the sideboard, Philippa took the

letter with more haste than grace and sat down in the nearest chair. ''Perhaps she has received word from young Beth and will have news of Jessalyn.'' Opening the missive, she read rapidly, her expression changing from curiosity to amazement to near-outrage.

''What is it?'' demanded Miss Pellerin. ''*Has* she heard something regarding that young scamp?''

Philippa looked up from the letter, her expression grim. ''Ellizabeth informs me that my darling stepdaughter has been her guest this past week and longer. It seems, if you please, that Miss Blandamore was given to understand that 'dearest Jessalyn' had my permission to assist her grace in the celebration of her recent birthday.''

—2—

THOUGH PHILIPPA HAD little concern after that for breaking her fast, she gave way to Miss Pellerin's insistence that she sustain herself against the coming storm. "For I have not the least doubt," said the older lady, "that you will set forth to collect the minx at once."

"I shall indeed," Philippa agreed, getting up to retrieve her plate and moving to take her place at the table. As she did, she spoke over her shoulder to the young footman, who was now holding her chair. "Stephen, you will relay instructions to the stables that my traveling carriage is to be brought round promptly at eleven o'clock, and see that someone fetches up two portmanteaux from the trunk room."

"Yes, m'lady." Pausing only long enough to pour out a cup of India tea for her and to refill Miss Pellerin's cup, Stephen departed upon his errand, leaving the two ladies alone.

"The duchess has kindly offered to put us up for the night," Philippa said, cutting a bite of ham before adding grimly, "Not that she had much choice in the matter once she had discovered Jessalyn's deception."

"What, precisely, does she say with regard to that matter?" inquired Miss Pellerin, lifting her cup to sip daintily at the hot tea.

"Her note is a brief one, which you may certainly read if you like, but the gist of the matter is that Jess and another child, one Lucinda Drake, decided off their own bat to accompany Lady Elizabeth Manners when she was called home to take part in her mother's birthday festivities. Aside from the bit about Miss Blandamore's having believed I had given Jessalyn my permission to make the excursion, she writes only that she will explain the whole upon our arrival, which she expects to be this afternoon."

"She must have routed that messenger out at an uncommonly early hour to get him here so quick," Miss Pellerin said, "particularly in view of the fact that when I looked outside this morning, everything appeared to be hidden by fog."

"Would you not do the same, ma'am, if you were to discover that a young lady visiting you was doing so under false pretenses? I daresay the messenger had his orders last night, for all that." She paused, then flashed a rueful smile at her companion. "I am dreadfully sorry, Cousin Adeliza, to be dragging you out upon the road again just when you've begun to settle in."

"Don't give it a thought, my dear. I shall be pleased to see Belvoir Castle again. Back in the days before it became unseemly to puff off one's skill in the French language, you know, we said the name properly. Now, calling it 'Beaver' as everyone does, one expects to find log dams cluttering the moat—or would if there were a moat. Isn't one, as I recall."

"No, ma'am. I suppose that means you haven't been there since the present duke married. Elizabeth said it had all been let go to rack and ruin, because of the dowager and most of the Manners preferring to live at Haddon Hall or Cheveley. The sporting men amongst them came to Belvoir to hunt, of course, and the others appeared for the occasional hunting-season house party, but that was all. Elizabeth, on the other hand, has made a near-crusade out of renovating the house and turning it into a real castle."

"Could be she thought her life would be less tumultuous away from her mother-in-law," suggested Miss Pellerin with a twinkle.

"If that was her intent, it didn't answer very well. The dowager spends more time there than ever she did before. But then, Eizabeth has made the place amazingly more comfortable, too, although she insists there is still much to be done. Her letters, even recently, have been as full of her plans for redoing the state apartments as of news of her infant son. You did know, did you not, that the duke has an heir at last? They had nearly despaired after fifteen years of marriage, three daughters, and I don't know how many stillbirths and miscarriages."

"Indeed, I did know there was a Marquess of Granby at last—born in August, was he not?"

"Yes. I daresay we shall be granted a peek at him, don't you think?"

"No doubt," agreed Miss Pellerin, setting down her cup. "However, if you mean to leave by eleven o'clock, we'd best stir our stumps, my dear. I've any number of chores that must be seen to, and you were meaning to speak to Weems about new gravel for the front drive and about setting someone to weeding those herbaceous borders. Ought to have been seen to last month, but I daresay there was rain the day they'd set aside for that particular chore."

Philippa chuckled at this sour reference to the chief excuse that had been tendered for nearly every lack spotted by Miss Pellerin's eagle eyes during the past week. Then her glance came to rest upon the duchess's letter again, and the laughter faded.

Miss Pellerin, shaking crumbs from her skirts, did not fail to note her changing expression. "Young Jessalyn wants a hearty scold for this mischief, I'm thinking."

"Indeed, ma'am, she deserves more than that. Only wait until I get my hands on that abominable girl."

Since her temper did not improve noticeably during the next two hours, it was as well for her coachman that he brought her traveling carriage to the door promptly at eleven o'clock, as ordered. The morning fog had lifted, and the sun had managed to break through gray clouds, giving a burnished golden look to the pale yellow brick walls of the house. Glancing about her as she gathered the pomona-green skirts of her traveling dress in preparation for accepting the footman's assistance to enter her silk-lined carriage, Philippa decided that the white gravel she had instructed Weems to order would be a distinct improvement over the gray that now decked the front drive. Her spirits lifted at the thought, and her gaze drifted to the lawn, where sunlight glinted on short, damp blades of grass, then further to the sparkling blue river below. Even the twin baroque towers of Wyvern looked welcoming, outlined as they seemed to be by gilded halos.

"You know, ma'am," she said when Miss Pellerin had clambered in behind her and settled voluminous dove-gray skirts neatly about her on the crimson velvet seat, "it has just struck my mind that the Lucinda Drake to whom the duchess made reference might well be some connection of the Earl of Wyvern."

"Got several daughters, the old earl has."

"Yes, but I hadn't realized he might have one so young. The two I have met are both older than I am. There is a son, too, is there not?"

"To be sure, young Viscount Rochford," said Miss Pellerin, bracing herself against the carriage's sudden lurch forward. "Not but what he's a good bit older than you are, too, of course. Must be in his thirties at least. Still and all, the countess didn't die till about seven years ago—maybe eight. No reason she mightn't have had a late-born child. Old Wyvern stopped going about when she passed on, and Rochford's been on the Continent, I believe, with Arthur Wellesley—Viscount Wellington, as they've chosen to style him since that dreadful battle at Talavera. Such a pity, all this fighting. Men, with all their opportunity for education, ought to recognize that war seldom serves any good purpose. Particularly war with France. Why, a gentleman must ever be better occupied chasing foxes than Frenchmen. He's a good deal less apt to get himself killed by a fox."

Chuckling, Philippa began to point out that not only had Lord Wellington enjoyed a great victory at Talavera, but also victories since at Vitoria and San Sebastían and, furthermore, that he had actually entered France at last, thereby causing many who might be counted upon to know about such things to predict Napoleon Bonaparte's impending defeat. However, she had got no further than midway through her second sentence when the carriage lurched into and out of a pothole, causing her to bite her tongue painfully. Further attempts at conversation were therefore abandoned while the carriage made its lumbering way down the rutted road, through the village of Whissendine, and beyond to the river crossing. As they made their way across the bridge less than a hundred yards northwest of the tall gray towers, however, Miss Pellerin observed that the Earl of Wyvern seemed to be in residence.

"Someone is, in any event. Flag flying."

There was indeed a green banner waving jauntily in the breeze from the left-hand tower. Philippa smiled at her companion.

"Perhaps you would care to stop and leave cards, ma'am. The earl is, after all, an eligible bachelor, and a warm one, I believe."

"Humph," said Miss Pellerin. "Warm in the pockets he may be, but if there's any warmth in his personality, I never heard tell of it. As crotchety an old recluse as one might find, by all I've heard. And one doesn't, as you know very well, Philippa, leave calling cards on single gentlemen."

"Well, no," that young lady conceded, enjoying herself, "but one might extend a gracious invitation to a neighbor to dine. That would be mere kindness, ma'am. He cannot be a recluse entirely, you know. I am certain he came to dine at least once or twice while I was here with Wakefield."

"Be that as it may, it would be no kindness if you mean to single him out," Miss Pellerin said severely. "I'll not have you matchmaking, Philippa. I should enjoy such meddling in my affairs no more than you do yourself."

'No, ma'am." Philippa was properly chastened. She certainly did not enjoy such meddling, even when she knew it to be well-intentioned, and she had been given no reason to think for a moment that Cousin Adeliza was not thoroughly content with her lot. To be sure, it had taken no coaxing on Philippa's part to convince her to act as companion. Miss Pellerin had fairly snatched at the opportunity, but her own explanation that it gave her something new to do seemed to be no more or less than the truth.

Conversation remained desultory at best, for even along the valley floor, the roads were in no great condition. They stopped for refreshment and to rest the horses in Waltham on the Wolds at the Grape and Saber, a charming little inn with a newly thatched roof and a jolly landlord, who insisted upon waiting upon them himself. After the jolting of the carriage, it was a welcome relief to be able to sit quietly in a private parlor for twenty minutes, but that was quite long enough for Philippa, who was anxious to reach Belvoir.

"Not that we shall arrive earlier than two o'clock or even half-past at this rate," she said, "but there is no use in attempting to convince Witheridge to push the horses beyond what he considers to be a dignified pace."

"Well, I, for one, prefer a sedate journey to one that

brings my hat bouncing down over my eyes every few minutes,", stated Miss Pellerin with a look that told Philippa without words what her companion's view would be of any attempt to urge the old coachman to greater speed. "We shall arrive looking like ladies, my dear, and since you intend to speak to your young stepdaughter on the very subject of ladylike behavior, I would suggest that you do nothing to make yourself appear nohow in the meantime."

Philippa wrinkled her nose, but her eyes were twinkling. "You sound just like my mama," she said.

"So I should think," replied Miss Pellerin, getting in the last word before settling herself more comfortably and closing her eyes.

She roused herself once more as the carriage began its upward journey through the dense woods that covered the hillside leading to the castle. Philippa had been enjoying the solitude and the passing scenery, and since the breezes had blown the clouds away, allowing the sun to shine brightly down upon the landscape, she was grateful for the shade of the winding tree-lined drive.

Belvoir as seen from a distance was imposing. The Napoleonic War had been a gold mine to the Manners family, as it had been to most of the landed gentry, and the Duchess Elizabeth had not had to stint her remodeling efforts. As the trees thinned and the carriage passed through the main gates, Philippa was conscious of a thought that the new French windows were perhaps a trifle delicate for the solid baronial walls surrounding them, but she did not so much as voice that thought, for her companion was waxing enthusiastic over the cheerful display of the fountains in the gardens, and before she had finished, the carriage arrived at the main entrance porch.

The steps were let down by an obliging footman in red-and-buff livery, and the ladies descended. They were now on a sort of terrace, and beyond the garden fountains the landscape fell away, providing a splendid view. Philippa had heard it said that on a particularly clear day one could see thirty miles in all directions from the mound of Belvoir, and today she could well believe it. She heard Miss Pellerin draw a long, satisfied breath and knew that she, too, was enamored of the panorama spread before them.

A scant moment later, Miss Pellerin recollected herself. "Well, my dear, shall we go in?"

The footman relinquished them to the porter, who in turn passed them on to Mr. Douglas, the duke's somber, portly butler, whom they followed along an entrance passage lined with arms for more than a hundred men.

Some moments later, they came to the guardroom, which served as the great entrance hall of the castle. The hall was built in gothic style with a large fireplace at each end and a floor of parqueted black-and-white Nottingham free-stone and contained yet another collection of arms and military equipment, including an impressive number of suits of armor.

"Mercy me," said Miss Pellerin, "I'd forgotten how much of this stuff the Manners family had collected over the years."

"They have been involved in a number of conflicts since the days of the Conqueror, after all," Philippa said *sotto voce*. "And there was the Marquess of Granby, as well, the present duke's grandfather, who organized the Leicestershire Twenty-first Light Dragoons entirely at his own expense."

" 'Tis a wonder they had this lot left over then, isn't it?" replied the irrepressible Miss Pellerin.

Philippa chuckled but changed the subject. "That portrait on the left at the half-flight of the great stair is Elizabeth, ma'am. The companion portrait of the duke is there on the right."

"Well, the artist did well enough by her—handsome, isn't she—but the duke ought to have known better than to allow himself to be got up like an Elizabethan knight. He'd have done better to be painted as he is, and so I shall tell him. Such affectation will merely lead his unfortunate descendants to confuse him with someone else, like as not."

The butler had said not a word, and Philippa followed him up the stairs, smiling as she wondered what her companion would say next. But Miss Pellerin was silent as they proceeded along a passage past a case containing decorations, seals, and other objects, including the ceremonial key to Staunton Tower, the stronghold of the castle. This key, Philippa knew, was ritually presented to any members of the royal family who might visit Belvoir.

At last they came to a pair of tall pedimented and pilastered doors which the butler opened with neat precision.

"Lady Philippa Raynard-Wakefield and Miss Pellerin, your grace," he said quietly, stepping aside to allow Philippa and her companion to enter what proved to be an elegant pink-and-gold saloon.

Its occupants, two ladies and a gentleman, were gathered around a cheerful fire that crackled beneath a pedimented carved marble chimneypiece. The younger woman, whose dark hair was twisted at the top of her head into a knot from which a number of curls had been allowed to trail becomingly over her ears, was neatly attired in a pale yellow frock with sensible long sleeves and a high neckline, while the older lady had plumped for the height of fashion with a deeply décolletaged lavender silk afternoon gown. The tiny puffed sleeves did little to enhance the lady's sagging upper arms, but the color very nearly matched her sparkling eyes, and her figure was still quite shapely and slim enough for the prevailing fashions. The dark-haired gentleman seated in a pink-silk-upholstered, gilt-trimmed Kent chair opposite them stood up in a leisurely fashion when Philippa and Miss Pellerin entered the room, but the younger of the two ladies leapt energetically to her feet.

"Philippa," she cried, "you are here at last! Was there ever such a coil? I declare, I could have strangled the lot of them when I discovered what they had been about, for I promise you, my Bethie was in the scheme right up to her little arched eyebrows."

Returning her gaze with some effort from the gentleman to her hostess, Philippa grasped the two warm hands that had been thrust into her own. "I have had some thoughts about what I shall do to them myself, Elizabeth. May I make you and her grace known to my cousin, Miss Adeliza Pellerin?"

"Oh, do you know, I believe we have met before, have we not," exclaimed the duchess, "for I remember your pretty name. 'Tis one of my favorites. We named Bethie after me and my papa, you know—Elizabeth Frederica. And little Emmeline is after my mama, with 'Charlotte' for the queen, who stood godmother to her, of course. And then tiny Katherine Isabella is after my dearest mama-in-law. But my next daughter, I promise you, I have already decided to name Adeliza, so someday you will likely have a namesake, Miss Pellerin."

"You ought to think yourself honored, Adeliza," said the dowager duchess in a tone that indicated she was quite tired of being ignored. "Usually when Elizabeth prattles as she is doing now, she talks of nothing but my wee handsome grandson."

"Oh, yes, Philippa, you must see Baby George. He is simply the most splendid baby. Prinny and York are to come for the christening, you know, and I simply insist that you and dear Adeliza—you will allow me to call you Adeliza, will you not?"

Miss Pellerin nodded, somewhat in a daze, and the duchess rattled on, "Well, you must agree to come to Belvoir for the festivities. Little George John Frederick Manners, Marquess of Granby—and isn't that a mouthful for such a little baby?—is to be christened on his papa's birthday, the fourth day of January, with Prinny and York to stand godfather. Her majesty has graciously consented to stand godmama, but only if Mama Isabella will stand in for her, for she cannot think the roads will be safe enough for travel in January, you know, but Prinny does not seem to mind. We had a letter straightaway from him by return post when dearest John wrote to inquire."

"Elizabeth, you are forgetting your manners," said the dowager duchess tartly. "Rochford has been standing like a marble piller and cannot think much of being ignored. I know I don't," she added candidly.

Recalled to her duty, Elizabeth performed the introductions, confirming Philippa's suspicion that the gentleman was the same Viscount Rochford whose father owned Wyvern Towers, and Philippa found herself gazing into a pair of fine light gray eyes set deeply into a craggy face. Rochford was above middle height but not so tall that he would be at a disadvantage in the saddle; and, with his harsh, weathered features, windblown dark hair, broad, muscular shoulders, and powerful thighs, he certainly had the look of a sporting man. Still, she noted, nothing could be found amiss with his attire. He was properly dressed for an afternoon in a lady's drawing room, in buff pantaloons that fit snugly over those powerful thighs and shapely calves, and a dark coat that rested upon the broad shoulders without a single crease to mar its fit. His linen was snowy white, and a dark amethyst glinted in the folds of his neatly tied neckcloth. His only other jewelry appeared to be the heavy ring on his right hand, a richly ornamented gold signet carved with the head of a dragon. Though his bearing was military rather than fashionable, it lacked the stiffness she had noted in many men who had recently sold out, as she assumed his lordship must have done.

She realized Elizabeth was speaking to her and turned, flushing when she noted a sudden spark of amusement in Rochford's light gray eyes. The man knew she had been staring at him, and his look now seemed to be no more than an invitation to continue her examination at her leisure. Aware of a sudden unfamiliar humming in her mind, she flushed deeper, focusing her attention upon the duchess with some difficulty. "I . . . I beg your pardon, Elizabeth. I fear I was not attending."

The young duchess's laughter rippled forth. "What were you thinking of, I wonder. I merely remarked that it was a pity the pair of you did not realize you were to come on the same errand. You might have shared a carriage. On the other hand," she went on without so much as pausing for breath, "you would have been prodigiously crowded with five in the carriage on the return journey, I daresay."

Philippa blinked in bewilderment and looked to Miss Pellerin for explanation. That lady's eyes were twinkling. "It appears we were correct in our surmise," she said gently. "The Lady Lucinda Drake is indeed Lord Rochford's youngest sister, and her grace was just explaining that he knew no more of the journey from Bath than you did. His errand is similar to our own, my dear."

Philippa turned back to his lordship to discover that he was smiling at her, showing strong white teeth. Though the humming in her mind seemed, most oddly, to descend to her midsection even as she returned his look, she soon took herself ruthlessly in hand, deciding that she had seen that look too often before. He looked, she told herself firmly, exactly like the preponderant number of gentlemen who had approached her throughout the past Season, and if that was not a predatory twinkle in those light gray eyes, one had wasted one's time learning to discern such looks. By and large, however, one was forced to concede that it was an attractive twinkle. Despite her wish to respond coolly, she found herself smiling back at the gentleman, noting as she did so that he stood a full head taller than herself.

Rochford bowed slightly and spoke in a pleasantly low-pitched voice. "It is a pleasure to make your acquaintance, Lady Philippa. But are you not the widow of Lord Wakefield, my father's late friend?"

"Indeed, sir," Philippa replied, stiffening.

The twinkle only deepened, and she realized the deep crags in his cheeks were crinkling as though in silent laughter. "I meant no offense, madam. I was merely curious as to why you are 'Lady Philippa' and not 'Lady Wakefield.' "

"Oh." Philippa relaxed, regarding him ruefully. " 'Twas a whim of my late husband's, I fear. He said that 'Lady Philippa Raynard-Wakefield' had a lilt to it that pleased him and that since he would no doubt predecease me, it would be as well for me to have a name of my own to distinguish me from whomever his son might choose to marry. My father is the Earl of Toddleigh, you see, so I was Lady Philippa Russell before I married. Then, too, the baron was proud of the Raynard-Wakefield name. The title came before the two families were joined as a requirement of the Raynard who gave his daughter to a Wakefield, along with Chase Charley, of course. He wished his name to remain with the estate."

"How very interesting, to be sure," said the dowager in bored tones, indicating the opposite. "Do you enjoy political discussion, I wonder, Lady Philippa?"

Philippa returned the sharp look she was getting with a calm one of her own. "I believe I can hold my own in such discussion, your grace. I allowed my interest to flag somewhat after my husband's death, but he—like many others, including yourself, I believe—had a great fascination for the intricacies of the political scene." Remembering, as she did now, some of the things Wakefield had told her of the dowager's more outrageous appearances in the gallery of the House of Lords, Philippa hoped the old lady would not take offense.

The dark blue eyes in the once beautiful face sharpened, but the dowager decided to take the remark as a compliment.

"I daresay I've kept a close watch over the gentlemen in power," she said on a note of satisfaction. "No doubt that is what keeps some of them up to snuff, for they know I have the Regent's ear, after all, and a number of other ears as well. I daresay that rotter Fox wished more than once that he had got on my good side from the outset, but he never did, and he lived to regret it."

Remembering Wakefield's tale of how the fourth Duchess of Rutland had roared "Damn Fox!" before a full house at the opera some thirty years before, Philippa was hard-pressed to conceal her merriment. Looking away from the dowager in self-defense, she found her gaze suddenly locked with that of the viscount. His twitching lips nearly led to her undoing.

Rochford seemed to realize she would be unable to control herself much longer. "Your grace," he said quietly, turning to the duchess and letting the twinkle fade away altogether, "I hesitate to disrupt this pleasant gathering, but I should like very much to have a word or two in private with my sister before the hour grows much more advanced."

"Oh, to be sure, I had forgotten why you had come, Rochford. How very silly of me, but I daresay 'twas all this pleasant company. You, too, Philippa, will be wishing to speak with Jessalyn. I shall arrange for you all to be shown to your bedchambers at once, and then I shall have your respective charges sent along to you straightaway. I expect they are not precisely looking forward to the interviews, poor chicks. Imagine telling dear, absurd Miss Blandamore that you had each written permission for them to accompany our Bethie when they had in fact written the letters themselves and signed your names. Dreadful children!" With that parting shot, she stepped lightly to the bell rope and gave it a couple of hearty yanks.

Philippa, glancing once again at Viscount Rochford, noted that his features had hardened and looked harsher than ever. As the light gray eyes met hers, she experienced a thrill of fear followed by a feeling of deep gratitude that she was not the person with whom he was annoyed. She even found it possible to feel compassion for the unfortunate Lady Lucinda.

—3—

PHILIPPA'S BEDCHAMBER WAS an elegant room despite clear and present evidence of the young duchess's desire to turn Belvoir into a real castle. Colorful Mortlake tapestries depicting hunting scenes draped two walls, the wide bed was hung with pale green-velvet curtains, and the large carved-walnut garderobe occupying a third wall displayed a cumbersome medieval appearance. When Philippa was shown into the room, she discovered a plump maidservant, attired in a blue dress with a white bib apron, flicking a feather duster across the carved windowsill. The duster whisked behind the girl's back as she dropped a curtsy.

"Good day, m'lady. I be Tilly, 'n I'm t' do fer ye, since ye've not brung yer own woman." A note in her voice indicated her low opinion of such frippery ways.

"Thank you, Tilly," Philippa said calmly. "I shall be glad of your assistance when I am ready to dress for dinner."

"Aye, m'lady. Just 'e ring, 'n I'll come up straightaway. I've put yer things away fer ye, then. D'ye require aught else?" When Philippa denied any further need for her services, Tilly reached to straighten one of the pale green velvet curtains, then left the room, holding her duster in a fold of her blue skirt as though it were not the done thing to let such an article be seen.

Philippa smiled and walked to the window. She was on the north side of the castle now, and thus had a clear view over the undulating green-and-gold checkerboard squares of the Vale of Belvoir. It really was wonderful, she thought, how much green there was. In Sussex, no matter what they did, the lawns at Wakefield Priory always seemed to have turned brown by now, but although many of the trees in the woods approaching Belvoir Castle had dropped their leaves, the lawns still displayed more green than brown, and the hedges contained as many green leaves as burnished golden ones.

A scratching at the door of the bedchamber interrupted her thoughts, and she turned from the window.

"Enter."

After a long moment, the door opened. Her stepdaughter paused warily on the threshold.

Philippa's lips thinned to a straight line, and her eyes narrowed. "Well, well," she said, "I wish I might say this meeting is a pleasure, Jessalyn."

Miss Jessalyn Raynard-Wakefield was a slender young lady with fine pale blond hair swept back from a high, rounded forehead and held in place at the moment by a pale pink ribbon that matched her high-waisted three-quarter-sleeved round gown and her beribboned satin slippers. She had thirteen summers behind her and a reputation for beauty and wit that usually gave her the confidence to carry off her pranks with a high hand; however, as she hesitated in the open doorway, it could be seen that her normally pink cheeks were pale, her blue eyes lacked their customary sparkle, and her expression was apprehensive. In the silence that followed her stepmother's words, she began nervously to chew her lower lip.

"Close the door," Philippa said, taking a seat upon the walnut dressing chair. "Then come here to me."

Jessalyn obeyed the first instruction but remained standing by the door. "What are you going to do?" she asked, swallowing hard.

Philippa folded her hands in her lap and eyed the miscreant solemnly for a long moment before answering sternly, "You know what you deserve for this outrage, do you not?"

Jessalyn dropped her gaze to the gold-and-white Axminster carpet. "Yes, ma'am," she said in a near-whisper, shifting her feet, "but I hope you will not."

"I believe you," Philippa said, repressing a sudden spark of amusement at what was clearly an understatement on the child's part and forcing an even sterner expression onto her face. She knew well from experience that to give even a hint of her amusement would be fatal to any lesson she meant to teach. "Moreover," she went on quietly, "as I have no wish to figure as a wicked stepmother, I shall certainly give you the opportunity to explain yourself before I pass sentence. Come over here, if you please, and tell me just what you were thinking of to have behaved so badly."

Jessalyn straightened her shoulders and lifted her chin. Her pink tongue darted out to lick her lips. Then she said, "I suppose we didn't think. Not sensibly, don't you know, or Lucy and I would still be in Bath. We certainly never thought you or Lord Rochford would be here," she went on more rapidly, "or we never would have done it."

"But I wrote to tell you I was coming into Leicestershire," Philippa said reasonably.

"When? We left Bath on the ninth, don't you know, since the duchess's birthday was celebrated upon the thirteenth."

"Then my letter must have reached Bath soon after you left," Philippa said, "which means Miss Blandamore knows by now what a dreadful trick you played her."

"How should she?" Jessalyn had moved closer, but she still kept a wary distance between herself and her stepmother.

"Don't be more of a goose than you already have been," was the impatient reply. "She will know perfectly well that had I written giving you permission to depart immediately for Belvoir, I should not have written again so soon, expecting my letter to find you in Bath."

"Oh."

"All that is beside the point, in any event, Jessalyn. I wish you will come over here to me, so that I do not feel as though I were shouting at you. Not," she added with a grimace, "that I do not feel a good deal like shouting. I presume that this little escapade was your notion from the outset."

Jessalyn bristled as though she would deny indignantly the possibility that she could have been responsible for anything, but after a second look at Philippa's stern face, she capitulated, moving toward her. "Bath was very dull," she said, hanging her head. But then she seemed to recollect herself, and her head came up again as she took another, impulsive step toward Philippa. "Really, ma'am, you can have no notion of how dreary it is in Bath in November. There is absolutely nothing to do."

"You have your schoolwork, surely."

"Oh, that." Jessalyn dismissed schoolwork with an indifferent shrug. "We just thought a birthday celebration for the duchess would be more amusing, don't you know." She looked at Philippa beseechingly, and catching the gleam of amusement that would no longer be suppressed, she sighed in relief. "I knew you would understand if I could but tell you. We—Beth and Lucy and I—had become such very good friends, don't you know, on account of us all having estates in Leicestershire, although we had none of us met here ever, only at school. So we thought—when Beth's mum wrote to tell her the carriage would collect her the following Tuesday—well, it just seemed like a splendid notion for us all to come. Lucy's father is drinking the waters at Leamington Spa and she quite thought her brother was still on the Continent, don't you know—and it is dreadfully unfair of him not to be, I think—but in any event," she went on rapidly when her stepmother's eyes narrowed ominously again, "I didn't know precisely where you were. When last you wrote, you were in London from Brighton but were thinking you might not stay as long as you had intended, so I thought the Priory, don't you know, only there wasn't time to send there or anywhere for proper permission, and Lucy's papa wouldn't care a rap, she said, and Beth was persuaded that no one would mind if we came with her, so we did." She ended out of breath, her hands folded tightly at her waist and her anxious gaze pinned to Philippa's face.

"Don't I know?" said her stepmother sardonically, unable to resist. "Really, Jessalyn, no matter how you might attempt to wrap this matter in white linen, you must know that what you did was very naughty."

"But how could I have asked you? Letters going back and forth would have taken weeks, which would not have answered the purpose at all, and I truly didn't know where you were."

"Well, that last point is clear enough. I don't believe you would have been so foolhardy as to come to Belvoir knowing I was fixed at Chase Charley, but you ought not to have come at all if you could not obtain my permission. Surely you must have known the duchess would make mention of your visit in her next letter to me."

"I didn't know she corresponded with you," Jessalyn said simply.

"Well, that doesn't matter. What you did, you and Lady Lucinda, was very bad, my dear. It is against the law, in fact, to sign a name not your own to a letter, or to anything else, for that matter."

Jessalyn bit her lip again. "I didn't know."

"You knew it was something you ought not to do." Philippa made the words a statement, not a question, and was unsurprised when Jessalyn remained silent. "You must apologize to the duke and duchess, my dear, and to the dowager duchess as well, for having involved all of them in your escapade."

"I did already," the child said, "when the duchess scolded us all for what we had done."

"How did she find you out?"

Jessalyn grimaced. "It was Lucinda'a fault. The duke mentioned the fact that her wretched brother was at Wyvern Towers, having heard the news from his master of hounds, and Lucy was so dismayed, she just cried out, 'Oh, no!' After that, our tale was told, don't you know, and things got rather confused until the old duchess ordered us off to our bedchambers. I think she was miffed because we had caused a scene, but I've noticed she likes causing them herself well enough."

"Jess!" Philippa had meant to call her to order for her disrespectful reference to Viscount Rochford, but the child had spoken too quickly for her to get a word in, and now it was all she could do to stifle a rising chuckle. Young Jessalyn had come to know the dowager rather quickly, for her grace was indeed one who didn't like scenes unless they were of her own creating. But when Jessalyn merely grimaced at the reproach in her stepmother's sharp use of her name, Philippa came back quickly to the issue at hand. "Very well," she said, "if you have already made your apology, you need say no more, but you must write to Miss Blandamore to explain precisely what you did and beg her pardon for deceiving her. You may," she went on sternly when Jessalyn's mouth flew open in protest, "begin your letter at once, for you are to keep to your bedchamber without company until we depart tomorrow morning. Is that clearly understood, Jessalyn?"

"Yes, ma'am." The tone was sulky, but after a moment when Philippa had said nothing further, Jessalyn brightened perceptibly. "Is that all?"

"That is all for now, young lady," Philippa corrected, "but we will speak of this matter at length when we reach home. I shall decide then what is to be done with you."

"Oh." The brightness dimmed.

"You may go now, Jessalyn."

Once the child had gone, Philippa soon became restless, uncertain that she had handled the matter as it should have been handled. She had not been a parent long enough to know the best way to cope with such problems and thought that perhaps she ought to have read the child a much more severe scold, or even to have used her as Jessalyn had clearly expected to be used. Philippa had no doubt that had Wakefield lived to see this day, he would have been furious with his daughter, but she was not by any means certain he would have whipped her. He had been, in Philippa's experience anyway, a comparatively gentle man. Her own father, by contrast, might well have soundly thrashed a young Philippa who had been guilty of perpetrating such an escapade. She grimaced. The Earl of Toddleigh had not been one to suffer mischief tolerantly.

She sighed, letting her thoughts drift to Viscount Rochford. Though her first thoughts were of a pair of fine gray eyes and an odd, unfamiliar humming in her mind, she soon brought herself to remember that the gentleman was undoubtedly enjoying—if such a word might be utilized in such a circumstance—a similar confrontation with his young sister. What if he discovered that it had been Jessalyn's bright idea to leave school? What if he thrashed poor Lucinda for her part in the matter and then discovered that the chief miscreant had been let off much more easily? Would he not demand to know what Lady Philippa was about to let her young charge off scot-free after Jess had led the other young women astray in such a dissolute fashion?

Philippa began to pace her room as her imagination ran

wild, and it was not long before she knew she had to have more space and air than the bedchamber's suddenly confining limits allowed her. Miss Pellerin having expressed the intention of taking a nap before dinner, she had no wish to disturb her, nor could she wish to submit herself to another spate of the young duchess's conversation, however charming. Accordingly, she slipped from her room, hoping she would meet no one, and was fortunate enough to find her way to a small north terrace without encountering a soul.

Philippa crossed the terrace to the crenellated stone parapet that surrounded it and stood gazing out over the Vale of Belvoir, breathing deeply of the chilled fresh air and relishing the quiet. Below her, at the edge of the lawn, two brown hares were nibbling the remains of some shrub or other in the border, and a little further on, several gardeners were engaged in planting a clump of what looked like paper birches. A pair of black-and-white magpies screeched at each other overhead, and as she looked up to try to catch sight of them, a voice spoke near enough to her right shoulder to startle her.

"Saw you from my bedchamber window. Dare I hope you have throttled your stepdaughter?"

She turned quickly to find the Viscount Rochford looking down at her from a point rather too near to be comfortable. 'I beg your pardon, sir, but I cannot have heard you correctly," she said stiffly, moving to put more distance between them and wishing that the startlement—for surely that was the cause of it—had not made her heart pound so rapidly.

Rochford appeared to be under the mistaken impression that she was merely making room for him at the parapet, for he stepped forward to stand directly beside her, and although he did not actually touch her, he was so close that she seemed to feel a prickling sensation all along her side. "You heard me well enough," he said, smiling rather grimly. "The last thing I anticipated having to cope with upon coming into Leicestershire was my youngest sister, I can promise you that much."

"I daresay." The sun, lowering toward the line of hills to the west, set auburn highlights dancing in his dark hair, and as she noticed these, she noticed also that a lock of hair toward the back of his head was lifting in the slight breeze, fluttering. Philippa was again conscious of a wish to try to widen the distance between them. Somehow his nearness was most disconcerting. He turned just then to gaze out upon the view, however, and she seemed able to breathe more naturally. "I collect, sir, that your presence in the county came as something of a shock to the Lady Lucinda."

He looked down at her again, and this time his smile was natural, even boyish. She found herself thinking that he might well have found time for mischief himself when he was a schoolboy. "Something of a shock," he repeated, savoring the phrase. "I believe you underestimate the tenderness of my sister's sensibilities, ma'am."

"Do I?"

"Indeed." He chuckled. "She knew perfectly well that my father was safely out of her way, and although she admits that my sister Margaret did inform her three months ago that she was sending for me, Lucy appears to think herself prodigiously ill-used for the simple reason that she thought it must take many months, if not years, for me to return."

"Dear me! Where did she think you had got to, sir?"

"The Lord only knows. She ought to have known I was in Portugal and had only to get on the first boat home, but her knowledge of geography appears to be scant at best. I cannot think the unfortunate Miss Blandamore has taught her very much."

Philippa's mind had taken another track. "I am a little acquainted with Lady Kegworth, sir. I trust she had no imperative reason for requesting your return."

"Well, my father is not in good health, if that is what you mean, but that has been the case for several years. Until now, however, he has taken an interest in running the estate. Margaret's reason for sending for me was that he no longer does so, and so when she and Kegworth agreed to accompany him to Leamington Spa, they decided at the same time that it was time I took the reins into my own hands. They picked the devil of a time for it, I must say," he added on a note of bitter amusement.

Philippa lifted an eyebrow. "You had more important matters in hand, sir?"

He did not misread the disapproval in her tone. This time

his smile was a rueful one. "Disobliging of me, was it not? The fact of the matter is, however, that the tide on the Continent has shifted to our favor. Wellington was on the point of entering France when I left, and I confess I should have liked very much to accompany him. Indeed, with the end in sight, as it is, I believe, I should like to be present when he routs Boney for good and all."

"I daresay that if he is as good as they say, Lord Wellington will manage nicely without you, sir," Philippa said, turning her attention once more to the vale.

When he had said nothing for several minutes, however, her curiosity got the better of her and she turned her head to look up at him, only to discover to her consternation that he was regarding her with measuring intent. She found she had become more accustomed to his nearness and rather liked looking at him, however, so when his gaze did not shift, she lifted that mobile eyebrow again.

Rochford seemed to recollect himself, but when he spoke he said nothing about Wellington. Instead, he said, "I have neglected to express my sympathies on your recent loss, ma'am."

She blinked, then gave herself a little shake and answered calmly, "Thank you, sir, but you need not reproach yourself. My loss took place nearly two years ago."

He nodded as though she had answered some question or other, and Philippa told herself there could be no difficulty in deducing what that question must be. She had seen that look on a number of masculine faces in the past months. No doubt Rochford was like the rest and had made it his business to discover during the time since she had been introduced to him that Lord Wakefield's widow, besides being well-favored and unattached, was quite amazingly wealthy.

She had not the least notion of how the Drake fortunes stood, but few men on the lookout for a wife would wish to pass up a young woman in her circumstances. Not only had Wakefield left her nearly every scrap of his unentailed property, but she had her dowry as well, a not inconsiderable amount, since she was Toddleigh's only daughter and the earl was a man of relatively deep pockets. That searching look and the remark about his sympathies could only mean that

Rochford wished to discover whether she still pined for her late lord before considering what strategy to use to win her hand. Philippa had seen the signs all too often, but never before had they so much disappointed her.

"You look grave, ma'am," he said gently. "I ought not to have mentioned your loss. Even after two years—"

"It was not that," she said impatiently.

"Well, then, it must be the children, but I trust you have not allowed yourself to be too disturbed by their mischief. I am persuaded that the duchess has chosen to look upon the matter in a flattering light—that they took such effort to attend her birthday celebration, you know."

Finding it easier to accept his interpretation of her feelings than to explain precisely what he had done to bring that grave look to her face, she managed a little smile and said, "You do not regard the matter so lightly as that, I believe."

"Certainly not. I informed my repellent sister that I should send a letter directly to Miss Blandamore instructing her to punish Lucinda as severely as she might."

Philippa could not help herself. She laughed outright, and when he looked down at her in bewilderment, she laughed harder until tears formed in her dark eyes.

Rochford smiled doubtfully. "Have I said something so funny, then?"

She shook her head. "Only it is clear that you have never met Miss Blandamore," she said, controlling her mirth with an effort.

"No, of course I have not. How should I?"

"Well, she reminds me of nothing so much as a cabbage, sir, with perhaps a little onion atop for the head. All ruffles and smiles and rippling flesh. She must have as many as four chins by now, like dewlaps."

"Good Lord!"

"Indeed, sir. I am persuaded the worst punishment she is capable of giving is a frown and perhaps a shake of her head, which would merely set all the ruffles and ribbons of whatever cap she is wearing at the time to moving in such a way as to distract a wrongdoer from all thought of her displeasure."

"How on earth does she manage to run a school for young ladies?" His eyes narrowed, and Philippa discovered within herself a sudden wish to defend the absent Miss Blandamore.

"Her breeding is excellent, I promise you," she said, "and the girls like her very much. Indeed, I am certain that had Lady Lucinda or Jessalyn thought for a moment that she might come to learn of their deceit and be saddened by it, they would have had second thoughts altogether."

"Then I wish they had thought of it," he said grimly. "Lucinda, for one, is certainly wishing now that she had thought more carefully before she acted."

"Oh, dear, were you very harsh with her?" Philippa asked anxiously, remembering her earlier thoughts upon the subject with some misgiving.

"She was treated to the rough edge of my tongue, certainly. She deserved no less."

"But you did not . . . that is, you—"

"I didn't beat the chit, if that is what you are trying to ask." It was he who looked away over the vale this time, and his next words came in a near-mutter. "Not that it mightn't have done us both some good if I had."

"Surely not, sir. Surely it is enough that she knows she has displeased you."

"Oh, she knows that much," he said. "I hope never to be the victim of such a flood of weeping again, I can tell you. I don't know where she found so many tears, but I am persuaded that anyone setting eyes upon her after she left the room must certainly think she had been mercilessly ill-used."

Though she hid a smile, Philippa was grateful that Jessalyn had not subjected her to such an appalling scene. Tears were not Jessalyn's way, however. That young lady was much more likely to indulge in coaxing and cajolery. Philippa felt a surge of compassion for Rochford, but it was very brief, lasting only until he gave it as his opinion in his very next breath that she had no doubt found it even more difficult dealing with her stepdaughter.

"Indeed," she said haughtily, "and why should I, sir?"

"Well, you must admit you are rather young for such a charge, my lady."

"I admit nothing of the sort. I have had charge of Jessalyn

since her eighth year, and in the general way of things, she and I get along very well. And I tell you, sir, that I bear also the responsibility for a young man in his first year at Oxford, and I do not find Edward to be any more cumbersome a burden than his sister."

"No doubt I misread the situation," he returned suavely. "Are you fixed in Leicestershire for some time, ma'am?"

"I do not know," she replied, looking away so that he would not read in her eyes the contempt she was feeling. Clearly his lordship had no wish to dispute any matter with her. No doubt, like so many of her would-be suitors, he would agree that the best horses were green if she were to express such an opinion. Truly, a gentleman intent upon pursuit could be a boring creature.

"You have no notion at all?" he persisted.

"I fear I have become something of a Gypsy over the past months," she told him honestly. "I suppose that having remained in Sussex for so long after Wakefield's death, I simply become bored now when I remain too long in one place. I came here seeking peace and quiet after the racket of Brighton and London, but so far peace is the last thing I have found."

"I see," he said slowly, "but surely you must have realized that Leicestershire during the hunting season is not known as a peaceful county."

Philippa shrugged. "I did not consider the sporting men," she said. "They cannot have reason to seek out my company when they are intent upon the fox."

"That is true, certainly, but they do not seek the fox at all hours of every day."

"Do they not?" She chuckled. "I well remember when my mama asked Lord Honeycutt about the hunting box he had hired for the season, whether it had a nice garden. His reply was that he hadn't got the slightest notion, since having never seen the place by daylight, he had never seen the garden."

Rochford smiled appreciatively. " 'Tis true enough, I suppose, that many men leave their houses before daylight to attend distant hunt meetings and don't return from their carousing before dark, but those must be the most dedicated, certainly, men who ride with more than one master."

"No doubt you know best, sir," Philippa agreed cordially, gathering her skirts as she prepared to take her leave. "You must forgive me if I leave you now, but I see that the sun is nearly sitting upon yonder hill, which must mean it is time and more to be dressing for dinner. I should not like to keep anyone awaiting my presence."

He bowed. "Yours would be a presence worth waiting for, I am certain, my lady."

She granted him a stiff smile to show him clearly that she had no liking for such broad compliments, and turned away. But even before she reached the door leading inside, she had a strange, tingling compulsion to look back at him, perhaps even to smile more warmly or to say something civil to show that she had not really disliked his words so much. Though she attempted to ignore the compulsion, thinking that any such action must give the viscount a false notion of her feelings toward him, the need to look back grew stronger until finally, unable to resist, she turned to discover a fine view of his back and those broad, muscular shoulders. The viscount had returned to his thoughtful contemplation of the vale.

—4—

TILLY WAS WAITING for her when she reached her bedchamber, and Philippa quickly changed to the green-and-gold evening dress she had brought to wear to dinner. The gown, cut low in the bodice to show off her high, well-rounded breasts, and short in the sleeves, was trimmed with gold lace that brought out golden flecks in her dark brown eyes. The skirt, though slim and straight in the front, was gored in the back, falling away to a demitrain from the high waist.

Tilly parted Philippa's hair neatly in the middle, then combed it smoothly into two clusters of curls above her ears. When she had finished, she stood back to await comment.

"Very nice, Tilly," Philippa said, regarding herself approvingly in the looking glass over the dressing table.

"Ye'll be wanting a touch of Sergis rouge, I'm thinkin', m'lady. Ye could do with a spot o' color in yer cheeks."

Philippa agreed. She had been out of the sun for a good many months, and her cheeks were pale. Warning the girl to go lightly, she watched anxiously to be sure she didn't end with two bright red spots on her cheeks. But Tilly was sparing with the stuff, and the results were acceptable. Indeed, it was difficult to tell that she had given nature any aid at all.

"I do hope the dowager doesn't disapprove," she said, smiling at the girl.

"That one? Not a chance, beggin' yer pardon, ma'am. The old duchess likes a bit o' paint 'erself. Says it livens up a dull complexion. She be gettin' on, though, 'n that's a fact. Some o' the younger gennulmen as should know better calls 'er 'Was-a-Bella.' Me, I'd like t' clap their 'eads t'gether, I would."

Philippa's smile widened. She was beginning to like Tilly. At that moment the door opened and Miss Pellerin entered.

"Oh, my dear, how splendid you look," said that lady. "That gown becomes you wondrous well. Do get up and let me look at you."

Philippa obeyed, turning to give the full effect. "Well, ma'am? You have seen this dress before, after all."

"Yes, indeed, but where are your jewels, Philippa?"

"Here." Philippa moved to open the case on the dressing table, removed a gold chain with a pendant emerald and matching earbobs. "No bracelets tonight, I think," she said, examining the rest of the contents. " 'Tis only a simple dinner, after all."

Miss Pellerin nodded, then moved to help her fasten her chain. Philippa picked up her gloves, pulled them on and smoothed them at elbows and wrists, and pronounced herself ready to go downstairs.

"And what of Jessalyn? Do we call for her?"

"We do not," Philippa said firmly. "If she goes supperless to bed, it will be no more than she deserves."

"Mercy me, then you have spoken with her. Was the discussion prodigiously uncomfortable?"

"Indeed, it was, ma'am, but no more so than his lordship's conversation with the Lady Lucinda, I'm told. I met him out on the terrace afterward. At least Jessalyn had the goodness not to subject me to a fit of the vapors such as that to which he said his sister subjected him."

"Well, no one has ever, with all her faults, accused Jessalyn of being vaporish," said Miss Pellerin with a smile, before adding more seriously, "You ought not to wander about by yourself, my dear. Had someone seen you with his lordship, an assignation might have been suspected."

"Oh, pooh," replied Philippa, grimacing. "Not but what his lordship mightn't have liked it to be an assignation. I fear he is like so many others, ma'am."

"Mercy me, on the catch for a wife, is he?"

"I don't doubt it. As you said before, he must be in his

mid-thirties, and he's been away for several years. He is not getting any younger, and there's the succession to be secured. Anyway, I recognized the look,'' she added a little sadly.

Miss Pellerin wisely said nothing more to the purpose than that she was sure they ought to be getting downstairs if they were not to keep the others waiting, and Philippa, with a guilty glance at the hovering Tilly, agreed. It took them some time to reach the pink-and-gold saloon where the household gathered before dinner, and when they entered they discovered that the others were indeed before them.

Philippa's appreciative gaze fell first upon the viscount, who was looking as much like a soldier as it was possible to look in proper evening attire. His light-colored breeches and dark coat were cut in such a fashion as to show his excellent figure to admiration, and his linen was so white it seemed to sparkle. He smiled at her, and she returned a tiny smile of her own that widened when her hostess spoke to her.

''Dear Philippa, you do remember Rutland, do you not?''

Philippa looked up at the fifth Duke of Rutland. ''Indeed, I do. How do you do, your grace?''

Rutland nodded, smiling at her. ''Well, thank you, Lady Philippa.'' He was a tall gentleman of a distinctly noble presence, but she stood in no awe of him, for he was a singularly courteous man who knew to a nicety how to put others at their ease. He talked with her for some moments more, then gestured toward the third and fourth gentlemen in the room, a short, plump, rather ugly young man dressed in the height of fashion, and another, handsomer man with a devil-may-care look about him. ''You know Lord Alvanley, of course, ma'am,'' the duke said, indicating the first gentleman, ''but have you met my brother, Lord Robert Manners?''

Philippa had not had that pleasure before, and she was pleased to meet Lord Robert, who proved to be a merry gentleman in his early thirties. The duchess broke in just then to demand to know if they were all to stand about staring at one another or if her husband meant to ring for refreshments. The demand being seconded by the dowager, who said that for her part she could do nicely with a glass of negus, thank you, the duke grinned at his brother, who went to pull the bell.

The fact that such action had not been necessary was proved by the immediate entrance of two footmen with silver trays laden with all manner of bottles and glasses. By the time each person had been served, Philippa discovered that Lord Rochford had maneuvered himself to a place by her side.

"I like that dress," he said simply.

"Thank you, sir. 'Tis one of my favorites."

"How refreshing that you do not claim it to be just whatever fell first to hand."

" 'Twould be most foolish to chance snatching up a gown that did not become one, would it not? I fear I have little interest in such games, sir."

"I say, Lady Philippa," Lord Robert broke in, moving to stand beside Rochford, "my mama tells me you have twice hunted with my brother's pack. Do you mean to do so again, now that you are here?"

Philippa dimpled at him, her cheeks reddening as she darted a glance toward the duke and discovered that he had overheard the question. "As to that, my lord, I cannot say. I have not been invited."

"Well, dash it, John, invite her," commanded his lordship. "Mama says she rides dashed well for a woman. Can't wish to sit by and watch if she can ride."

"No, indeed," agreed Rutland. "You must join us here at Belvoir whenever you like, Lady Philippa. We should be pleased to have you ride out with the family."

"You permit women to ride with your pack?" Rochford inquired with a lazy smile. "You are more daring than most, duke."

Rutland chuckled but avoided his mother's eye. "I have been given little choice in the matter, Rochford. No more, in fact, than my father before me. Have your sisters never demanded the chance to ride with the Wyvern pack, then?"

"Much good it would have done them," the viscount said, grinning. "Neither my father nor I would be like to permit such a thing. The company is scarcely suitable, and the country is a deal too rough."

"You have your own pack, sir?" Philippa inquired, interested despite her determination to set him at a distance.

"My father's pack, actually. But then, I daresay it comes to the same thing."

"Alvanley has been kind enough to say that the Wyvern pack is as well-bred as our own," said Rutland, smiling at that gentleman.

"Young Alvanley," said the dowager in stern tones, "would like any pack of hounds that could run fast enough to avoid being run down by him. His lordship," she added, shooting that gentleman a challenging look, as though she dared him to disagree with her, "is a crammer and heads his fox as often as not, if he don't overrun him."

"Alwayth did thay," Lord Alvanley lisped, unabashed by these strictures, "hunting would be a dashed thight more fun were it not for the damned houndth alwayth getting in the way."

"That means," said Rochford near Philippa's ear, "that he cares only for the hard riding and nothing much for the hunt itself. Alvanley rides neck-or-nothing, and if he doesn't turn the fox away from the course, he rides past him, or did you follow that exchange without my translation?"

She smiled at him but stepped a little away. "I knew about overrunning, of course, and I daresay I knew that Duchess Isabella was expressing disapproval, but I am not fully alive to all the slang of the sport, I fear."

"No reason any gently bred female ought to be," he replied, but his tone was even and his smile took offense from the words.

Indeed, his smile was so warm that Philippa found herself responding to it yet again. A moment later, disconcerted to find herself still staring into his gray eyes, she sought a way to break the spell and grasped at the question that had been plaguing her since young Quinlan's visit. "Please, sir, can you tell me why the scent is poor in Leicestershire in November?"

"Is it, by God? First I ever heard of it. Here, Duke"—he turned toward Rutland—"has the scent fallen off since I was last here in November?"

Rutland stepped closer to them, but they had everyone's attention now, and it was the dowager who answered first.

"Nonsense. Pure poppycock. Who's been filling your head with such rubbish, sir?"

"Why, Lady Philippa tells me she has heard the news from some quarter or other."

All eyes were on Philippa now, and she found to her dismay that she was blushing deeply. "I . . . I really know nothing about it," she said. "Someone merely made the statement—"

"Someone who had a bad day's hunting one November, no doubt," said Rutland gently. "That is generally how such tales get about. Though the height of the season hereabouts is more likely to be December and January, one can get good runs in November as well. The scent is higher in the shires than elsewhere because of all the grass and because we don't permit all our farm animals to run loose fouling it. It is generally breast-high, meaning the hounds don't stoop to it, or very good—'burning' or 'screaming,' in the language of the hunt—but we have our flighty days, too, when the scent is variable. Because the weather is more uncertain in November than in the later months, more likely to present us with quick freezes, it is possible to have more variable days. No doubt that is what your informant meant. Won't you let me refill your glass before we go in to dinner?"

Philippa nodded, not because she wanted more ratafia but because it gave her the chance to follow Rutland a little away from the others, a chance to catch her breath. By the time she turned back, the members of the party had rearranged themselves, and the duchess was telling a humorous anecdote in her rattling way. The company was still laughing when Mr. Douglas entered to announce that dinner was ready.

Conversation at the table was general but turned at last, as indeed all conversations in Leicestershire inevitably turn, to hunting. Lord Robert Manners was reminded by something his mother said about some lord or other of a tale concerning that same gentleman in the hunting field. This tale was topped by one related by the duke, and soon everyone but Philippa and Miss Pellerin was exchanging tale for tale. After well nigh a half-hour of this conversation, the young duchess laughed ruefully and spoke across her brother-in-law and

Alvanley to Philippa, who was sitting at Rutland's right hand, across from Miss Pellerin.

"You must forgive them, my dear. Once the subject raises its head, nothing can stop them. I am persuaded you find such conversation tedious, but I promise you, the more one hears of it, the less boring it becomes."

"You needn't fret about me, Elizabeth," Philippa said, smiling. "I grew quite accustomed to such talk at Wakefield's table, although I suppose I did not really attend to it, or I would be able to understand more of what is being said now. The niceties of the sport elude me, but I do like a good fast run with the hounds."

"I'd forgotten," said the dowager, "that you stayed in Leicestershire with Wakefield through the hunting season. That must have been dull for you. I know that his first wife flatly refused to leave Sussex in the wintertime."

"Well, I enjoyed myself," said Philippa, smiling. "Not that I was able to hunt other than when we visited here, of course, for I fear Wakefield was a trifle old-fashioned in that regard."

"All Leicestershire is a trifle old-fashioned in that regard," said the dowager tartly.

"Why, how can *you* say so, ma'am, when the duke has very kindly permitted me twice to hunt with the Belvoir? Indeed, he has invited me to do so again," she added, turning her smile upon Rutland.

His eyes crinkled at the corners, but though he said nothing, his brother was not so reticent. "Dash it all, why should she not hunt with us occasionally?" Lord Robert inquired. "Not at all the thing to do with the Quorn or Cottesmore, of course. All those rowdy young sprouts riding neck-or-nothing, and not a courtesy to be found amongst the lot of them. But when Mama rides with the Belvoir, not a word of language does one hear that one ought not to hear. The very thing for you, Lady Philippa."

Alvanley was grimacing, and it was as much to forestall any words he might utter that would set the dowager off that Philippa said quickly, "I shall enjoy it, of all things, I promise you, sir, but you must know that I shan't often be able to travel so far. 'Tis all of seventeen miles from Chase

Charley to Belvoir, and I fear I am not sporting enough to enjoy getting up in the dark and returning in the dark."

"But you must stay here when you hunt, of course," said the duchess, laughing. "How absurd you are, Philippa, to think we should expect you to ride here and back in a single day, and hunt as well."

"But that is what the men do, is it not? They hire horrid little houses in Melton Mowbray so as to be as near the three great hunts as possible. Then they ride to Charnwood Forest to hunt with the Quorn on Monday—or is that the Friday hunt? Not that it signifies, of course," she added, shaking her head. "For the next day, they are off to Belvoir or to Oakham to ride with your pack or the Cottesmore. They are not such poor honeys as to need to rack up overnight."

General laughter followed her description of the Melton men, but no one contradicted what she said of them, although Lord Alvanley took exception to her description of the horrid little houses.

"I darethay my house ought not to incur your disdain, Lady Philippa. A very cozy box, I promith you."

"Yes, I have heard that you purchased that charming little house across from the George, my lord. I've no doubt you find it quite comfortable."

"Having spent a small fortune to make it so, he dashed well ought to find it comfortable," said Lord Robert with a wink.

"Money," groaned Alvanley. "Mutht we alwayth talk of money?"

"Not rolled up yet, are you?" asked Rochford.

"Not yet," admitted his lordship, "but if my uncle don't path on soon, it will be bellowth to mend with me, I promith you."

"We will have no such vulgar talk at this table," said the dowager severely.

Philippa looked quickly down at her plate, for as the old lady spoke, she had no difficulty seeing her in her mind's eye as she must have been that night at the opera when she had damned Fox before the entire *beau monde*. No vulgar talk, indeed. When she had herself in hand well enough to venture looking up, she was unfortunate enough to look directly into

Rochford's eyes. Was it her imagination or was there a twinkle lurking there? Not daring to look long enough to make sure, she turned quickly to the duke.

"You were saying earlier, sir, that the Wyvern hounds are considered to be as fine as your own?"

Rutland smiled. "Perhaps not *as* fine, ma'am, but fine enough. I think I may say without fear of contradiction that the Wyvern color is not so perfect as the Belvoir, but then, our hounds are particularly well-noted for their bright yellow color. And it is true, also," he added, raising his voice with just the suggestion of a provocative note, "that their cry is more musical to the discerning ear."

"They are as fast," declared Alvanley before Rochford might take up the lightly veiled challenge, "and that ith more important. Who careth what they thound like. Hounds serve no purpose other than to give us a direction in which to point our horses' headth, after all."

Lord Robert Manners and Rochford both entered enthusiastically into argument with Alvanley over this piece of impertinence, just as though there had been no ladies present, Philippa thought.

"At this rate," said the duke to her in an undertone, "you will have learned a great deal about hunting, and certainly a good deal more of the language of sport, before you return to hunt with us, my lady."

Philippa chuckled. "I shall, indeed, sir. I must confess, however, that I share Lord Alvanley's belief that the riding is the best part of the hunt. I was not in at the kill when I was here before, nor do I have any desire to be there in the future. To see any small animal suffering must be repugnant to me. But the chase itself—ah, the hard riding and the jumping—there is the thrill, I think."

"There are many who agree with you," replied the duke, "and here in Leicestershire, I daresay as many foxes go free as are caught. There are those of us who believe that a fox who successfully avoids the pack long enough to go to ground will be around for a second day's sport, you see. 'Tis a pity you will not be here often. My mother would enjoy your company. Even on the days she rides, there are few ladies to accompany her."

"Well, I confess I should much prefer to find a hunt nearer to Chase Charley, so that I might hunt whenever I wished. It seems a pity to me that more women do not hunt in the shires. I know many who would like to, many who have hunted with their family packs over pretty dull ground."

"Perhaps they prefer what you call dull ground," the duke said gently. "Leicestershire hunting sets an incredibly fast pace, you know, not one for gently bred females."

"I think gently bred females can often ride just as well as gently bred males," Philippa said firmly, "and I can tell you, sir, I mean to discover whether Mr. Assheton-Smith or Lord Lonsdale can be convinced to agree with me."

"Well, good luck to you," said the duke, "but I fear you will have little success."

"Then I shall ask Rochford to permit me to hunt with the Wyvern," said Philippa matter-of-factly, only to be dismayed when she realized that the argument had ended and the others had fallen silent. They had all heard what she had said. She looked at Rochford, feeling warmth surge into her cheeks at sight of the mocking glint in his eyes.

"Well, Rochford?" The dowager regarded him challengingly. "What have you to say to that, sir?"

"I say 'tis an interesting proposition," replied his lordship promptly, "and one that deserves careful consideration."

"Humph," said the dowager, sharply signaling to her daughter-in-law that it was time to leave the gentlemen to their port.

But Philippa took heart from the fact that the viscount had not delivered a flat negative, and as she followed the other ladies back to the pink saloon, she told herself that if she could not contrive to convince Assheton-Smith or Lord Lonsdale, she would bring Rochford round her little finger, one way or another.

Conversation in the saloon turned to household affairs and children, and the duchess took this opportunity to send for the latest addition to her nursery. There was sufficient time for the other ladies to coo over the young Marquess of Granby and to tell his proud mama how very like his handsome papa he looked before the gentlemen entered the room and the nursemaid was directed to take his young lordship back to his crib.

Lord Robert was speaking as the gentlemen came in, and he seemed to be distressed. Clearly, Philippa thought, the conversation was one begun in the passageway, for they would not ordinarily have carried their port talk to the saloon. "I say, Rutland," said Lord Robert, "you will have your hands full if someone else gets up to William's tricks."

"What's that you say?" demanded the dowager. "Has someone threatened to post his land, Rutland?"

"Not yet, madam," replied her eldest son calmly. "I merely expressed the hope that this season would see no more of that nonsense."

"Well, so I should hope." Seeing the bewildered looks on Philippa's and Miss Pellerin's faces, she added impatiently, " 'Tis all nonsense, just as he says. Three years ago, Sir William Manners, a kinsman who is no longer welcome in this house, got a bee in his head and came to the conclusion that Rutland had robbed him of his due electoral influence at Grantham. All poppycock, as I said before, and the details are of no consequence to anyone. But the idiotish man retaliated by stopping the duke from hunting over his land and got thirty-five farmers to bring actions for trespass against the Belvoir hunt."

"Mercy me!" exclaimed Miss Pellerin, her hands fluttering in her lap. "Did he actually find a magistrate who would hear such a case?"

"Man'th got a right to hunt damn well anywhere he liketh," said Alvanley in mellow tones, indicating that he had enjoyed perhaps a bit more than his share of the ducal port. "Destroying pestilential beasth, after all. Doing everyone a dashed favor."

"Coming it too strong, there, Alvanley," said Rochford with a lazy smile. " 'Tis absurd in this day and age to argue that people feel it is their duty to hunt foxes solely in order to destroy noxious animals. No one will believe, no matter how you might choose to stretch their imaginations, that clergymen descend from their pulpits, bankers neglect their counting houses, brewers run away from their breweries, or that tradesmen, clerks, and others desert London for six full months of the year in order to rid the poor overrun farmers of Leicestershire of their foxes."

"Indeed, Alvanley," said Lord Robert, "considering that you yourself fined one of the gamekeepers at your manor house in Cheshire last year for killing two foxes before they could be hunted, you can hardly claim that there is any object other than our own amusement to be had out of the sport."

"But can you actually be sued for trespass?" Philippa asked.

'Yes," replied Rutland with a wry grimace. "A case in London four years ago set the precedent, and my dear cousin took advantage of it the following year."

"Then he won his action?"

"He did not," declared the dowager.

"Well, that is not precisely the case, you know," said the duchess before her husband could speak, "for Rutland paid what Sir William demanded, and the row ended before it was well begun."

"Didn't want to chance losing the sport," said Rutland with his gentle smile. "There was quite a rash of suits at the time, but they've subsided."

"The threat still exists," said his brother, rather grimly, Philippa thought. "Never know but what I'll scrabble through a bullfinch just for the fun of finding a damned 'No Trespassing' sign on the other side. Excuse me, Mama, but 'tis more than a fellow can stomach. What is one to do if the fox don't read the sign?"

"Well, you know, Robert," said the duchess, "we really needn't worry too much here in Leicestershire, for our tenants all have reason to support the hunt. 'Tis only in more hostile territory, where the tenants' good offices have not been so carefully cultivated, that hunters need keep a lookout for signs. I daresay you'll not find a single one in all of these three counties."

"Perhaps not," retorted her brother-in-law, "but I for one don't like knowing the possibility even exists."

"You are a justice of the peace, Alvanley," said Rochford. "Surely you ought to be able to find a precedent that will supersede the London decision. I was not in England at the time, of course, but there must have been some opposition to their case."

"Humph," said the dowager, who had remained silent longer than was her custom. " 'Tis all very well to call that young man a justice, but that don't make him a man of law any more than his having been a captain in the Fiftieth Foot and a member of the Coldstream Guards makes him a soldier."

"Well, ath to that," said the short, round baron, "I liked the uniform, don't you know, and a man mutht eat. But I do recall that the London case wath brought by disgruntled landowners who didn't like the hunterth tramping down all their newly sown wheat. Called it 'intolerable damage on valuable land,' as I recall it. It wath the Old Berkeley Hunt they wath after, and the OBH rethponded thtupidly by treating the whole with indignation, thaying it wath all private pique and perthonal resentment. They also inthisted they had the right to hunt and went tho far as to smash the top rail of a gate to let their mathter get to hith houndth after he had been warned off by Lord Essex's gamekeeper. 'Twath Essex who brought the action."

"Of course, Essex himself is a hunter, so it was easy for him to convince the court that he didn't oppose hunting in general but only the conduct of the OBH in particular," said Rutland. "Made it difficult for the rest of us when the suits began flying fast and furious."

"Theems to me," said Alvanley, who had clearly been thinking furiously as a result of the dowager's setdown, "that since all land came originally from the crown, 'tith the crown which held hunting rights over all of England. Logically then, the king—or in point of prethent fact, the Regent—should hand over these rights to the local pack. Then hunting would have a prethise, legal status."

The duchess's gurgling laughter burst forth. "Cannot you see his face, Rutland, if you were to request that Prinny grant you the hunting rights for the Belvoir hunt over that part of the three counties you are most like to cover?"

The duke smilingly suggested it would be as well for the success of the forthcoming christening festivities if the subject did not come up, and even Lord Alvanley joined in the laughter that followed. It was quite well known that the

Prince Regent, despite his oft-avowed love of sport, was more apt to respond to such a suggestion in the manner of a superannuated baby than in that of a dignified monarch ruling on a point of law. He was, at the best of times, a good deal more likely to sulk, wheedle, simper, or throw tantrums than he was to act decisively.

Since none of them was foolish enough to insult the Regent outright in such company, the conversation soon turned to other matters, and it was not long before the party broke up and its members made their way back to their separate bedchambers. As Philippa and Miss Pellerin walked together along the passageway leading to their rooms, Philippa congratulated herself upon having so neatly set matters in train that would presently allow her to hunt.

" 'Tis a very good thing," she told her companion, "that I may rely upon Rochford if the others fail me, for I am persuaded that even men who might otherwise follow me to my doorstep will have no interest in wealthy widows on the hunting field."

"Rochford did not say you might hunt with the Wyvern," Miss Pellerin pointed out gently.

"No, he did not, but neither did he say he would not permit it, and I believe he does have a wish to please me, you know," Philippa replied with a knowing smile.

"Philippa, such immodesty does not become you."

"No, ma'am, to be sure, it does not. I beg your pardon." After a brief pause, she essayed another topic. "I like the duke very much, do not you?"

"Indeed, Rutland is very kind. He seems to lay his money out rather recklessly in building and no doubt for his hunting, but I believe he does not game or squander his funds idly," opined Miss Pellerin before adding conversationally, "I knew him better when he was younger, of course. I daresay the forthcoming christening will provide much the same ill-conceived hilarity as did his coming of age. I was a guest at that celebration, which took place at Haddon Hall, and besides the seventy-odd gentlemen who dined and the hundred other ladies and gentlemen who attended the ball that evening, there were some two hundred fifty tenants and another ten thousand or so residents of Leicestershire, Lincolnshire, and

Rutlandshire who came to wish him well. I believe all who wished to be drunk were so, which comprised a considerable number, as you may imagine."

"Goodness," said Philippa, but her thoughts were already wandering. Although the thought of hunting while she was in Leicestershire had previously been a vague notion at best, she was rapidly coming to believe that she would like nothing better than to fling herself onto a good strong horse and follow the field neck and crop over every ditch and rail, pounding after the baying yellow hounds with the wind blowing in her hair and her skirts flying. Ah, it was a delicious thought, indeed. Now, if only Rochford or one of the others might prove to be sufficiently conciliating to answer her purpose.

—5—

BY THE TIME Philippa had been two days back at Chase Charley, she had decided it would be all the better to ride with the Quorn or the Cottesmore if such an opportunity might be arranged than to put herself under an obligation to Lord Rochford by cajoling him into allowing her to ride with the Wyvern. Accordingly, on the third day, a dismal, very cold Monday, having set Jessalyn to the disagreeable task of memorizing a number of improving verses in their absence, she dressed herself in a fashionable carriage dress of gray-and-brown Spanish kerseymere with Cordovan half-boots and York tan gloves and, accompanied by her ever-obliging companion, sallied forth to Quorndon Hall.

It was a journey of slightly under fifteen miles, for the hall was situated a mile and a half southeast of Loughborough, which itself lay to the west of Melton Mowbray. Thus it was that, at ten o'clock, greeted by the chimes in St. Mary's church tower, Philippa's carriage entered Melton Mowbray by the Oakham Road, one of the six main roads which formed the popular town. These roads were flanked by stone and stucco houses, mostly residences of the townspeople, some of which were more than a century old and nearly all of which were discreet and modest within their walled gardens.

The lodges, or hunting boxes, which had sprung up everywhere during the past fifteen to twenty years as a result of the near-mania for hunting in Leicestershire, were considered by those same residents to be a vast disfigurement upon the landscape, for the pretentious, overgrown red-brick villas, each with stabling for twenty to thirty horses, simply sprawled without rhyme or reason around the outskirts of the little town. Their general architectural style might tactfully be described as Elizabethan Gothic—the residents were more likely to call them just plain ugly—but in any event, they were badly planned, with rooms that were dark and gloomy. Their alternatives, the George Inn and the Harborough Arms, could in no way be described as first-class; yet, for such accommodations as these, for six months out of the year, the highest and mightiest of the land left their more accommodating estates and flocked to Melton Mowbray to live in discomfort so that they might chase the wily fox.

As the carriage passed the beautiful little church known as much for its lovely Georgian pews and gallery as for the melodious chimes in its tower, and entered the central square where the six roads converged, Philippa was relieved to discover that Melton Mowbray was bustling with nattily dressed sporting gentlemen. She had feared she would find Mr. Assheton-Smith away from home, since Monday was a day particularly set aside for the Quorn's fastest, most popular hunts; however, she had had it on the authority of her young footman Stephen, a hunting enthusiast, that no one would wish to hunt with the ground frozen hard, as it seemed to have been overnight.

"Won't carry a scent," he had said loftily at the breakfast table that morning. " 'Tis one thing after a slow freeze, m'lady, but quite another when the fields freeze over quickly after being soaked through, like they've been. November scent be right flighty, they say."

Of course, it was entirely possible that so intrepid a hunter as Mr. Thomas Assheton-Smith was known to be might have gone out regardless. But Philippa was ready to take the chance he had not, in order to speak with him.

Their coachman followed the Nottingham Road to Grimston, then crossed the river to turn south through Barrow-upon-Soar to Quorndon Hall. The hall itself would have been pretty, Philippa thought as the carriage passed through the entrance gates, were it not surrounded by kennels and stables. That it was, was not particularly surprising, of course, since according to her knowledgeable footman, the Quorn's kennels were the second most extensive in all England, and one of the stables alone held twenty-eight horses so arranged that when a spectator stood in the center of it his eye commanded each individual animal. The young footman had further informed her that the stables were provided with seats and lighted by powerful lamps, so as to form a high treat to the eye of any sportsman on a winter's evening. In addition to this, he assured her, there were any number of loose boxes, and even an exercise ride under cover, for bad weather.

"I do hope Mr. Assheton-Smith is at home," she said now to her companion. "He is said to be nearly as determined a hunter as Squire Osbaldeston, you know, but Stephen Footman assured me that he would not go out upon such a day as today."

She looked pointedly at the young footman, who had swung down from his perch at the back of the carriage when it stopped and was at that moment opening the carriage door and letting down the steps. His twinkling eyes told her he had heard her, but his expression was properly blank as he extended his hand to assist her from the carriage.

He hurried ahead of them, so that by the time they had ascended the broad white steps of Quorndon Hall, the front door had been opened wide, and a butler who looked quite elderly enough to have been passed along with the property to the various Masters of the Quorn bowed low and admitted them to the entrance hall.

The ladies were guided at once into a drawing room that, despite the clear lack of a feminine touch, was perfectly comfortable. They were not offered refreshment, only the information that their host would be along shortly.

Mr. Thomas Assheton-Smith, at thirty-seven, was not a man noted for his mastery of the social graces nor for the evenness of his temper, but he was cordial enough when he entered his drawing room, and if he was astonished to find that masculine chamber in the possession of two ladies of quality, he gave no more sign of his emotion than a slight tightening of his narrow lower jaw and a wary glint in his deep-set blue eyes. He was tall for a hunting man, being a shade over five-foot-ten in his boots, but he was very thin—not more than ten stone—and built like whipcord, with hands that looked a size too large for the rest of him. His dark hair was neatly though not fashionably styled, and his well-cut brown coat hung loosely from his lanky shoulders. Even his buckskins fit him loosely, as though he could not bear to be confined in modern, tight fashions. If his bow was casual, it did not lack polish, for Mr. Assheton-Smith was a man of breeding, having descended from an excellent family and having, moreover, enjoyed the benefits of an Eton-and-Oxford education. His general manner, however, was more that of a curt country squire than that of a gentleman, and he seemed, once Philippa and Miss Pellerin had introduced themselves, to be under the impression that they had come to collect a subscription for the church poor box at Barrow-upon-Soar.

"Always glad to dig into m' pockets for a worthy cause, ladies. How much d'ye need?"

Philippa chuckled, extending her hand to him as he stepped nearer. "I cannot blame you for thinking we have come to dun you, sir,' she said, "for I cannot believe you have had many ladies approach you with the object I have in mind."

"And what object might that be, ma'am?" he asked, just touching her hand with two fingers of his own.

"Why, to hunt with the Quorn, sir. I should account it a great privilege if you would allow me to join the meet for your Friday hunt," she added, rushing her fence.

"Ladies don't hunt in Leicestershire," Mr. Assheton-Smith said flatly.

"To be sure, 'tis not the fashion to do so at present, sir, but I have a fancy to set a new fashion. I ride very well," she went on quickly when she saw his eyes narrow, "so I shall not disgrace you, and I have hunted twice with the Belvoir without coming to grief."

"If you have never fallen, I cannot think you much of a hunter, ma'am," Assheton-Smith retorted, adding without a trace of false modesty, "I am accounted the best rider in the shires, you know. Rode cheap, small horses when I came here seven years ago and rode just as well on them as I do now on the living best, and I can tell you, ma'am, I have fallen in every field in Leicestershire. Once I fell eight times in a single run. Falling is a fine art, for there is no place you cannot get over with a fall, but if you have never fallen, then you have never learned to throw your heart over so that your horse may follow it. In short, ma'am, there is no place for you in my hunt."

"But surely," Philippa protested, "whether I come to harm should be my own concern, sir. You do not require that a gentleman must have fallen in a hunt before you allow him to ride with the Quorn."

"Different matter," he said shortly. He had not taken a seat but remained standing, glowering down at them. There was a small silence; then he repeated in even firmer tones, "Entirely different matter. Fact is, m'lady, a Melton hunt ain't no place for a woman. The fields are rowdy, and the men don't watch their language as they would in a drawing room. The pace is faster than anywhere else, and the riding rougher. Fact is," he added, glaring at her now, "the right place for a woman is a sofa, not a saddle, and that's the whole of it, rump and stump."

Though she longed to hit him, Philippa took leave of Mr. Assheton-Smith shortly thereafter with as much haughty dignity as she could muster. Thick silence ensued in the carriage until they had passed well beyond the gates of Quorndon Hall, and then, unable to contain herself a moment longer, she said explosively, "Dreadful man!"

"Well, do you know, I do not believe he is commonly accounted so," said Miss Pellerin conversationally. "He is very wealthy, you know, and he disapproves strongly of gambling and drinking, which must set a good example for all those young sportsmen who gather in Melton Mowbray to cut such capers every year. They say, too, that he goes to church every Sunday, and on foot, too, which accounts for his being so willing to donate his money when he thought we were seeking aid for the poor."

"They say," retorted her companion in minatory tones, "that he once kicked a sheepdog and then threatened to fight the shepherd merely for daring to get in the way of his precious hounds. So much for his setting a good example. He cannot even catch a wife, which is scarcely cause for astonishment when his appalling temper is legendary and his reputation for settling every dispute with his fists, I venture to say, is a good deal more widely known than his Sunday principles."

"No doubt you are in the right of it, my love, but I daresay you will find few people who will take your side in this matter. Though it made you angry to hear Mr. Assheton-Smith say so, most men, I fear, will agree with him and refuse to allow a woman in the hunting field."

"Pooh," retorted Philippa rudely. "Many women hunt with their families, all over England, just as I did at Toddleigh. 'Tis only in the shires that men are so fusty."

"But the society of true huntsmen is not such that a well-bred woman would seek to join them," said her companion in some distress. "Truly, my dear, you would not wish to sit with gentlemen over their port after dinner, as they say that dreadful Harriette Wilson did when she came into Leicestershire, and I am persuaded that sporting gentlemen behave much more disagreeably on the hunting field. You know perfectly well that gentlemen in gentlemen's company use language and manners which must only offend a lady."

"Then they must learn to behave better."

"Oh, but surely one would not wish them to be civilized all the time, as we poor females must be, for that would be to change them quite beyond recognition. I daresay any gentleman forced to maintain for an unlimited span of time that elevated standard set by polite society as acceptable to females would soon be driven to distraction."

"No doubt," said Philippa dryly, "but I do not desire to inflict my presence on them indefinitely, after all. I wish merely to share the excitement of the hunt. I do not even wish to be in at the kill, for one can imagine nothing so disgusting, nor yet so damaging to one's sensibilities—not to mention to the poor fox—as to watch a pack of hounds reaping the reward of a successful chase. I but long for activity—strenuous activity. I was used as a girl to ride hard and long on my father's estates in Yorkshire, which is much rougher ground, I promise you, than these grassy fields. Why, every field in Leicestershire is closely examined several times a week for holes down which an enterprising fox might dive at the height of the chase, and when such holes are discovered, they are immediately stopped up. In Yorkshire, one must always be as wary of the terrain underfoot as of what lies ahead."

"Well, as to that, I do not know, but they do say that

Leicestershire is hard-riding country. Perhaps," she added rapidly and in more conciliatory tones, "if you truly wish to ride with a field, you will indeed contrive to convince Rochford to allow you to ride with the Wyvern from time to time. That would be much wiser, I'm thinking, than to ride with the Quorn. Why, mercy me, my love, they say there can be as many as three hundred riders in a single field with Mr. Assheton-Smith. You cannot wish to ride in such a crush as that."

"Well, I am not by any means certain, either, that I wish to be beholden to Viscount Rochford," said Philippa. "I have thought about it, ma'am, and if he should be on the lookout for a wife, I can think of nothing more uncomfortable than to put myself in a position where he might believe me willing to pay serious heed to his addresses."

"But, my dear, you have only met the gentleman once."

"Once was enough, ma'am, truly. You must confess I have had a deal of experience in that regard, whatever my experience with hunting may be. At first he was merely polite, if you recall, when we met him with their graces in the saloon, but he did make a point at that time of establishing my relationship to Wakefield. Later, on the terrace, after I had spoken to Jessalyn and he had had words with his sister, he was much more affable." For a moment, involuntarily, she fell silent as she remembered the odd sensations that had taken hold of her body when he had smiled down at her, and it was almost as though Rochford were again beside her, right there in the carriage. Her skin tingled warmly at the thought of him, as though she expected to feel his touch. Really, she thought, the sensation was most disconcerting. Then, realizing that her companion must be expecting her to explain herself with somewhat more clarity, she added hastily, "You must see, ma'am, that not immediately having realized the full extent of my eligibility, he must have made inquiries in the meantime and discovered that I am completely worthy of his interest. Oh, dear, I sound exactly like a conceited schoolgirl, do I not?"

Miss Pellerin smiled gently, neither agreeing nor denying. "Mightn't he merely have spoken as he would, in a quite friendly fashion, to anyone who had been caught in such a coil as the two of you were caught up in, my dear?''

Philippa paused, considering this possibility. ''I suppose he might at that,'' she agreed slowly. ''I confess I should like to discover that I have misjudged him. Still, in the event that my first impression was the correct one, I believe I shall approach Lord Lonsdale tomorrow in the hope that it will not then be necessary to put myself under obligation to Rochford.''

''I do not believe your luck will be any the better with the Cottesmore than with the Quorn,'' replied her companion. '' 'Tis a smaller hunt, I believe, but I have never heard of any lady riding with it, although Letty Lade may have done so. You will not look to her to be a pattern card for your own behavior, however.''

''No, of course not. I should not like anyone to think of me in the same thought as Sir John Lade's wife or Miss Wilson, I promise you.'' Not that either thing would be likely, she told herself. Not when Harriette Wilson was an infamous courtesan and when Letty Lade's greatest claim to fame was the intriguing fact that she had once been mistress to a notorious highwayman with the interesting name of Sixteen-String Jack, who had perished—laughing, by all accounts—on the gallows at Tyburn Hill. Still, the thought put Philippa in mind of something else. ''Truly, ma'am, I have no wish to be thought fast—or to be the only female in the field, for that matter.''

''Well, I hope you are not expecting me to join you, Philippa, for I tell you to your face that I cannot consider such a thing at my age.''

Philippa glanced at the plump figure beside her and, with laughing eyes, declared that the exercise might do her companion a great deal of good.

Miss Pellerin replied placidly, ''No doubt it would, but I should infinitely prefer a daily walk round the garden if it is all the same to you, my dear.''

Philippa chuckled, but her mind was already occupied with the possibility of discovering other females who would support her cause. Surely there must be wives or daughters in some of the many hunting boxes around Melton Mowbray who would enjoy riding with the hunt.

''In any event,'' she said a moment later, as though there

had been no change in the course of their conversation, "I daresay I was acting out of some sort of ridiculous pride when I approached Mr. Assheton-Smith, for although they meet often at Melton, they are just as like to meet at Quorndon Hall, or Charnwood Forest, or even Ashby de la Zouch, which would make my joining them as inconvenient as riding with the Belvoir. After all, the Belvoir also meets at Melton occasionally. 'Tis clear I should have gone to Lord Lonsdale in the first place, Cottesmore Hall being little more than four miles from Chase Charley. The two estates march side by side, you know, with Wyvern running to the north of us both."

"I still believe you would be more comfortable with the Wyvern if his lordship will permit," opined Miss Pellerin. "After all, there is no telling but what his sisters may visit Wyvern Towers over Christmas, and they are no doubt excellent horsewomen. I must advise you against riding as the lone female with any hunt, Philippa. You would not like it at all."

"No," agreed Philippa slowly, "but I am persuaded that if Lord Lonsdale will agree to allow ladies to ride with the Cottesmore, a good number of others will turn out. If they do not, of course, that will be another matter."

Unfortunately for her plans, Lord Lonsdale, when she managed, with her ubiquitous companion in tow, to run him to earth the following day, proved as obdurate as Mr. Assheton-Smith in his refusal to contemplate the notion of allowing women to inflict their presence upon his hunt.

"All them skirts flying about'd frighten the horses," he declared. "Not the thing, Lady Philippa, not the thing at all." He was a bluff, hearty man of very good humor for the most part, but most unfortunately he stood some four inches shorter than Philippa herself, and he seemed to feel the difference sharply when first they met. Accordingly, his good temper deteriorated during the course of the conversation until, goaded by her insistence that he ought to give her an opportunity to prove herself before refusing his consent so arbitrarily, he began to speak in a very curt way indeed.

"I tell you, m'lady, you've not the least notion of what you would be about. A Melton man ain't no fit companion for a female. He don't want one around when he is enjoying his sport. Leastways," he amended, "not in the field, and the sort he enjoys afterward ain't respectable ladies like yourself. By God, ma'am, half the men you'd meet ain't even respectable themselves. Anyone can join a hunt, after all."

Philippa knew that much to be true. At Melton one's birth, looks, manners, or morals, within very broad limits, didn't matter. In any given hunt, an earl might as easily find himself riding neck and neck with a well-heeled local butcher or greengrocer as with a squire.

"There's no one more gay or reckless than the Melton man, m'lady," Lord Lonsdale said more gently, seeing her disappointment. "He cares neither for purse nor neck, reputation nor digestion. He's but spending a few years of golden youth before settling down in that state of life to which it has pleased Providence to call him, with happy memories of all the wicked things he believes he did in those glorious days when he hunted from Melton. 'Twould be to deny him those memories an I let a woman join the Cottesmore."

"Mercy me," Miss Pellerin said few minutes later in the carriage, "his lordship made all those dreadful young men sound very nearly saintly, did he not?"

Philippa's mouth had been drawn into a tight, thin line from the time they had taken their leave of Lonsdale, but at these words her angry expression relaxed and her lips actually twitched. When she glanced at Miss Pellerin, her eyes were twinkling. "He certainly did. One almost wished to weep at the thought of denying them their precious memories, like denying a puppy his mama's milk." She gave a little choke of laughter. "If the truth be known, his precious Melton men are, collectively, a mob of snobs without manners or morals—noisy, ignorant, and bad sportsmen."

" 'Tis a melancholy reflection and quite past common understanding," said her companion, "that the same gentlemen who behave so outrageously as to be the despair of the local people would in most cases individually regard the throwing of a sofa cushion when at home or being drunk in the presence of ladies as a deplorable breach of decorum."

"Very bad *ton*," said Philippa, still twinkling. But she sobered at once. "Those gentlemen of whom he speaks so fondly do indeed render themselves odious to the local people. Mr. Weems, my bailiff, was telling me that only last year a group of them offered the local cobbler a lift on their coach, and when the poor unfortunate man was halfway up, they started the team at a mad gallop with the poor wretch hanging on to the back as best he could until he was flung off into the road. On another occasion some so-called *gentleman* entered the village shop, which is kept by Mrs. Haversett, a charming old lady with gray ringlets. Weems said the gentleman ordered a pint of treacle and told her to put it into his hat. Mrs. Haversett told him the treacle would soil his hat but finally yielded to his insistence, whereupon he clapped the hat onto the dear old woman's head and ran out shrieking with laughter. Melton is often terrified by such hooligan tactics, Weems says. To my way of thinking, Lord Lonsdale's precious gentlemen could well do with a woman in their midst if it would curb such dreadful behavior."

"I am persuaded that you mean well, Philippa," said Miss Pellerin with a small shake of her head, "but I hope you do not think to change the ways of the Melton men all by yourself. You are frequently inclined, I fear, to leap into things without thinking them through, and in this case it will not do."

Philippa recalled that Wakefield had often said the same thing of her. Indeed, he had frequently compelled her to write out separate lists of the positive and negative aspects of any decision she might make regarding matters of business. But since it would be foolish to consider personal desires in the same fashion that one considered more important matters of business, her companion's words brought no more than another chuckle before Philippa said contritely, "I believe I have frightened you, Cousin Adeliza, but indeed I never meant to. My papa would say I've got a flea in my wig, and he would no doubt rant and rave and very likely succumb to the apoplexy he insisted my antics would bring upon him, but I beg you will not fall into the same error, for while I detest being told I cannot do something I wish to do, I have no true desire to force myself upon such a group as the one we have been discussing."

"So you will not hunt, after all, my dear. That is too bad, but indeed, I believe it is for the best."

"Not hunt?" Philippa regarded her wide-eyed. "Oh, no, ma'am, that is not what I meant at all. I do see now that it would be improper for me to foist myself on a large hunt when I should not have so much as the protection of its master, but there can be no harm to my joining the Wyvern if Rochford will look out for me."

"But he has not said he would," Miss Pellerin protested, looking flustered.

"No more he has," agreed Philippa. "However, I mean to write a civil note to him the minute we reach the house, asking him to bring his sister to dine with us tomorrow. Once he is sitting at my dining table, he can scarcely refuse to grant me one tiny favor, can he?"

She was to have her answer sooner than that, however, for when they arrived at Chase Charley, they were greeted by the information that Viscount Rochford had called and was awaiting their convenience in the library.

—6—

FEELING UNACCOUNTABLY EXCITED by the news of the viscount's presence, Philippa pulled off her hat and moved quickly to examine her reflection in the pier glass over the side table near the common-parlor door. Stripping her gloves from her hands and giving them into a footman's keeping along with her hat, she tucked a loose strand of golden hair into her otherwise smooth coiffure and decided she was presentable. With Miss Pellerin but a step behind her, she passed quickly through the parlor to the library, where she discovered Rochford in buckskins, riding boots, and a dark coat, sitting at his ease before a crackling fire, a leather-bound book lying open on his knee. When he saw them, he closed the book and got to his feet with leisurely grace.

"Good day, ladies. I trust I have not called at an inconvenient time. My little sister wished to visit with Miss Raynard-Wakefield, and as your butler seemed to believe you would arrive momentarily, I took the liberty of accepting his invitation to help myself to the books in here. A tolerable library, I must say."

"Thank you, sir," Philippa said, giving him her hand. "My late husband collected many of the books here, although with the exception of those volumes about hunting and Leicestershire history, he liked them more for the splendid show they make than for their content, I fear."

Rochford smiled. "My uncle, who is shortly coming to visit me, would count it a privilege to see this library, ma'am. He comes into Leicestershire, he says, for the hunting, but his nose is forever in a book, and our collection at Wyvern cannot match this one."

Taking her seat in a leather Kent chair on the other end of the hearth, Philippa said, "Your uncle is welcome at any time, sir. It would be our honor to receive him."

"Indeed it would," said Miss Pellerin, entering the conversation for the first time as she took her seat in a straight-backed chair that the viscount drew forward for her. "I believe you speak of the Honorable Mr. Archibald Drake, do you not?" When Rochford nodded, she continued enthusiastically as he sat down again, "Mr. Drake is accounted a very fine scholar, Philippa. I have never been privileged to meet him, but I once read a monograph he wrote on Elizabeth Woodville—Henry the Seventh's queen, you know—and I am persuaded that Mr. Drake's mind is infinitely superior to those of most gentlemen."

"He can become a curst bore on the subject of the fifteenth and sixteenth centuries if he's given his head, Miss Pellerin, and so I must caution you," said Mr. Drake's undutiful nephew, crossing one leg over the other.

" 'Tis only fair that I caution you in return, my lord," Philippa said in a confiding tone, her dark eyes atwinkle, "that such warning will but whet her appetite. I fear my dear cousin treads near the brink of being stigmatized for a bluestocking. She has to put a firm guard on her tongue in polite society in order to avoid giving herself away."

"Philippa!" Miss Pellerin was scandalized.

"But it is true, ma'am, and I daresay that ten minutes in Mr. Drake's company will unmask you, so it is as well that his lordship be warned."

"Very true," said Rochford, smiling at the older lady in such a way as might have caused a younger heart to leap in response, "though I must tell you, ma'am, that I find nothing amiss in a lady's having a well-informed mind. I have always thought such prejudice to be foolish beyond permission."

"Then you are an oddity, my lord," said Miss Pellerin flatly. "A female in this day and age who reveals even the most innocent knowledge of Greek or Latin, not to mention of history or philosophy, must have windmills in her head. My mother was used to wince whenever I would speak of things about which a female was expected to know nothing, and she believed to her dying day that my spinsterhood was due to my having too often revealed the depth of my studies."

"And was that the cause, ma'am?"

Philippa looked at him swiftly, suspecting impertinence, but Rochford looked merely interested and not at all as though he were roasting Miss Pellerin. The older lady also regarded him for a moment or two, solemnly, before she replied to his question.

"I do not believe so," she said then, slowly, "although it would be wrong to say that my education was not at all to blame. I received a number of eligible offers, though my papa did not agree with my mama's notion of what gentlemen were eligible, of course. You must know, sir, that Papa was the one who provided the books and encouraged my studies, for he believed that most young men and all young women waste their time in school. In principle I agreed with him, but had I met a gentleman who showed a modicum of common sense, and for whom I might have developed a tenderness, I daresay I might have married even had I not believed his learning equal to mine. In any event, though it was not to be, my life has been an interesting one and I do not repine. After all, had I been married with a family of my own, I should not have been at hand when dear Philippa had need of me."

"Indeed," said Philippa, "though I sound selfish to say it, ma'am, I am delighted that things worked out so that I might have you to myself."

Miss Pellerin regarded her fondly. "We rub along together tolerably well, do we not? Indeed, with this wonderful library and all the tasks we have to keep us busy, you need not trouble your head over such minor setbacks as you have encountered these past two days."

"Setbacks? How is this?" Rochford turned to Philippa, his harsh features softening as he looked upon her.

She felt warmth flooding her cheeks, both from the admiration she read in his gaze and the conscious hope that her companion had not prematurely introduced what might prove to be a ticklish subject. Careful to keep her tone light, she said, "Oh, 'tis the most bothersome thing, but I daresay Lord Lonsdale is in the right of it, that it would be more convenient, not to say more proper, for me to hunt with a private hunting party than with all the rowdy, devil-may-care Melton men who ride with the Cottesmore."

"Certainly, it would be most improper for you or any gently nurtured female to ride with the Cottesmore," agreed Rochford.

Scarcely what she had hoped he would say, but Philippa refused to be put off by so insignificant a detail as that. "Gently nurtured females ride with the Belvoir," she pointed out, smiling.

"I hope I have better manners than to contradict a lady, ma'am, but I believe that if you reconsider your statement you must admit that they do not ride with the open fields. As I recall the matter, Rutland did not extend an invitation to you to join them when the Belvoir meets at Melton."

"Will he never do so, then?" This possibility had not, in fact, occurred to her.

"No indeed. When you hunted with his pack, I daresay you saw no one you did not know in the field, or if there was a stranger, he was one who might properly be introduced to you; whereas, in a general hunt, one often has not the least notion who the man riding next to one may be."

"Well, I daresay you are perfectly right," Philippa said amicably, "which shows very clearly how wrong I was to apply to Mr. Assheton-Smith and to Lord Lonsdale at all, when I ought from the outset to have applied to you, sir. It becomes perfectly clear that the Wyvern is the hunt for me, for I am persuaded, sir, that you are rather more nice in your notions than to allow the scaff and raff to fling themselves into your runs. I may certainly rely upon you to invite only those gentlemen who may be trusted to treat a lady as they should."

Rochford's eyes gleamed in appreciation of her tactics, but he shook his head. "No, Lady Philippa," he said gently.

"No?" She bit her lip, then cocked her head a little to one side. "Do you mean to say, sir, that there are those amongst your friends who cannot be trusted to keep the line? For if that is the case, I promise you that I have had a vast amount of experience in dealing with such gentlemen. I do not fear them."

"No." This time the note in his voice was firmer. The gleam of amusement had faded.

They looked at each other, and Philippa found herself thinking that his features were not precisely harsh, after all, but merely weathered, no doubt as a result of his having spent so large a portion of the past years under the open sky. As he had been a soldier, one must expect that such had been the case. He was really rather pleasant-looking, actually. She had liked seeing amusement in his eyes. It was a pity it had gone, a pity, too, that he meant to be difficult. Really, the men of Leicestershire were proving to be an altogether obstinate lot. Or perhaps widowhood had dulled her feminine wiles. She had not been used to have such difficulty in persuading gentlemen to her wishes in the past, and she would, she knew, be particularly annoyed should the viscount prove to be immune to her wiles.

She dimpled, letting her smile come slowly as she raised her hands to fold them between her full, round breasts before leaning coaxingly toward him. "My lord," she said gently, "surely you cannot mean that you will not allow me to ride even the distance of a few fields with your hunt."

"I mean precisely that, however." He responded to her smile, but his own was rueful and his voice was bare of laughter when he continued, "I fear you still have little understanding of what hunting in this county is all about, my lady. 'Tis the pace that kills, not only the fox and horse, but also the nerve of the rider. I have no doubt that you have acquitted yourself well with the Belvoir pack on those days that Rutland allowed his mama or his duchess and her friends to ride with him, or that you have acquired more than a modicum of skill if you have hunted in Yorkshire, which is scarcely humbug country. But for those not brought up to hunting in Leicestershire, the fast pace and hard riding bring little pleasure. After suffering a few crumplers, galloping at a thorn-filled ditch ceases to be fun, whilst any other method of taking it would be suicide. Even the infamous Melton men come and go quickly. Only the most intrepid amongst them lasts more than three or four seasons before his banker's nerve fails, or he takes a wife, enters Parliament, succeeds to the family estates, or takes his own local hounds. After that, he may return to Melton occasionally, but twenty minutes of a clipping run is all the hunt he wants by then."

"But you are speaking once again of the general breed," she objected. "I have been told that one finds three hundred men or more in a field with the Quorn and at least half that many with the Cottesmore. The Wyvern is not so big, surely?"

"No, of course not. I have my pack out for my own pleasure and that of my particular friends, but that does not mean for a moment that riding with the Wyvern would be suitable for a woman. The runs are by far too dangerous and the pace too fast. I do not wish to alienate your friendship, however," he added, smiling again, "or to give you cause to compare me unfavorably with the duke, so if the idea finds favor, I shall undertake to promise that if my sisters should honor Wyvern Towers with their presence at Christmas as I believe they intend to do, I shall arrange a hunt for your pleasure and theirs as well. Will that satisfy you, ma'am?"

"Oh, how very kind," Miss Pellerin said, looking anxiously at Philippa. "You will like that prodigiously, my dear."

Philippa was not at all satisfied by such a compromise, but she realized that she would only put his back up if she pressed her argument any further. That he had not immediately agreed to grant her wish was disappointing but scarcely sufficient cause to cast her into the dismals. She would come about. Therefore, she smiled sunnily at him and assured him that she would above all things enjoy riding out with his sisters.

"Did you say that you had brought the Lady Lucinda to call?" she asked then. "That was kind of you, sir. I know poor Jessalyn has been feeling moped all the weekend, thinking herself sadly neglected one moment and ill-used the next. Nor was she happy to be left with orders to improve her mind by memorizing improving verses both yesterday and today. I fear I am in danger of becoming known as a strict, uncaring stepmother."

"Nonsense," replied the viscount stoutly. " 'Tis no more than either of those young ladies deserves after serving us all such a trick as they did. I should not have succumbed to Lucinda's entreaties today, except that I was of a mind to call here in any event, and I could not very well leave her behind. At present, Wyvern Towers is scarcely a proper abode for a very young lady."

"Is it not?" But even as the words were spoken, Philippa realized what he meant. "To be sure, sir, without cither of your elder sisters in residence, there can be no proper female to bear her company."

"She does not even have her own maid," said Rochford, "I have instructed one of the maidservants to attend her, but the girl is a local and hardly what Lucy is accustomed to. I must arrange to send her back to Bath as soon as possible, and that is why I have come to you. It occurred to me that you might have some notion of how we could send them back together. I have my chaise, but unless I send my own man as well as the maid, I have no servant I would trust with such a minx as Lucinda. I thought perhaps you might know of someone who would answer the purpose."

"I don't," Philippa said frankly. "Moreover, I must tell you, sir, that when I broached the subject of her return to Jessalyn, she pointed out that they will be but turning round again to come back here for Christmas. The Lady Elizabeth Manners is to remain at Belvoir until the new year, you see, which has put it into Jessalyn's head to insist that she wishes to do likewise. Angry though I am with her, I cannot but see that it is the sensible course to follow."

Rochford grimaced. "Very likely, but I can tell you it would mean putting my household at sixes and sevens to accommodate Lucinda."

"I suppose she could come to stay here," Philippa said slowly. She had not intended that her peaceful interlude should be disturbed by the antics of one young lady playing truant from school, let alone two.

But Rochford was already shaking his head. "That would not do, though you are kindness itself to offer. Such a plan would cut up all your peace. I suppose the sensible thing would be for me to hire a governess-companion for my sister, a good, strict one who would know how to keep her out of mischief. My father will be at Wyvern for Christmas, and will expect to see her there as well, so there can be no great objection to her remaining now if she might be properly attended. How do you suppose one goes about finding a governess in Leicestershire at this time of year?"

"I suppose we might inquire of the Duchess of Rutland. If she does not know of someone herself, I daresay she can tell us how to go about the business."

"I could give them lessons, you know," suggested Miss Pellerin calmly.

Philippa chuckled. "You would no doubt do them a great deal of good, ma'am, but if the Lady Lucinda is anything like our Jessalyn, they would be a sad trial to you. I doubt that Jess has two thoughts to rub together in that head of hers that do not have to do with young men and her future prospects."

"Lucy, too," said Rochford with a sigh. "A sillier chit I hope never to meet. Her ignorance would appall you, ma'am."

"On the other hand," said Philippa thoughtfully, "there is no reason that the pair of us could not undertake to instruct both girls in the sort of lessons they would have had at school. I am quite a dab at sketching, and I play the pianoforte well enough to help them with their practicing . . . that is, unless the Lady Lucinda plays upon the harp or some other instrument, sir. I confess I should be of little assistance to her in such a case."

"I'm not by any means certain she plays a musical instrument at all," said his lordship, grinning. "But, my dear ma'am, I have already said that I do not wish to impose upon your good nature, or Miss Pellerin's, in such a way."

"No, you said that you did not wish to burden me with your sister's continued presence in my house," Philippa said, smiling back at him and thinking it a pleasant exercise. "You see, sir, that I do not scruple to contradict a gentleman. My manners are not so nice as yours, I fear."

"You choose to treat this matter lightly, Lady Philippa, but I do not see any reason for inflicting my sister upon you in any way."

"Oh, but you are wrong, sir. Truly, if Jessalyn remains in Leicestershire, you would be doing me a favor to send the Lady Lucinda to us for lessons. Otherwise, I shall be my stepdaughter's sole source of entertainment, and that, I must tell you, would not suit me at all. If Lucinda is here to bear her company, Jessalyn's presence will be a pleasure. If she is to mope about, complaining that there is nothing to do, she will drive me demented."

"Then you leave me with no more to say," Rochford told her, his gray eyes resting warmly upon her, "for I should certainly not care to figure as your ticket to Bedlam. What do you propose?"

Finding it difficult to meet that gaze directly, she focused her eyes upon the uppermost button of his waistcoat and said briskly, rather as though she were relaying instructions to her footman, "If you can contrive to deliver Lucinda to us each morning and collect her again in the afternoon, I shall do my possible to see that her time with us is not ill-spent. Between us, Cousin Adeliza and I ought certainly to be able to set lessons for the girls in deportment, sketching, music, and perhaps even some botany, though what they will study outdoors at this time of year, I'm sure I cannot tell you."

"Oh, I brought a lovely book that will serve us well in that regard," said Miss Pellerin enthusiastically. "I showed it to you only the other day, Philippa, Mr. Culpepper's *Herbal*. You will remember—a delightful book with the most detailed drawings of all manner of plants and flowers. The girls will be fascinated."

Rochford chuckled. "You may contrive to fascinate Lucy with the pictures, ma'am, but if you can get her to read the text, you will truly have worked something of a miracle. I do not think she has read anything except for those dreadful romantic novels girls somehow contrive to get their hands upon no matter what precautions their elders take to prevent their doing so."

"Nonsense, Rochford," said Philippa in rallying tones, her amusement making it possible for her to meet his gaze again. "Surely she has read *La Belle Assemblée* and the *Ladies' Monthly*."

He grinned at her. "Indeed, ma'am, you are very right, and two sillier magazines for a fourteen-year-old chit I cannot conceive of. Only last evening she was informing me that I simply must send for a modiste to make her a pink gauze tunic dress to wear to parties. The one she showed to me within the pages of *La Belle Assemblée* would be quite amazingly improper on a married woman, let alone on a chit from the schoolroom."

Philippa sighed, twinkling at him. "I know how it is, sir, for I promise you that Jessalyn can be quite as ridiculous. But, in point of fact, that is how young girls develop sartorial taste, you know. They will not distress me by poring over such stuff as that."

"No, indeed," said Miss Pellerin, "for you are quite correct, Philippa. In such a manner do they learn what is suitable and what is not. And if they enjoy magazines, my dear sir, I shall be only too happy to share my *Literary Quarterly* with them. There are excellent tales to be read there, and every one of unexceptionable quality, I assure you."

"I do not doubt it, Miss Pellerin, but I fear that even if you could convince Lucy to poke her nose into such a work, she would not understand the half of what she read."

"Mercy me," said Miss Pellerin.

"Just so," returned his lordship with a grimace.

"Never mind all that," Philippa put in, laughing at both of them. "There is no cause to repine, after all, for have we not just been saying that it does a lady little good to stuff her head full of great literature and learning? Both Jessalyn and Lucinda will do very well for themselves if we can but contrive to bring them to a better sense of what is acceptable behavior and what is not. We can do that very well, Cousin, and so you must admit."

"Yes, of course, though it does seem a pity that they might never delve into anything more complex than a lady's magazine," said Miss Pellerin sadly.

"I think," Rochford said with gentle tact, "that my sister will benefit merely by being sometimes in your company, ma'am."

"Why, what a pretty compliment!" Miss Pellerin, flustered, smiled at him, then looked away as though she had been caught quite off her guard. "I venture to say, sir, that no one has said such a thing to me in thirty years. You are very kind."

"Nothing of the sort," he retorted, chuckling as he turned his quizzing gaze upon Philippa. "Only ask Lady Philippa if

I am kind. I suspect that she is still at outs with me over that little matter of the hunt. I hope, however, that she will find it in her heart to forgive me before many days have passed."

"Don't be absurd, sir, there is nothing to forgive save ignorance of my capabilities." Since she had attempted to cover her surprise at such an accurate reading of her state of mind by speaking dampingly, she found it annoying to hear her words tumble over one another as if they were in a great rush to be said. Still, she could not seem to stop the spate, and went on, saying even more quickly, "I do not bear a grudge, however, and to prove it to you, I hope very much that you do not mean to go away immediately, but will stay—you and your sister both, of course—to take supper with us. We dine early, so you may be assured of getting back to Wyvern Towers soon after dark."

He looked at her for rather a long moment, long enough in fact to bring a flush to her cheeks again, but then he grinned, succumbing to the invitation without a struggle. "To tell the truth," he said ruefully, "my sister has put a rub in the way of my social activities. I can scarcely go hunting or even drive into Melton Mowbray for an evening's revelry if it means leaving her to her own devices without so much as a sensible female to look out for her. Alvanley took supper with me last evening, so I have not been cut off entirely, but I must find someone soon—not a governess now, of course, for I do accept your generous offer and think it will answer very well—but someone whom I can trust to keep the chit out of mischief when I cannot be home of an evening."

"Or when you are entertaining, sir," Philippa said, dimpling. "It would not suit your notions of propriety, I venture to say, to look up from your carousing to find your sister, bright-eyed and fascinated, perched upon the stairway peeping between the balusters."

"Indeed, it would not," he admitted, adding gently, "but I do not carouse, my lady."

"Then you have nothing to fear," she retorted.

"Really, Philippa, you must not allow your sense of fun to lead you into making such improper statements," said Miss Pellerin, shaking her head in amused exasperation. "Lord Rochford will think you raised in a cow byre. I am persuaded, my lord, that if you were to inquire at the village shop of Mrs. Thing—what was her name, Philippa, the old lady with the ringlets?"

Rochford chuckled. "Mrs. Haversett, of course, and a very good notion that is, ma'am, for I am sure she will know of someone who would come to the Towers to look after Lucy when I am not by, or when I am, for all that," he added, grinning at Philippa.

"I must tell Bickerstaff that there will be extra covers to set," she said, rising.

Miss Pellerin sighed "Indeed, and I hope there will be no need for him to discuss the matter at length with Cook, my dear."

Rochford looked at her, then back at Philippa. "Lucy and I would be pleased to stay to supper, but I hope that does not mean we will be putting anyone out."

"No, no," Philippa reassured him, laughing again. " 'Tis only that we have a new cook, and she is very jealous of her dignity. Would you believe it, sir, she insisted upon having a room of her own instead of sharing with the kitchen maid, who is a very good sort of girl, and Cook wanted her meals served to her in the housekeeper's room, which of course did not suit Mrs. Bickerstaff's notions of what was due to her exalted station."

"Good Lord," said Rochford, fascinated. "What did you do?"

"I simply informed Cook that she would take her meals in the kitchen in order that I might be assured that the rest of the staff was well looked after by someone they could respect, and I pointed out that Mr. and Mrs. Bickerstaff have been so accustomed to dining in privacy that I was persuaded she would feel out of place no matter what pains they took to make her welcome."

Rochford nodded, his eyes crinkling with amusement. "I make you my compliments, ma'am. A neat solution."

"Well, I do not scruple to tell you that it taxed my patience, sir. I do not like Cheltenham drama amongst my servants, and I was sorely tempted to send Cook packing, but one does not do in Leicestershire that which one would have no qualm about doing in London. I do not like to cook."

"Gracious, do you know how?"

She nodded. "My mama had some odd notions about how daughters ought to be raised, you see. I daresay it comes of being kin to Cousin Adeliza, for they are first cousins, you know. But Mama insisted I should know as much as any of my house servants about managing a house. So I can cook and do plain sewing as well as fancy stichery, and I even know a weed from a flower in my garden, though I confess I do not know much more."

"That sounds like quite a lot to me," said Rochford. "My papa and your mama might have a few things in common, for he insisted that I should know all about our estates, and said that I could scarcely order a groom to do a chore that I knew not how to accomplish myself."

"Well," Philippa said with a laugh, "when Wakefield taught me to manage his affairs, he did not go so far as that, I am thankful to say, but I do know that gentlemen are often taught such things."

"Yes," agreed her cousin, "and you, my dear, were fortunate to have such a wise mama, for I have always thought it the oddest of circumstances that women who wish to marry their daughters off to dukes or earls have never given them the least notion of how to manage a great estate. Imagine if Rutland had married a silly wench with no more notion of how to go on than most, instead of Elizabeth Howard, who although she must have deplored her papa's tyrannical ways, must always be grateful that she received the benefit of his deep interest in farming and land management. Why, Rutland would scarcely have time for his hunting if all the burden of renovating Belvoir and running three large estates had fallen to his shoulders alone. Not but what, with his mama for an example, he would be most unlikely to have been attracted to a girl with no gumption."

"No, indeed, ma'am," said Rochford, his eyes twinkling. "Believe me when I say that I should take it most kindly if you were able to instill some notions of household management and habits of economy into my sister whilst you have the opportunity. One thing I did not mention about that gown from the magazine is that it would cost three hundred guineas, if it cost a shilling, to have it made up. She has informed me, moreover, that the allowance Papa makes her is too small to allow her to contrive at school. What on earth can she find to spend money on in Bath?"

Both Philippa and Miss Pellerin laughed heartily at his confounded look and proceeded to list for him those things which a young lady in Bath might certainly wish to buy. As she aided her cousin in this endeavor, Philippa remembered at last to pull the bell and inform Bickerstaff that there would be guests for dinner. When the butler had gone away again, the conversation continued in an amiable vein until they were joined by the two younger ladies, who exclaimed their excitement at learning that they were not, after all, to be returned to their seminary but might, if they were good, remain in Leicestershire until after Christmas. After that, it was not long before Bickerstaff stepped into the library to announce that dinner had been served in the dining room.

Altogether, Philippa decided as Alice, her abigail, helped her to prepare for bed that night, the afternoon and evening had gone very well. The viscount and his sister had proved to be excellent company. Indeed, she could not remember having enjoyed a more relaxed, more amusing occasion. As she pulled the eider quilt up to her chin, she recalled the way the viscount's gaze had so often and so tenderly come to rest upon her, and she lay back against her pillow, believing that time would be her friend. Not for long would such a warmhearted man be able to deny her her greatest wish.

—7—

DESPITE HEAVY RAINS and strong winds during the night, Wednesday morning dawned bright and sunny, and warm enough so that when Philippa stepped out onto the park-front terrace before breakfast there was steam rising from the lawn and a strong scent in the air of decaying leaves from the borders and the nearby park. Gathering the train of her russet-colored riding habit, she hurried down the gray stone steps to the gravel path that led across the northwest corner of the garden to the stable pavilion. She had sent word ahead that she wished to ride, so her groom, Jake Pottersby, had her covert hack saddled and ready for her.

"Good morning, Jake," she said, smiling, "and good morning to you, too, Mr. Weems," she added, speaking to the older, rather stout man who had been speaking to Pottersby. Both men removed their caps and returned her greeting, Pottersby cheerfully, Weems with his customary doleful reserve.

"Expect the wheat's done been drowned in its fields, m'lady," the older man said, "what with that downpour 'n all. First, there be so little rain a man might fear t' see 'is wells go dry, and puts off plantin' 'is winter crops. Then, 'e no sooner gets the seed in the ground than it be washed away."

Philippa shook her head at him, twinkling. "Truly, Mr. Weems, I don't think the wetting it got last night was enough to do any damage. We must be grateful rain came with that wind so that all the loosened topsoil wasn't blown away. And I daresay," she added thoughtfully, "that there is a deal more damage to the wheat from the hunters always riding through the fields than from the elements, when all is said and done."

Weems regarded her as though he knew not what to make of a woman who could speak so glibly of topsoil, let alone anything more complicated, and Philippa struggled to suppress her amusement. She had realized a week before, within moments of letting her bailiff know she would be taking a strong interest in his activities, that he didn't know quite how to deal with her. She smiled at him when he remained silent. "Come now, Mr. Weems, you know very well that you tend to look on the gloomy side of things. Confess that you are not truly fretting over the wheat at all but have come to discuss with Jake here whether today will be a good one for the hunters. 'Tis all you Leicestershire men think about, I'll warrant."

"Not all, m'lady," Weems said, but his attitude was a little less stiff. "Like as not, yer in the right of it about them fields. Right in the path t' the Whissendine crossing that north wheatfield be. Be right more than Tom Giles can do t' keep that field in seed. Not with upward of three hundred hunters a-crossin' of it two and three times in a week."

"Gracious, then I cannot think why he sows that field at all!" Philippa exclaimed. "I collect that Mr. Giles is the tenant for that particular farm, but I must say that to sow and resow seems a dreadful waste of his manpower and my money."

"Damages," said the bailiff succinctly, exchanging a look with the groom.

Jake Pottersby nodded wisely. "Aye, sithee, mistress, 'e bahn make a sight more off t' damages nor ye gain from t' wheat. Happen ye got other fields fer wheat. That north field be t' only one by way o' being in direct line o' the crossing, howsomever."

"You mean to say we plant a field just so that we can claim damages from the hunts each year?"

"Aye, m'lady, that's near enough the mark," said Weems.

"Well, I cannot approve of that," Philippa said, shaking her head. "Surely Tom Giles need not plant that field at all but can put it to grass to pasture some of our dairy cattle."

"Can't do that," said Weems, looking scandalized. "Fouls the scent. We keeps the cattle in barns through the winter, m'lady. Agreement with the hunts, ye ken."

Philippa bit her lip. "Of course. I had forgotten we had

such an agreement, but I still think we ought to let that north field go to grass until spring, Mr. Weems."

"Ye'll 'ave t' speak with Giles, then, m'lady, 'n 'e ain't goin' t' like the notion, I'm thinking. He goes shares on the damages, half and half with the old lord . . . that is, wi' yerself, I expect."

"With the estate, you mean," Philippa said. "I see, so Mr. Giles augments his income by claiming damages from the hunt, is that right?"

'Aye," said Weems, showing relief that she understood the matter at last.

"Then you are to give Mr. Giles no more seed," Philippa said firmly. "He may claim whatever damages he thinks fair, but to plant and replant under the circumstances is not sensible. I daresay he will not be able to collect for more than one crop in the field, in any event."

Weems shrugged. "Kin claim nigh well what 'e wants t' claim, m'lady. Hunt allus pays. Can't afford to set up any backs by refusin'."

Philippa remembered the Duke of Rutland saying much the same thing when he explained why he had paid his cousin rather than battle him in court. She shook her head again and asked Pottersby if her mount was indeed ready.

"Aye, mistress, and full o' gig." He stepped nearer the tall roan gelding and patted its cheek. The roan tossed its head and pawed nervously at the ground, whickering. Pottersby smiled. "Always like this after a storm. Nobbut all-alive 'n framing t' fratch. Ye'll want to keep a sharp eye and a firm rein, look how."

Nodding, Philippa turned back to Weems. "On my way here this morning I noticed that the pond by the entrance to the park is spilling over its banks. Today is as good a day as any if you have some young men to put to cleaning it. I daresay there's a good bit of silt built up by now if it hasn't been attended to these two years or more."

The bailiff nodded. "Set 'em to it immediate, ma'am. Can't rightly say when the last time was it was done. I've put a couple of lads onto thinning out that ash coppice north o' the park, too. Ye'll 'ave a good bit o' firewood out o' that fer the big house, as well as fer the kitchens."

He turned away a moment later, clapping his cap back onto his head and striding purposefully from the stableyard. Philippa allowed Pottersby to give her a leg up into her saddle, then waited for him to mount his own horse.

"Where to, this mornin', mistress?"

"Toward Melton, I think. I want a gallop. What sort of hunters have we got in the stables, Jake?"

"Got two cobby young'uns the young lord sent up from Oxford," Pottersby replied, raising his voice as she turned toward the drive and urged her mount to a trot. "Noan so much trained, I'm thinkin', though me 'n young Ned Owen been workin' 'em. Got a couple of older fellows, too, but happen ye'll do better t' sell 'em or use 'em fer cover hacks than to hunt 'em."

"Well, I need at least two good hunters who can be trained to carry a sidesaddle, Jake, and I need them as soon as possible."

The groom rode up alongside her. "Two, m'lady?"

She nodded, looking straight ahead of her. She had known Jake Pottersby since her childhood in Yorkshire, and she did not wish to give him the impression that she would listen with any patience to remonstrations from him.

He took the hint. "Happen it'd be best an ye get Leicestershire hunters, born 'n bred, then, Miss Philippa. Can't do better nor that, look 'e how. Happen ye could find a rare nesh nag or two through Lord Lonsdale or Mr. Assheton-Smith."

"No, thank you, Jake. Not unless there is no other way. I daresay they might even refuse to sell me one, just out of masculine contrariness."

"I'll ask about, then, shall I and all, Miss Philippa?"

She nodded, and then as they came to the Oakham Road, she touched the roan's flank with her spur, leaned forward slightly, and dropped her hands. The roan was quick to take her meaning, and his stride lengthened smoothly and quickly until he was galloping full out.

By the time they returned to Chase Charley, the steam was off the grass and tiny white clouds were gathering over the western horizon. Just wisps, they were, but Philippa found herself hoping they were not precursors of another storm. She was looking forward to playing governess, and the Lady

Lucinda Drake was expected to arrive for her first lessons with Miss Raynard-Wakefield at half-past ten. Another downpour might prevent her from coming.

Philippa found that her fears were being echoed in the breakfast parlor when she joined her cousin and stepdaughter there a half-hour later, having changed from her habit into a becoming morning gown of fawn tabinette with cherry satin ribbons tied at the high waist and threaded through the blond lace trim at the bodice edge.

"Do you think it will rain again, ma'am?" Jessalyn asked anxiously around a mouthful of well-buttered apple muffin. "Cousin Adeliza says it will not, but there are clouds forming on the horizon, don't you know, and it did rain ever so hard last night, so it may very well do so again, and if it does, then Lucy might not come, after all."

"Goodness, Jessalyn, draw breath!" Philippa exclaimed, laughing. "You prattle like a bagpipe, child."

"Do let your stepmama fill her plate, at least, before you press her for a weather report, Jessalyn," said Miss Pellerin with a wry grimace, "and have the goodness to remember to wait until you have quite finished what you are chewing before you speak. A lady does not talk with her mouth full of food."

Jessalyn swallowed hastily. "But I fear that Lord Rochford will not allow Lucy to come to us if it comes on even to mizzle, and certainly he will not do so if we get another storm like we had last night. It well nigh blew the house down."

"Hardly that," Philippa said, taking her seat and nodding to Stephen to fill her coffee cup before adding shrewdly, "I daresay his lordship is keeping just as anxious an eye on the weather as you are, my dear. He will see that the Lady Lucinda gets to Chase Charley though there be a snowstorm, I believe." She glanced at her cousin. "Do you not think so, ma'am?"

Miss Pellerin smiled at her. "I do, indeed," she said. "He seemed most anxious to provide her ladyship with proper companionship, so I have not the least doubt that half-past ten will see her on our doorstep."

Her prediction proved to be an accurate one, for Lady

Lucinda Drake arrived punctually, accompanied by her brother, who was looking precise to a pin despite the fact that he was dressed for riding rather than for paying morning calls, in buff leather breeches and top boots. His dark blue coat had been cut by a master, and he wore a proper neckcloth rather than the Belcher handkerchief preferred by most of the young bloods of sport. He carried a riding whip, but as he explained to the ladies in the stone hall, where they had been sitting by the fire, though he had indeed ridden over, he did not intend to leave the carriage for his sister's convenience.

"I don't care for being clapped up in a coach when I might ride instead," he said, smiling at Philippa, "but I've only the one carriage at my disposal at the moment, and I mean to see if I cannot find some respectable female through the worthy Mrs. Haversett today. I don't doubt I shall make a better impression if I call to see her in a carriage rather than on horseback. Then, too, my uncle is arriving today, and though he will bring his traveling carriage, I should rather ride in my own, which is not nearly so old and musty, and I should—with your kind permission—like to bring him to call this afternoon when I return to collect Lucy."

They agreed that it would be pleasant to meet the Honorable Archibald Drake, and Rochford soon took his leave after adjuring his sister to be on her best behavior.

Philippa turned her attention to the two young ladies. They provided quite a contrast in appearance, for whereas Jessalyn was flaxen-haired and deceptively fragile-looking, the Lady Lucinda had glossy black shoulder-length ringlets, a delicate white complexion, deep blue eyes, and rosy red lips. She was an inch or two shorter than Jessalyn and prettily plump instead of willowy slim. But both girls possessed the same mischievous twinkle, and both appeared to be under the impression that they had been rather clever.

"We shall have our lessons in the morning room, I think," Philippa said to them. Then, as the two looked at each other and giggled, she added sternly, "I do hope that you, neither of you, think you have achieved something marvelous by contriving to remain in Leicestershire instead of being sent back to school in disgrace as you should have been."

Jessalyn bit her lower lip and regarded the black-and-white

pattern in the stone hall floor as though she had discovered something there of abounding interest, but Lucinda looked up at Philippa in dismay.

"Oh, dear Lady Philippa, are you still at outs with us? I promise, I at least shall never do such a thing again. I . . . I shouldn't dare." Her voice caught on the last words, and Philippa, remembering Rochford's description of the confrontation he had had with his sister at Belvoir, found herself hoping the girl wouldn't burst into tears on the spot.

"I collect that your brother gave you a severe scold," she said matter-of-factly, "just as I gave one to Jessalyn—and just as you both deserved, I might add. But the matter is behind us now, Lucinda, and there is little to be achieved by dwelling on the past. You would do better to put your mind to what you mean to accomplish now."

"Accomplish?" Lucinda looked at her now as though Philippa had suddenly begun to speak a foreign tongue.

Miss Pellerin, speaking for the first time since Rochford's departure, said dryiy, "Indeed, Lady Lucinda, you have come here for lessons, you know."

'Oh, yes, of course, but I quite thought . . . well, you see, I thought that perhaps Jessie and I would merely take our sketchbooks out and sketch trees and plants like we did with Miss Blandamore, or rather with Miss Cynthia, for Miss Blandamore don't like to walk about the gardens when she can sit with her cup of tea, don't you know, and . . ." But here Lady Lucinda seemed to lose the thread of what she had been saying, and she broke off to look toward Jessalyn for help.

Jessalyn rose to the occasion by saying earnestly to Philippa, "We are very good at sketching, ma'am. I daresay our efforts may astonish you."

"No doubt," Philippa replied, exchanging a look with Miss Pellerin. "We shall repair to the morning room, however, where I shall explain to you just what schedule I mean for you to follow. You may take your sketchbooks outside this afternoon if the weather remains clement."

As it turned out, the lessons were not as much of a loss as Philippa feared they might be after this inauspicious beginning. Both Jessalyn and Lucinda were well-behaved and attended to what was said to them, and although Miss Pellerin might indeed have winced a time or two when they betrayed their ignorance, she also discovered in herself a talent for relating information in such a way as to fascinate two young ladies who had never had the benefit of truly academic lessons before. No one, however, was more astonished than Lord Rochford later that afternoon when his sister greeted his entrance into the yellow drawing room, where the ladies had gathered after the promised sketching expedition, with the enthusiastic announcement that she had been learning the relationship of all the Norse gods, one to the other.

"And," she added in the tone of one confiding astonishing news, "tomorrow Miss Pellerin is going to tell us all about the Valkyrie, who sound as though they must have been quite the most fascinating ladies, Andrew, truly!"

"If," said the older gentleman who had come into the yellow drawing room with the viscount, "your Miss Pellerin has a clear understanding of how all those gods and goddesses are related to each other, I for one would like to meet her."

"Well, this is her—I mean, this is she," said Lucinda, correcting herself hastily.

"That is scarcely a proper introduction," her brother informed her gently.

"Never mind that," said the older gentleman, turning to bow toward Miss Pellerin. The slight squeak that accompanied this action gave Philippa at least to realize that the Honorable Archibald Drake was confined in that contraption known as the Brummell Bodice, a whalebone corset worn by many dandies of the period in the hope that it would force their bodies into a shape more like that of the great arbiter of fashion himself. In Mr. Drake's case, the hope was a forlorn one. No amount of lacing could conceal the roundness of his stomach. Nor did the padding in the shoulders of his superfine coat succeed in making his own shoulders look anything but a trifle lumpy. Certainly they were not of a breadth or strength to compare with his nephew's, Philippa thought, letting her eyes stray to the viscount's magnificent shoulders. A moment later, when she realized that Rochford had caught her staring, she blushed and turned quickly back to Mr. Drake, who had stepped forward to clasp Miss Pellerin's plump, beringed little hands between his own. "You, good lady, have truly been explaining the descendants of Odin, Vili, and Ve to these children?"

"Uncle Archibald, we are not children!"

"Hush, Lucinda," said her brother. "A lady does not contradict." He turned to Philippa, his eyes gleaming. "Does she, Lady Philippa?"

"No, indeed not, sir," Philippa replied without a blink, wondering suddenly how it was that she should feel as though she had known him since her early childhood. The thought was disconcerting, and she found herself sounding rather more shatterbrained than usual when she said, "Will you allow me to ring for refreshment? Oh, there is no need, for here is Bickerstaff with the tray now. How quick you are, Bickerstaff. Will you take a glass of Madeira, Mr. Drake, or perhaps some claret?"

"Madeira," replied Mr. Drake tersely, taking a seat by Miss Pellerin. He had not taken his eyes from her face and was still examining her as though he had discovered some rare specimen. "You have not replied, dear lady," he said now. "Do you indeed expect to explain such things to these . . . these young ladies?"

"Certainly," said Miss Pellerin, folding her hands primly in her lap, but looking adorably self-conscious as she did so. "There is no particular mystery, you know, if one but approaches the Eddas logically. It is interesting, sir, that you refer to the descendants of Vili and Ve, as well as of Odin, for most persons, you know, think of them all simply as Odin's descendants."

Philippa, realizing that the conversation was about to enter realms that would leave the rest of them behind, turned to Rochford with a grin. "I daresay we ought to leave them to it, sir. Will you sit? Jessalyn," she added, looking at that young lady, "perhaps you will prefer to take Lady Lucinda up to the morning room, where you may order some cakes and ratafia for yourselves, if you like."

Rochford, accepting a glass of Madeira from Bickerstaff's tray but declining interest in cakes or sandwiches, had taken a seat on a yellow-satin-covered gilt chair near Philippa's. He stretched out his long legs before him and sipped from his glass, watching her while she spoke to her stepdaughter. When she caught his look, she smiled ruefully.

"Ought I not to have sent them away, sir? I didn't even ask you, but I realize now that you might well have wished for Lucinda to stay."

"No, why should I?"

"Well, because you would not then have to await her convenience when you are ready to take your departure, of course."

He grinned at her. "But I should have to endure her conversations instead. I infinitely prefer her absence."

She shook her head at him. "Unnatural brother. Her conversation is not precisely stimulating, perhaps—"

His choke of laughter stopped her. "I beg your pardon," he said when he could speak again, "but your choice of words was more than my sense of the ridiculous would tolerate. Tell me, ma'am," he added on a more provocative note, "did you put your cousin up to this Norse-mythology business?"

Philippa stared at him. "What on earth would put such an idea into your head, sir?"

"Why, the mention of the Valkyrie, of course," he murmured, his gray eyes glinting wickedly.

"I cannot think what you mean," Philippa said tartly. "I cannot even, at the moment, recall precisely what—"

He cut in without apology. "Oh, no, fair lady, that will not wash. I may acquit you of intent, but I cannot believe you do not see that some benefit might be drawn by filling my idiotish sister's head with notions of young virgins, armed most ridiculously with helmets and spears, riding bravely into battle—no doubt upon hunters of the very first quality."

Philippa chuckled. "You must indeed acquit me of intent, sir, but I don't pretend that the idea would never have entered my mind once Cousin Adeliza had begun to describe the Valkyrie. Truly, the notion of entertaining the girls with Norse mythology was hers alone. She is of the opinion that such tales are a good way to introduce young minds to history, and she approves of the Norse myths over those of the Greeks and Romans, because she thinks for some reason that they are more suitable for innocent ears. She will call the

Valkyrie young warrior maidens, I do not doubt, not virgins. And now that I bring it to mind, were not the Valkyrie choosers of those who would enter Valhalla, rather than warriors themselves?''

''Indeed, and they are thought to be responsible for the aurora borealis as well,'' said Rochford, clearly enjoying himself. ''Their armor supposedly sheds a strange flickering light which flashes from time to time across the northern night skies.'' He sipped again, then glanced at his uncle and Miss Pellerin before looking back at Philippa. ''Are you quite certain you did not urge her on to tell that tale in order to bring my sister into your quest to join the hunt, ma'am?''

''I would not do such a thing,'' Philippa replied, on her dignity. ''I do not scruple to tell you to your head, sir, that I believe you ought to encourage your sister and other ladies of the area to ride with the Wyvern for the excellent reason that such exercise would be good for them. There is no need to encourage them to go beyond the first two or three fields, nor would they wish to do so, but to deny them the pleasure is wrong.''

He smiled at her. ''I apologize if I offended you. Such was never my intention. You will be pleased to know that I have written to assure that both my sisters mean to honor us at Christmas. If they do, I assure you I shall organize a family hunt to which you and Miss Raynard-Wakefield will certainly be invited.''

''You are kind, sir. Jessalyn adores to ride and will be overjoyed by such an invitation. She is really too young to join in social gatherings, but since it will be a family occasion and since Lucinda will also take part, there can be no objection, I am certain.''

He smiled again, and she found herself responding warmly. Indeed, he was a kind man and a gentle one. No doubt, all he needed was a certain amount of intelligent coaxing before he would be brought round to seeing matters as clearly as she did herself.

Accordingly, in the days that followed, Philippa put her feminine wiles to work. Lady Lucinda arrived each morning in her brother's carriage, accompanied by the young maid who served her, but she was collected nearly every afternoon, after the day's hunt, by her brother and her uncle, which gave Philippa ample opportunity for her efforts, particularly since Mr. Drake seemed interested in conversing only with Miss Pellerin. Philippa was encouraged by the fact that Rochford made little secret of his liking for her. Though he did not precisely state that he had sown most of his wild oats on the Continent and was now ready to settle down with a wife, she was nearly certain from the omnipresent twinkle in his eyes and his increasing warmth of manner that he would make her an offer before she left Leicestershire. And though she told herself that she would be no more inclined then than she had ever been to accept such an offer from any man, she could not very often bring herself to ignore his flirtation. Likewise, although when it crossed her mind to do so, she made every effort to dampen his pretensions by setting him at a distance, she could not in all honesty say she had made a great effort to discourage him. Still, her fondest hope was that his own wish to please her would best serve her particular purpose in the end.

Rochford seemed intrigued by her attitude toward him, but she had little doubt that he had rarely encountered difficulty in attracting members of the fair sex. He was certainly handsome, poised, and possessed of undeniable charm, and when he began to increase his efforts, Philippa realized that he had set himself to charm her. No doubt, she told Miss Pellerin when they had entered upon the second week of their new routine, Lord Rochford saw her as something of a challenge to his talents for seduction.

"I think he is an excellent young man," said Miss Pellerin, frowning slightly. "I cannot think why you make such odd attempts to keep him at arm's length, my dear."

"Well, I do not think them odd at all, and I intend to go right on as I have begun," said Philippa, who would have found it difficult by then, if pressed, to give a sensible reason for her behavior. Rochford's company was by no means repugnant to her. Indeed, she had come to look forward to his visits and to feel prodigious disappointment on those days when he chose to hunt some distance from home and thus did not appear at Chase Charley in time to escort his sister home. Nonetheless, before very long she was certain her goal was in sight, and so she told Miss Pellerin. "I am quite certain, ma'am, that only a perfect ninny would fail to take advantage of the situation as it stands. I daresay if the matter is handled properly, Rochford's desire to please me will stop him from making any strenuous objection to my joining his hunt."

"Oh, my dear, I believe you underestimate the strength of his prejudices in this matter," said Miss Pellerin with a worried frown. "I cannot believe that he will change his mind just because you ask it of him."

"Well, I do not intend to ask him," Philippa said with studied unconcern. "I have quite decided that I should be much the wiser to present him with a *fait accompli*."

—8—

DISCOVERING WHEN THE viscount would next be taking his pack out was not difficult. All Philippa had to do was to inquire of her gamekeeper, Sam Cudlipp, who was responsible for stopping earths—those bolt holes down which a fox might run to ground—for any hunt that wished to cross Raynard-Wakefield land. For this signal service, Cudlipp was paid a tidy sum by each of the shire hunts, and since new earths must be stopped the night before a hunt, Sam would surely know when the Wyvern would next be out.

Accordingly, the very next morning before breakfast, Philippa and Pottersby rode through the parkland behind the house to the keeper's cottage, which stood in a narrow hollow of the woodland, overshadowed by a mighty Spanish chestnut tree. The exterior of the cottage was thatched and gabled, with walls three feet thick to keep out the cold of winter and the heat of summer. Such walls, as Philippa had discovered through Wakefield's conversation, were not solid masonry, but two shells filled up between with rubble and mortar rammed down hard.

The visitors were met in the cottage yard by two barking retrievers, and within moments a buxom, vivacious, middle-aged woman appeared at the door. Calling to the dogs, who were by then gamboling about Philippa as she slid unaided to the ground from her saddle, the woman bobbed a curtsy. "Good day t' ye, m'lady."

"Good morning, Mrs. Cudlipp." Handing her reins up to Pottersby, Philippa gathered the train of her habit over her left arm. "Is Cudlipp at home?"

"He be down t' the kennels, m'lady, but back in a pair o'

minutes 'e said. Will ye honor the house, mum?'' Then, to Philippa's astonishment, she added sharply, ''Get ye gone now, but mind 'e make yer manners to 'er ladyship!'' Mrs. Cudlipp's words were explained, however, when two small children, a boy and a girl, slipped out from behind her skirts, executed awkward bobs, and ran giggling away with the dogs. Smiling, Philippa accepted her hostess's invitation to step inside.

The brick floor of the low-pitched sitting room was a step below the level of the ground, and there was a peculiar but not altogether unpleasant odor that seemed to come from the fire, where roots burned, hissing as sap exuded from them and boiled in the fierce heat. The cottage was exquisitely clean, with not a speck of dust to be seen.

Mrs. Cudlipp turned to Philippa with smiling, respectful dignity, desirous of pleasing, yet quite at her ease. ''Will ye take a cuppa, m'lady?''

''Thank you,'' Philippa said, adding as her eye was attracted to a rug of some beautiful fur lying across the sofa, ''Those stripes are familiar, but surely that is not a tigerskin!''

Mrs. Cudlipp chuckled. ''Not hardly, mum. That be catskin, my special, 'n only jest sewed together. It be a-dryin' now. That be t' first I done only o' tabby, though I done one afore that was all black, 'n right handsome it was, too.''

Fortunately for Philippa's future standing in that household, Cudlipp chose that moment to push the heavy door open and step inside. Thus she was spared the necessity of forming a polite response, and could turn her attention immediately to the purpose of her visit.

Sam Cudlipp wore buskins, baggy homespun breeches, and a duffel coat with his dog whistle hanging from a buttonhole and his keys clinking from a ring at his wide leather belt. He would have been a tall man but for a slight stoop acquired in the passage of the years, no doubt as much from the weight of his gun or his game bag as from hours of walking. There was still plenty of power in his long sinewy arms, brown hands, and bull neck, however, and there was intense vital energy in his bright blue eyes as he nodded at his visitor.

''The bairns come baying that 'er ladyship be in t' cottage, 'n I seen Jake Pottersby in t' yard. Welcome, m'lady." He spoke from the depths of his broad chest, as men will who shout often across the fields and through the copses, and the sound filled the small room. There was solidity in his footsteps as he moved forward, and he met her eye fully and unshirkingly, yet without insolence, putting Philippa forcibly in mind of what men must have been like in feudal days when they all had had an affinity for the woods. There was something, too, in his overwhelming masculinity that reminded her suddenly and disconcertingly of Rochford.

That straying thought caused her to stumble over her greeting. "G-good day, Cudlipp. I have come to . . . that is, I must know . . . Oh, dear." She shook her head in comic dismay. "My words seem to have got jumbled on my tongue." Gratefully she accepted a cup of hot, strong peppermint tea from Mrs. Cudlipp just then and sank down upon the sofa, only to start and sit very straight when she realized she had nearly leaned back against the catskin rug. "Oh, this tea is delicious," she said appreciatively. "I must apologize for appearing to be such a zany." She looked up at Cudlipp, who still stood rock solid where he had stood since entering the cottage.

"What be ye wishful of, m'lady?"

"Why, 'tis the simplest thing," she said lightly. "I wish only to know when Lord Rochford means to hunt the Wyvern pack over our land. I know he must inform you, Cudlipp, because if he does not ride north, he will almost surely have to ride onto our property, and he will wish you to stop the earths for him."

"Aye, 'n see yon drains put to, as well," the keeper responded. He looked at her searchingly, and for a moment Philippa dreaded that he would ask her why she wished to know and then would refuse to tell her. She was not by any means sure she would be able to come the mistress over the servant with this man. Fortunately, however, Cudlipp made no such demand. It appeared he had merely been thinking. "That be Tuesday next," he said at last. "We got t' Quorn on Monday, 'n t' Cottesmore on Thursday, so it be Wyvern on Tuesday."

Philippa allowed a small sigh of relief to escape her. During the next few moments she managed to elicit his opinion with regard to the direction the Wyvern pack was most likely to take, and soon after that she bade her hosts farewell in the yard and allowed Jake Pottersby to fling her into the saddle.

The morning sun's warmth had penetrated the parkland by the time they crossed back over the narrow stream, and the damp steam that floated upward from the peaty soil and sodden masses of decaying leaves beneath the horses' hooves was the reverse of pleasant, but Philippa paid little heed, for her nostrils soon accustomed themselves and her thoughts were busy.

As they approached the stables, she spoke over her shoulder to Jake Pottersby. "Have you looked about for a suitable hunter or two, Jake?"

"Aye, mistress, I have and all. Happen there be two nags available from young Lord Ponsonby in Melton. Eh, but they say he's run off 'is legs and be needful t' sell off 'is young'uns. Leicestershire born 'n bred, the pair of 'em be. Ain't reetly seen 'em m'self, but hear tell they be prime bits o' blood 'n bone."

"Then get them for me at once, Jake. If they are so good as that, they won't be on the market long. Go today, and don't haggle. Pay whatever the man wants for them if you think them good enough for us."

"Sithee, Miss Philippa," said Pottersby to her back, "be ye meanin' t' ride these nags yerself, think on, or be ye purchasin' 'em fer the young lord?"

"Don't be absurd, Jake. I told you before that I want them trained to a lady's saddle, and I shouldn't take it upon myself to purchase a hunter for Wakefield, in any event. He would be sure to take a pet. Moreover, did you not say there are already two young horses he's sent up from Oxford?"

"Aye, and a pair of fratchin' cocktails, they be, look how. Still 'n all, ye ride a feather. Happen ye oughtn't to have more nag than ye can handle."

"I want good mounts, Jake, with strength and staying power, and I'll have none of your nonsense. It will do me no good to have some gentle prad who won't take a fence standing or any other way. I want to hunt, and I want to be able to stay at the front of the field if I wish to do so. Do you understand me?'' She turned to glare at him.

Pottersby nodded. ''Aye, happen I do, think on, 'n I'll wager t' old earl'd take on mortal bad an 'e knew what yer gettin' up to. Bad enow, we got t' keep our glims peeled fer any mischief young miss might be framin' to—''

''What so you mean, Jake? Has Miss Jessalyn been creating ructions in the stables?''

''Not to say ructions, Miss Philippa. Happen she did come down yesterday, a-saying that she and her young ladyship'd be framin' t' ride, but I told her we ain't got but one lady's saddle, 'n that'un was yours.''

Silence fell between them as Philippa gave this new matter some thought, and they had passed into the stableyard before she spoke again. Then, as he was helping her dismount, she said, ''Lord Rochford means to invite her to hunt at Christmas, so I think it would be as well if you were to purchase proper ladies' saddles and two more horses for the stables, Jake, horses with some hunting skills but suitable for Miss Jessalyn and the Lady Lucinda to ride. Try, if you can, to find some with a bit of spirit but small enough for them to handle easily. Jessalyn, at least, is an excellent horsewoman, but I don't want her on Wakefield's hunters or either of the two you mean to purchase for me.''

Jake nodded, and half an hour later, in the breakfast parlor, Philippa informed Jessalyn that she had arranged for her to have her own mount. ''But mind, Jess, you are not to ride any of the horses in the stable unless Jake Pottersby says you may, and you are not to go out without a proper groom to attend you, not even if you go with Lucinda.''

Jessalyn regarded her speculatively for a moment, but she must have realized from Philippa's firm expression that there would be no coaxing her to let the young ladies ride before Jake had found suitable mounts for them. Fortunately, he was able to do so within very few days, and their first excursion was—as Jessalyn laughingly told Philippa and Miss Pellerin afterward—to the gamekeeper's cottage to see the catskin rug, for although Philippa had not mentioned the real reason for her visit to the cottage, she had been unable to resist describing the rug.

Pottersby succeeded in acquiring the two hunters from Lord Ponsonby the afternoon following their discussion, and Philippa spent the following days working with them. She was very pleased with both of them. They had beautiful manners, good soft mouths, powerful shoulders and haunches, and strong, well-formed legs. After an afternoon of larking first with one and then the other, she announced excitedly to Pottersby that they were exactly what she had had in mind.

"Aye," he returned morosely, " 'n better nor like, ye'll end wi' a broken neck, m'lady."

"Pooh," she retorted. "Why, Cupid—the bay, you know, for he goes as though he had wings—is so light of foot that he fairly sailed over that double oxer at the end of the north wheatfield. You know, it is not merely a hedge and two rails but a ditch as well, and nearly an in-and-out rather than a mere oxer, but he treated it as though it were nothing. And the black is the best over water I've ever seen, though he can be contrary when it comes to hedges, I've noticed. With Cupid there is no checking or crashing, just smooth as be-damned—as Wakefield would say."

Pottersby shook his head. "Not old Wakefield wouldn't say it, Miss Philippa, 'n if yer of a road t' take yer language from Oxford brats, I'm by way o' thinkin'—"

"Oh, Jake, for mercy's sake," Philippa said, chuckling, "you can be as uncivil as Papa. I promise I shan't say anything to make you blush when I hunt."

"Happen that means yer aimin' fer me t' join the hunt along o' yerself, Miss Philippa, and that's a thing I'm not meanin' to do."

"Well, you've got to," Philippa said flatly. "No matter how much I want to prove myself to Rochford, I'm not such a ninnyhammer as to ride into a field of I don't know how many men without protection, and since I can scarcely ask another lady to abet me in this particular venture, you are all I have, Jake, so you must ride Ponsonby's Black Nestor, for I doubt any other horse we have can keep up with Cupid here, and I don't want to lose you."

"Old baron'd turn me off, sure," said Jake, turning the corners of his thin mouth downward.

"Well, the old baron isn't here, and neither is Papa," said Philippa incontrovertibly. "You won't let me down, will you, Jake?"

The only response she received was a growl, but it was enough. She knew he would not fail her if for no other reason than his fear that she might go alone if he didn't go with her. As a result, the following Tuesday morning, she found him awaiting her in the stable, both hunters saddled and ready to ride.

Fog lay heavily on the countryside, and there was a curious stillness in the air, broken only by the scratching clip-clop of the horses' shoes on the new white gravel drive. It was early, and the only humans in sight were a pair of gardener's boys dressing the barren grapevines at the far end of the kitchen garden. The air was chilly, too, and Philippa wondered if her dark green wool habit would suffice to keep her from freezing before she could get into action. She had chosen it for its unremarkable color, not for its material, for she knew that although she welcomed the warmth of the wool now, it might well become unbearably hot later on, during the chase.

The fog hid Wyvern Towers from view, and she wondered if the meet had begun. In Melton, she knew, there would be groups of hunters setting out about now in different directions to meet different packs of hounds. Each sportsman would, much earlier yet, have sent two horses ahead of him. On one would be mounted a very light but extremely well-dressed lad, who would later return home on his master's cover hack. On the other would be the second-horse man, riding the mount that would carry his master during the second half of the hunt.

Had they been hunting in the Midlands or the Provinces, the hunters might well have been carried to their assorted meets by a stylish carriage and four, but here in Leicestershire, the byroads being bad for wheels, the cover hack was considered by nearly all to be the better conveyance. One reason Philippa had started early herself was that she had no wish to encounter any of these gentlemen en route.

She led the way across the Eye Brook at the Whissendine ford and on through the north wheatfield to a sycamore copse some three miles beyond, having carefully selected the location several days before. According to Sam Cudlipp, the best coverts for the Wyvern pack were to be found to the east of that point at which the Eye Brook curved and became a river. Once drawn, the fox would most likely run away from the water toward the Stamford Road. Therefore, if the hunters were lucky, they would get a run of nearly ten miles before they would head the fox back toward Wyvern and the Whissendine.

The copse she had selected had not been thinned yet, and its density provided good cover for Philippa, Pottersby, and their horses. It was not until they had been waiting for some time that it occurred to Philippa that it would also provide good cover for the fox, which was no doubt why it had been encouraged to grow in the first place and had not yet been thinned. Since it was no part of her plan to be challenged by the hounds before she could join the hunters, she urged her mount further to the northeast end of the copse, no easy task, for the soft mist condensed on the boughs, and the trees seemed to drip continuously. Whenever she had to push a low-hanging branch out of her way, it had a tendency to fly back, sending a cold shower down her neck.

Jake Pottersby had pulled up his coat collar, but she knew he was as uncomfortable as she was, and it was with great relief that she heard the cry of the pack less than half an hour later. Any longer, waiting in that damp chill, and she knew she would have had to give up and go home.

The baying of the hounds acted upon her like a tonic, however, and she urged Cupid forward almost to the edge of the copse. The mist, she noticed, was beginning to lift, for she could see the hunters like gray ghosts riding toward her, packed together, sailing almost as one man over a post-and-rails fence two fields away. At first she could not see the fox, but once she had located the pack, it was but a moment before she saw the brush flying, as Mister Reynard scrabbled this way and that over the grassy field, heading straight for the copse.

The fox scrambled through the next obstacle, which was a

thorn hedge, and the hounds followed, jumping and scrambling to get over or through. Close behind came the hunters. The hounds saw the copse at once and, to Philippa's relief, headed the fox to the north of it, so there was scarcely a check in the noisy surge of baying hounds, thundering horses, and cheering riders, although the latter slowed their mounts to avoid overriding the hounds, which was a thing that was simply not done by any but the veriest thrusters.

She looked for the viscount, but most of the gentlemen were dressed in similar clothing, and although she was very nearly certain that she recognized him as one of the frontmost riders, she could not be certain. Not, she told herself firmly, that it mattered in the slightest, for he would see her soon enough.

Nibbling nervously at her lower lip, she waited with forced patience until the field was past before giving Cupid the office to start. The powerful horse needed little urging then, but gathered his legs beneath him and shot out of the copse after the others so sharply that Philippa had all she could do for the first few moments to retain her seat and not lose her hat. When she did manage to look over her shoulder at last, she saw to her relief that Jake was only a few yards behind her.

Keeping well to the rear of the field, she held Cupid in at first when he showed a wish to come up with the others. Despite her practicing, Philippa found that she had to concentrate very hard each time she came to an obstacle, lest she disgrace herself, and it was not until she had cleared an oxer, a thorn-filled ditch, and two timber fences that she gained sufficient confidence to urge Cupid to a faster pace. No sooner did she drop her hands, however, than he put on a sharp burst of speed, and within minutes she was passing the first of the men and riding toward a gap between two others. She caught them by taking an in-an-out with more speed than grace, then dashing across the next field, letting Cupid run full out.

She had not given thought to Jake Pottersby since the first oxer, but now she spared a glance over her shoulder and was encouraged to find him still behind her, his expression grim but excitement showing in every other line of his wiry body. Philippa shot him a saucy grin, then turned her attention back to her own mount and the necessity for making her way between two more hunters before reaching the next obstacle, another oxer.

The men were beginning to notice her now, and heads turned as she flashed past the two riders and felt Cupid gather beneath her for the jump. There was a water-filled ditch on the other side, but as usual, the powerful horse was flying and cleared the whole without so much as a check upon landing. Philippa laughed aloud, so exhilarated did she feel.

At that moment, a rider who had been beside her before the jump came down prematurely with a splash and a shout of chagrined dismay, and when next she looked back, over her left shoulder, it was to see him straining to pull his horse from the ditch. Then, as she was about to look forward again, she caught a motion from the right in her peripheral vision that appeared to be Jake waving like a madman. Twisting back around in order to see him better, she saw instead that which made a clearer view of Pottersby unnecessary. Rochford, astride a black even bigger than Black Nestor, was but ten yards to her right, and he had seen her.

Having been certain she would find him at the front of the field, Philippa had not made a serious effort to identify the viscount among the others, and having managed to convince herself that she would amaze and astonish him when she rode up beside him, she had not troubled to examine that conviction any further. Now one look at the expression on his face was enough to tell her she had erred badly in her judgment of how he would react to her *fait accompli*.

Her stomach tensed as her gaze locked momentarily with his, and she knew in that instant that despite any gentlemanly wish he might have to please her, he was not going to dismiss her action lightly. Nor, by the look of him, was he likely at some point comfortably distant in the future to settle for a quiet discussion of what she had done. There was little to be seen in his wrath-filled expression of the warmhearted gentleman she had counted upon to be amused by and thus forgiving of her tactics. Instead, if she was any judge of such matters, his lordship was in a flaming rage and ripe for murder.

Philippa's breath caught raggedly in her throat, but she swallowed determinedly and touched Cupid's flank with her whip. Though she had not thought before that the splendid horse could go faster, he proved her wrong, and it seemed by his speed that his hooves could not be touching the ground. But when she dared to look back a moment later, she saw to her dismay that Rochford was less than twenty feet behind her.

Then—almost worse—when she looked forward again, she realized she had been covering ground so rapidly that she had passed the other hunters. The hounds were practically under Cupid's feet.

The big horse swung to the right of his own accord to avoid trampling them, and as one the hounds swerved left almost at the same time. A moment later they were behind, and as she approached the next fence, she saw plowed ground beyond and knew that if she took the jump, the soft earth might slow Cupid enough to allow Rochford to catch her.

Frantically she turned her horse with a sharp jerk of the rein, observing only as she did so that they had somehow got ahead of the fox. But Mister Reynard, seeing the huge horse looming above him, did what any sensible fox would do. He skidded to a halt, doubled back on himself, and shot directly toward the oncoming field. Then, recognizing his error, he adjusted his course in order to avoid both the hounds and hunters, and hightailed it toward a nearby spinney.

The hounds, confused first by the riot of hoofbeats and then by the fox's evasive action, had checked and were scrabbling this way and that, casting for the scent that seemed to them to have stopped in thin air. The fox having disappeared into the spinney, Philippa urged Cupid over a timber fence into a field of stubble and brush, then across a small brook, riding as hard as she dared, certain that Rochford was still behind her. A moment later, she heard the cry of the hounds in the distance and knew they had come upon the scent again, but it no longer mattered to her which direction the fox had taken. All that mattered now was that she escape from the viscount, or at least lead him far enough from the other hunters that he might vent his fury with her in privacy.

She had heard him shout at her once. His words faded before reaching her ears, but his tone convinced her that she didn't want to hear him. By the time Cupid had cleared two more timber fences and a thorn hedge, she thought they must be well away from the hunt. Before the thought had been completed, however, they topped a low rise and quite suddenly, directly ahead, she saw an overgrown hedge, a bullfinch, one so large and so thick that the sight of it caused her to check. A glance over her shoulder served to spur her on again, however, for Rochford looked even angrier than he had looked before, and there appeared to be several riders behind him. Instantly she rejected all thought of stopping to face him and, in near-panic, gave Cupid his head, praying the big bay would find an opening through the dreadful hedge and that—since she had not had the forethought to provide herself with a veil—she would be able to protect her face and still retain her seat. It would do her dignity no good at such a time as this to have to ask Rochford to rescue her from a thorn hedge. Indeed, the very thought made her shudder.

Fortunately, Cupid still had his wits about him and found a gap large enough to accommodate him. Holding one arm protectively across her face, Philippa scarcely felt the branches brushing and tugging at her before she was through and into an open field. At nearly the same moment that she realized she was on her own land, she realized, too, that the innocent-looking rail and hedge ahead of her was in fact the double oxer she and Cupid had practiced jumping some days before. Two rails with a thorn hedge between and a ditch on the far side that she remembered being rather a wide one. As she neared the jump, she touched Cupid lightly with the whip, just enough to remind him to give his best effort, and a moment later she was safely over and conscious of gratitude for the fact that she had not chosen to ride Black Nestor, who might easily have sensed her tension and refused to take such a jump at all.

She was perspiring now, and Cupid seemed not quite so full of energy as he had been. Flecks of moisture beaded on his neck, and she could hear his breath blowing hard from his nostrils, a sound that she had not heard before.

Seconds later a tremendous, thudding crash behind her put all thought of Cupid's distress straight out of her head and caused her to jerk hard on the reins, bringing the bay to a plunging halt. Fear washed over her even before she turned, and when she looked back, she was unable to suppress the cry of horror that sprang to her lips.

Rochford's black, half in and half out of the ditch, was struggling to his feet. His master lay several feet away on the grass, unmoving.

—9—

FLINGING HERSELF TO the ground, Philippa hurried to Rochford's side. When he began to stir, she felt a surge of relief, but when he did not immediately open his eyes, panic threatened to claim her again.

"Oh, Rochford . . . oh, my lord, wake up. Do, please, wake up."

At the sound of hoofbeats on the other side of the treacherous jump, she leapt to her feet, snatched off her hat, and began waving it.

"Here!" she called. "Over here. Oh, do come quickly. Oh, Jake," she cried when she saw the first rider, " 'tis his lordship, and I fear he has injured himself quite seriously. He barely stirs."

As she was speaking, Jake found a gate in the hedge and using that end of his whip made especially for the purpose, opened it without dismounting and let himself through. He was followed by several gentlemen, of whom Philippa at first recognized only Lord Alvanley. That gentleman's presence was scarcely calculated to please her, but for the moment she paid him little heed, having thought only for Rochford.

"Oh, Jake, do come look at him, He does not open his eyes, and I am persuaded he must have hit his head when he fell. Please, God, he has not broken his neck."

Rochford groaned just then, and she hurried back to him.

"Rochford! Oh, please open your eyes."

"Step back, Miss Philippa, 'n cease thy fatching," Jake said, dismounting beside her. "Happen I'll see to 'im."

"Never mind that, my man," said a stern voice behind them. "Let the sawbones through. Here, Dr. Livesey, we've a body for you to practice on, man. Look sharp."

Philippa looked up at the man who spoke. He was dressed much as Rochford and Alvanley were, in creamy, snug-fitting buckskins and a well-cut dark coat, but there was a distinct note of elegance in his attire that was somehow lacking in the others, although she had not come to notice the fact before. He carried himself with the same easy confidence as the others, and his manner, like theirs, was one of casual, even amused, arrrogance, but his gleaming top boots boasted glossy white tops, and his neckcloth was more intricately tied than theirs. She had thought his voice familiar, although the note of command in it when he spoke to Jake was not, but that one look at him was enough to bring a deep flush of embarrassment to her cheeks.

She got slowly to her feet, allowing the small, thin gentleman who was clearly Dr. Livesey to move briskly past her to kneel beside Rochford. Suddenly, but for her worry about the viscount, she might have wished herself a million miles away, for surely the tale of her escapade would now be spread from the Channel to the Scottish border by the following morning.

"I did not know you numbered amongst Rochford's guests, Mr. Brummell," she said, gathering her dignity and meeting the ironic glint in his silver-gray eyes as steadily as she could.

Mr. George Bryan "Beau" Brummell, known even more widely for his cutting tongue than for his sartorial dictatorship, bowed from his saddle. "I do not have that precise honor at present, Lady Philippa, but have taken up my customary residence at Melton Old Club."

She nodded, for once feeling no amusement at the thought of a club that was restricted by the number of its bedchambers to having only four members at a time. Over a period of years, she knew, a number of the very best gentlemen had been members, and there was, in truth, something highly respectable in everything connected with Melton Old Club. There were said to be no ostentatious displays at table, though everything was as good of its kind as a first-rate cook and the finest wine cellars could produce. It was said, too, that the club's members and former members were remarkable for their ability to live together on terms of the strictest harmony and friendship. Looking up at the gentleman presently accounted the club's most famous member, Philippa could hope only that he would somehow find it in his heart to forget to mention to all and sundry her part in the day's activities.

Then Rochford groaned again and she forgot her own troubles when she saw that his eyes were open at last. Indeed, his gaze was fastened upon her in a manner that could only be described as ominous, but she made no attempt to evade it, for she was too concerned with what the doctor might say.

Livesey was indeed muttering something, but she could not make out his words. She did hear Rochford's reply, and the strength of his voice filled her with relief.

"Thought I'd thrown myself clear," he said, his deep tones carrying easily to her ears despite the increasing murmur of masculine voices behind her. "Landed on my right foot, and my ankle gave way. Then—I don't know—I must have gone top over tail. My head aches like fury, I do know that."

"And no wonder," said the doctor acidly, "with the bump you've got forming there. Must have hit a rock, my lord, and 'tis no more than you deserve after overriding the fox as you did and spoiling the chase."

"Glad to see you ain't stuck your spoon in the wall, Rochford," said one of the three other men who had followed them. "Daresay you'll like to know the black did no more than strain a hock."

The three men had been talking among themselves while one of them examined the big horse, and Philippa was nearly as conscious of their disapproval as she was of Brummell's and Alvanley's, not to mention Rochford's. It was Alvanley, however, who first put the general opinion into words.

"Wouldn't be a wonder if he *had* thtuck his thpoon in the wall, riding neck-or-nothing like he wath," he said suddenly. "Lady Philippa, whatever were you about to ride into the field like that? You might both have been killed, you know."

"Nobody was killed,' said the Beau in damping tones, "though Livesey is quite correct in noting that her ladyship's impetuous behavior ruined a fine run."

"Much you care for that, Brummell," said Alvanley, changing line with the quickness for which he was noted and grinning puckishly. "You never ride beyond the first few fieldth anyway. Darethay you'd have drawn up two or three miles back, were it not for her ladyship's having added a note of piquanth to the adventure."

The other gentlemen laughed then, and Brummell looked sourly at the young baron, eleven years his junior and already possessed of a reputation nearly as great as his own for quickness of wit. "Thought you meant to hunt with the Quorn today, my lad."

Alvanley pulled a long face. "Fortunately, I dithcovered Assheton-Smith meant to hunt Charnwood Forest, and one can never thee those dashed great granite stones amongst all the rotting fernth. Only consolation to hunting that ground ith that if you are killed you have your gravestone there beside you."

The others laughed more heartily than ever, and Brummell, chuckling in spite of himself, said, "Damme, Alvanley, I wish I had said that."

"Don't worry, you will," snapped Rochford wryly from the ground.

"If you have all quite finished," said Dr. Livesey, brushing impatiently at his pants legs and glaring at the others, who except for the Beau were now slapping their knees in merriment, "I suggest we set about getting his lordship off the ground and into bed, where he belongs."

"Nonsense," grumbled Rochford, beginning to sit up. "I can . . ."

The doctor managed to catch him by the shoulder, thus saving him from cracking his head against the ground as he slumped dizzily backward. "Certainly, my lord, and you will dance the quadrille after dinner as well. Now, if my patient is of a mind to be sensible, surely someone might send for a wagon to convey him to his home."

"Good gracious," said Philippa, "it must be all of five miles or more to Wyvern Towers from here. If he has a headache now, I shudder to think how he will feel by the time he has bounced all that way in a farm wagon."

"Have you a better suggestion, my lady?" asked the doctor. "I confess it will be a sad trial for him. Besides the headache, he is much bruised, and that left ankle is certainly swelling inside his boot."

"That settles it, then," Philippa said firmly. "It cannot be but a half-mile or so to my house from here, and although it is uphill, surely these men can carry him that far."

" 'Tis as good as done, ma'am," said one of the three men whom she did not know. "We can use the gate there to carry him on, or two of us can make a chair for him with our hands, you know. Better than to create riot and rumpus by sending for a carriage or any such thing."

So it was arranged, with everyone but Dr. Livesey and Philippa taking it in turns to make the chair. Even the Beau took his turn, and if the distance proved to be closer to a mile and a half than a half-mile, the men did not complain, except for Rochford, who insisted that he could perfectly well ride a horse if they would only let him. The others, treating the whole business as a lark, informed him that it was best to keep his injured ankle elevated and that he had, moreover, already proved himself incapable of sitting a horse.

"Indeed, my lord," said the doctor, attempting to soften the effect of these last words, "dizzy as you are, you might well find it difficult to maintain your balance. Moreover, your own mount is lamed. I cannot think you would prefer to ride pillion."

Rochford said nothing further after that, but Philippa, riding at that moment between Jake and Mr. Brummell, could not think that these proceedings or the accompanying merriment were likely to improve the viscount's temper. Nor did she think it would be improved when, a half-hour later, having turned her horse over to Jake and given orders that the other mounts should be seen to, she led the cavalcade into the stone hall, only to find Miss Jessalyn Raynard-Wakefield and the Lady Lucinda Drake hanging over the gallery rail in a most unladylike manner to see what was going forward.

"Good gracious!" wailed Lucinda. "What happened to Andrew? Is he badly hurt?"

"Was there an accident?" inquired Jessalyn of nobody in particular.

No one replied to these questions. Instead, the doctor turned to Philippa, raising his eyebrows. "Is it necessary to take him upstairs, my lady?"

"No, indeed, Dr. Livesey. This way, gentlemen." She led them through the great stair hall, past the service stair, and through the dressing room to the blue damask bedchamber in the southeast corner of the house, overlooking the park. "The bed was made up fresh yesterday. Is there anything else you will require, doctor?"

"Rid me of his merry escort, my lady, and you will be doing me a signal service. Then, if you have a manservant who can help me get him undressed, I would appreciate your sending him along straightaway."

"Very well, sir." She went to pull the bell, and the butler entered with magnificent promptitude. "Do you send Stephen Footman to assist the doctor, Bickerstaff, and then see that these gentlemen are provided with refreshment in the yellow drawing room."

"Yes, my lady. At once, my lady."

"Don't go, Philippa." It was Rochford, speaking from the bed where he had been placed by his escort with exaggerated gentleness and many ribald remarks. The ominous light had not yet faded from his eyes, and Philippa was grateful for the doctor's prompt intervention.

"Of course she must go, Rochford. Don't be daft, man. I mean to examine you from top to toe, and you'll not want her here for that, I'm thinking."

The viscount glared and seemed about to contradict him when Brummell said gently, "Don't be a bore, Andrew."

Rochford looked away then, and Philippa made good her escape as soon as she had directed the other gentlemen into the yellow drawing room, situated immediately to the west of the bedchamber. Leaving them to enjoy whatever refreshment Bickerstaff saw fit to serve them, she hastened upstairs to the morning room, where she found her cousin and the two girls. Even as she spared a prayer of gratitude to whichever almighty being—Greek, Roman, Norse, or English—had stopped Jessalyn and Lucinda from descending to the lower floor, she discovered that it had been no easy task. To judge by the pelter of questions that greeted her entrance to the room, they had been forcibly restrained.

"What happened, ma'am? Cousin Adeliza would not let us go downstairs."

"Is Andrew badly hurt? Oh, please, will he live, ma'am?"

"Philippa, what on earth are you about, to have brought all

those gentlemen into this house? The girls inform me that there are at least a dozen of them racketing about belowstairs."

Setting her whip down upon the deal table and stripping off her riding gloves, she answered Miss Pellerin first with a rueful smile. "Not quite a dozen, ma'am, though I fear I have truly brought the Fates down upon us this time—or is it the Furies? I never can keep them all straight."

Miss Pellerin smiled dryly. "I believe you must mean the Furies, my love. I daresay the daughters of the just heavens have less to do with what you've brought upon yourself than have the avenging spirits. The Furies concern themselves, as you must know if you will but consider the matter, with retribution. And retribution, I believe, is what you fear at the moment."

"What are you talking about?" demanded Jessalyn. "Why did they have to carry Lord Rochford into the house, and why was it into *this* house?"

"Yes, please, and how badly is he hurt?" begged Lucinda, her eyes spilling over with tears.

"Mercy me, Philippa, answer the girl before she floods the place," said Miss Pellerin with acerbity. "I never saw such a one for watering up."

"Lucinda, your brother will be perfectly all right," Philippa said bracingly. "He took a tumble and bumped his head. All the commotion comes about merely because his friends were by to see him do it and cannot resist the opportunity to roast him. Such is the way with gentlemen, as you will learn. They are at this moment making merry in the yellow drawing room, whilst Dr. Livesey attempts to make Rochford comfortable in the blue damask bedchamber."

"I want to see him," said Lucinda woefully.

"Not just now," Philippa told her, wincing at the thought of what Rochford's reaction must be to his sister's weeping presence at his bedside. "You will do better to wait until he is feeling more the thing. However," she added quickly when Lucinda sniffled, about to give way entirely to her tears, "since he will very likely remain here overnight if not longer, I am persuaded he would feel better to know you are under the same roof, so if you will oblige me by writing out a list of what you will require, I will send someone to carry it to

Wyvern. We must tell your uncle and your companion what has occurred, after all."

"But I thought Uncle Archibald had ridden out with them." said Lucinda on a note of protest, ignoring the reference to the worthy dame whom Rochford had hired to bear her company at Wyvern.

Philippa smiled at her. "He may have done so. Not everyone was at hand when your brother had his accident. We had taken a different direction, so the riders were separated into two groups."

"How very odd," said Lucinda. "Was there not but one fox?"

"Yes, well, in any event," said Philippa hastily when she saw her stepdaughter's mouth opening to pursue this interesting topic, "you may stay here for as long as Rochford wishes you to do so, Lucinda. Merely instruct your maid to bring the things you will need."

Bickerstaff entered the morning room just then to inform her that the doctor wished to speak with her.

"Thank you, I shall go down to him."

"And how many extra covers do you anticipate for dinner, my lady?" asked the butler without a blink.

"Extra covers? Oh, good gracious, I hadn't thought. Surely not all of them." Pulling off her hat, she ran a slim hand through the disordered tresses, then shook her head with a rueful grimace. "Tell Cook she must manage, whatever happens, Bickerstaff. I haven't the slightest intention of inviting any of them to remain, but I shouldn't wish to wager that we won't have company nonetheless."

"No, my lady. If I might venture to say so, his lordship may well desire one or two of the gentlemen to share his meal with him."

She nodded. "Keep a sharp ear to the ground, Bickerstaff. I shall depend upon you, and upon Mrs. Bickerstaff as well, to see that Cook does not fall into flat despair."

With that, she hurried down the great stair and was thankful to find the doctor awaiting her in the stair hall. Sounds of revelry came from the drawing room, and she would not have liked to have to seek him out among the others.

"How is he, Doctor?" Her tone sounded anxious, even to

her own ears, and she could not be surprised that the doctor felt compelled to speak to her with gentle sympathy.

"He'll do, my lady," he said, smiling kindly. "He's very strong, you know, and if he hadn't hit his head, I'd have said you might see the back of him and the rest of that lot by suppertime. But he is suffering from concussion, I believe, and if he isn't already as sore as be-da—that is, as sore as he can be—he will be by morning. I don't think he's broken anything, although his shoulder is severely bruised and he may have cracked his clavicle—the collarbone, you know—and his ankle was badly twisted. I've left a paper of instructions on the table in the bedchamber for his man, for I know you will send for him. There's nothing much to be done, barring giving him a drop of laudanum to help him sleep and putting cold compresses to the ankle." He smiled more broadly. "I doubt you'll get him to take the laudanum. Not if he knows it, in any event."

She nodded sagely. "I take your meaning, sir. We'll see that he gets the rest he needs. How soon will he be up and about?"

"Couple of days should do it. He oughtn't to ride or to be banged about in a carriage until he can stand and move about without feeling dizzy, though, so if you can contrive to keep him still for two days at least, you will have done him a service." He coughed delicately behind his hand. "Uh, he has expressed a strong desire to speak with you, by the by, which is why I've ordered that lot to stay out of the bedchamber for now. Afterward, you can let them in if you must, but don't let them stay long. I don't like concussion."

Philippa had scarcely heard anything he said after the bit about Rochford's wanting to speak to her, but she nodded and thanked him for his assistance. The doctor regarded her speculatively for a moment, then said gently, "There truly is no reason to fret, you know, Lady Philippa. He'll be fit as a fiddle in no time at all, and you may send for me at any hour. My house is the second you come to on the Nottingham Road in Melton. Any of your local lads'll know where to find me."

"Yes, of course, Doctor," Philippa said vaguely. "Won't you have a glass of Madeira before you go?"

"Don't mind if I do."

She watched him enter the drawing room and heard the surge of masculine voices that greeted him, then turned toward the back of the stair hall. A moment later she entered the blue damask bedchamber, hoping she looked more composed than she felt and wondering just how mussed her hair was.

Rochford was propped against a number of pillows. The bedclothes came only to his waist, but he was wearing a gray woolen dressing gown that she recognized as belonging to the late baron. His eyes were closed, but when he opened them as she shut the door behind her, Philippa swallowed uncomfortably and, for some odd reason, remembered her confrontation at Belvoir Castle with Jessalyn. She hadn't felt like this, she thought unhappily, since before she had married.

Rather than let the silence grow, she said "Dr. Livesey said you wished to speak to me."

"I do." He straightened a little, wincing in the process. "I should like to say a good many things to you, my girl."

She had seen the pain in his expression and experienced a flashing memory of the fear she had felt when she had seen him lying unconscious on the ground. That memory was followed by an increasing sense of guilt. Stepping a little closer to the bed, she said contritely, "I never meant anyone to be hurt, sir. We had become friends, I thought, and I was persuaded that you would not be really angry if I joined your hunt in progress. I meant to depart before the kill, you know, and no one would have thought anything more than that I had ridden in and out for a bit of a lark."

"You never believed for a moment that I would approve of such an action," he said so coldly that a chill raced up her spine, causing her to feel instant empathy for any subaltern who had chanced, during the course of Rochford's military career, to incur his displeasure.

He waited now for a response, and she felt her dignity deserting her. "I . . . I was persuaded—"

"You persuaded yourself is what you mean to say, Philippa, and a damned idiotic thing it was to have done," he said harshly. "Had you truly believed I should not object to such a course, you would, at the very least, have joined us at the meet, not midway through the first run. And certainly you would not have taken flight as you so stupidly did the moment you realized I had seen you.''

''I was frightened,'' she said in a small voice that could be controlled only with effort. ''You . . . you looked so fierce.''

'I was angry. I *am* angry, for a more ill-advised stunt I cannot imagine. You must have mush for brains, madam, or you would know that much yourself. You might have been killed or have brought harm to someone else, for you hadn't the least notion of what you were doing. Have you even considered what might have happened if the fox had contrived to go to ground in whatever copse you chose for hiding? You'd have had the hounds rioting at least, and God only knows what else would have occurred. As it was, only luck prevented your mount from stumbling when he overran the hounds and headed the fox. Lord, what a mess that was! And riding as you did, without thought for line or obstacle, you might have been blinded in that bullfinch if your horse hadn't found an opening. I won't say what you deserve for this day's work, my girl, but you may count yourself fortunate that I am not your father, for I should not then be satisfied with mere words, I promise you.''

He was not satisfied by so few words as these, of course, and continued in blistering form for some minutes longer, his accusations bleak and pointed, his opinions harsh and cutting. Fighting an overwhelming urge to burst into tears, Philippa listened meekly, having no wish to defend herself. She well knew that little though she liked what she was hearing, she deserved to hear every angry word. Indeed, her own guilt threatened to bring her more pain than any words he might choose to say, even though his temper caused him to say hurtful things, things that exaggerated the truth. Such things, she knew, were but the result of temper. Then, too, how it must gall his pride to know he had failed to take a jump that she had cleared easily.

Nonetheless, despite her continued self-reassurance that it was pain and temper causing him to hurl the angry words at her, by the time he was finished Philippa's eyes were burning from unshed tears, and a lump had filled her throat, refusing to be swallowed. When he paused at last, she tried to speak, but the words would not come.

Clearly thinking she meant to defend herself, Rochford said sharply, "There is little you can say to your credit, I fear, for your actions were both foolhardy and inexcusable. 'Tis no wonder your stepdaughter misbehaves, madam, with you for her example. And my own sister—"

But Philippa heard no more, for with a gasp of hurt dismay and tears spilling down her cheeks at last, she whirled about and hurried from the room, pausing only to close the door to the dressing room behind her. By taking the service stairs, she avoided the morning room and was able to enter her bedchamber through her dressing room. There, by telling herself several more times that he had not meant the half of what he had said, that he had been speaking out of temper, she managed to calm herself at last and to sit in quiet reflection until Miss Pellerin came to find her to tell her that dinner would soon be served.

"Do we dine alone, ma'am, or in company?"

"Mr. Brummell and Lord Alvanley dine with his lordship," Miss Pellerin said, regarding her narrowly, "but Bickerstaff has already served them in his lordship's bedchamber and Mr. Brummell promised faithfully that they would not stay long afterward or wait upon ceremony with you. I assured him that you would not expect them to do so."

"Thank you, ma'am. I do not believe I can cope with either of them tonight. Has his lordship's man arrived?"

"Yes, and he has everything well in hand, for Bickerstaff set up a cot for him in the dressing room, you know. And Lucy's maid has come, but not her companion, which is just as well, for I am persuaded we should neither of us know what to do with her. I put Lucy in with Jessalyn, thinking that was what you would like."

"Yes, for aside from Edward's bedchamber, there is no other suitable room downstairs, not that I think for a moment that Rochford would want her near him."

Miss Pellerin cocked her head to one side. "Are you all right, Philippa?"

"Oh, yes." Philippa managed a smile. " 'Tis merely a crisis of the nerves, ma'am, for you must know that Rochford rang a rare peal over me. Not that one can blame him, of course, though he rather outdid himself in some of the more cutting things he said."

Miss Pellerin nodded as though it was no more than she had expected to hear, but then she said gently, "If he lost his temper, my dear, he will be sorry for it. You will see."

Philippa nodded, not believing her but able to think of nothing to say. After her dinner, she contrived to arrange a conference with Brooksby, the viscount's able valet, in consequence of which a toddy ordered from the kitchen was augmented with a liberal dose from the bottle of laudanum left by Dr. Livesey. Thus did the viscount sleep soundly through the night, and the following morning when Philippa went, a little apprehensively, to visit his lordship and inquire how he did, she was greeted by a rueful smile and what could only be described as a wary look in his lordship's gray eyes.

"I certainly gave my tongue full rein, didn't I?" he said with a wry twist to his lips.

"As to that, I cannot say, sir," she replied, smiling back at him quite naturally in her relief that he was not still angry with her, "but I must hope you have not thought of any worse accusations to fling at my head."

"I haven't." He glanced down, then up at her again. "To be truthful, I cannot even recall all I said yesterday, but I am certain that I overrode the necessary, and if my temper led me to say anything of a particularly offensive nature, I hope you can forgive me."

"Handsomely said, my lord, and I do not bear a grudge, so you may be easy. Have you everything you require?"

"I am bored to distraction and aching in every limb, if you would have the truth of the matter."

She chuckled, well in charity with him again and glad to see that now his temper had run its course, he had regained his customary good humor. For the rest of that day she exerted herself to see that he was entertained, even going so far as to encourage the young ladies to take some of their lessons in his company, and when he laughed aloud at a tale related to them by Miss Pellerin, Philippa knew she had found the perfect medicine for what ailed him. That evening he insisted upon joining them in the library after supper and managed to do so without seeming to suffer unduly, although he leaned heavily on his valet's arm and gritted his teeth each time his left foot touched the floor.

The following morning Rochford informed Philippa when she stepped in to wish him good day that he was determined to return to Wyvern Towers that day. "For although I still have my share of aches and pains, and the company is such that only a fool would make complaint, I am certainly well enough to sustain a carriage ride of less than five miles and must not trespass longer upon your goodness."

Taking heart from his easy manner and twenty-four hours of good feeling between them, Philippa dared to tease him a little. "I daresay it will take longer for your pride to heal, sir, than your head or your ankle. Lord Alvanley and the others will surely continue to roast you until some other amongst them diverts their attention."

He laughed ruefully. "I hold you personally to blame for all my discomfiture at their hands, madam, and shall have to think up a suitable punishment."

When his eyes glinted with a purpose she could not fathom, the look was enough to make her retort rather rapidly, "I was not the one who came a cropper, my lord, and if anything good may be said to have come from this dreadful business, at least you must now agree that I ride well enough to join your hunt."

He frowned but kept his voice under rigid control. "We have already plucked that crow, have we not? Surely you must realize that the very fact that an expert rider like myself can take such a dangerous fall merely proves that Leicestershire hunting is entirely too dangerous for a woman. You were very lucky, Philippa, to have escaped injury. A fragile female, after all, is not so likely to recover from a fall as quickly as I have done. There is good reason for the old Melton saying that the right place for a woman is upon a sofa, not a saddle."

—10—

Forgetting the odd look in his eyes that had fluttered her nerves but a moment before, Philippa now had all she could do to control her leaping temper. Having convinced herself that once the viscount had come down from his high ropes he would see reason, her reason, she wanted nothing so much now as to favor him with a few home truths of her own. Had she not generously undertaken to entertain his little sister every weekday so that he might indulge in whatever took his fancy without having to fret over whether Lucinda was properly looked after? Had she not greeted him warmly whenever he chose to honor Chase Charley with his visits, although her butler had orders to deny her to other gentleman callers? Moreover, had she not included his uncle in her hospitality despite the fact that the old gentleman scarcely ever saw fit to speak more than a word or two to her?

Though Mr. Drake had indeed called to see how his nephew did, he had taken less than a moment to wonder why Rochford should have chosen to run counter to the fox and to tell him he ought to have watched himself more carefully, before briefly albeit punctiliously thanking Philippa for her care of the viscount. Then he had turned his attention to Miss Pellerin, and it was to her that he had addressed whatever else he had had to say upon that occasion.

And had Philippa not provided nursing for his lordship when he needed it, and a bed for him to sleep in that he might be spared the torturous journey to Wyvern Towers? And had she not seen to it that his slumber each night was undisturbed? To be sure, she had behaved very well, and for her trouble she received gratuitous insults. Gathering her dignity close about her, she suppressed her baser instincts and wished Rochford a chilly good day, leaving him once more to his solitude.

An hour later, when she received a hastily scrawled but gracefully apologetic request for her company, her first inclination was to refuse to see him. Therefore, having graciously risen above such ungenerous behavior, she was astonished when, gray eyes atwinkle, he asked whether she had got over her miff yet. "We ought not to be so quick to set each other at odds this way," he said, smiling, "but I daresay that with our emotions so near the surface, as they are, no more may be expected of us."

"Our emotions, sir?" she said softly, suspicions alerted.

"Come, Philippa, you cannot have been insensible to the growing warmth of feeling between us these past weeks. My fury on the hunting field was no more than reaction to fear for the safety of one who has become dear to me."

She stared at him, dismayed. "Rochford, you are not being so daft as to make me an offer, are you?"

He returned her look with a bewildered one of his own. "But I thought—"

"What *I* thought," she informed him awfully, "was that we had become friends, that you were different from the others, but you proved me wrong on the first count when you chased me from the hunt, and now you prove me wrong on the second. Surely I have told you that I have no wish to burden myself with another husband."

"Yes," he said quietly, even sadly, "you said as much, but I thought you had come to know your own feelings, and mine, in the meantime. 'Tis a pity you cannot see what is so clear to others."

Her breast swelled with indignation, but the angry words she wished to say died away in the back of her throat when her gaze encountered the steady look in his light gray eyes. Though she could not speak, neither could she stay to listen, so once again she left him, and thenceforth spoke not another word to him before he took his departure in his own well-sprung carriage later that afternoon. His sister accompanied him, for although Jessalyn had begged that Lucinda might be allowed to stay with her, Philippa had not seconded the invitation, and Rochford did not hesitate to refuse permission.

"I am certain that your stepmama's peace has been cut up quite enough for a day or two," he said, glancing at Philippa briefly before returning his attention to Jessalyn. "I think it would be as well, for that matter, if Lucy were to remain at home until Monday, for I shan't be able to ride out until then, in any event, so I daresay she will be no trouble to me. How will that suit you, ma'am?"

"I am sure Lucinda is welcome whenever she chooses to come here," Philippa said stiffly.

"Mercy me," said Miss Pellerin, gazing in bewilderment from one to the other, "his lordship must realize that much by now, my dear, and is merely expressing his concern, as anyone might, for your well-being. So kind and generous are you to be giving lessons every day to the girls, but it will not harm them to have a day off, and I am persuaded it will do you a great deal of good to have several days all to yourself. That, no doubt, is what his lordship intends."

"Just so," said Rochford gently.

"As though butter wouldn't melt in his mouth," Philippa muttered a few moments later as they watched the carriage rattle away down the drive.

"Philippa!" exclaimed Miss Pellerin with a warning gesture toward Jessalyn, who was standing a little to one side, her eyes still on the departing carriage.

"Well, I'm sorry if it ill becomes me to speak so, Cousin, but you don't know all that man has said to me. His behavior today alone has been unforgivable."

"Mercy me, I had thought the quarrel between you all over and done," said Miss Pellerin, shaking her head woefully. "Do you mean to say that he ripped up at you again, my dear?"

"Oh, no, ma'am. First he informed me that a woman belongs on a sofa, not on a saddle, and then, if you please, he as good as asked me to marry him, as if *that* would make all right again. Oh, Wakefield was right to warn me to beware of even the most charming of gentlemen," she added, her voice rising in increasing agitation. "Not that Rochford is that, of course. Imagine his telling me I belong on a sofa—setting myself to please men, is what he meant, no doubt—as though I had been Harriette Wilson or that big-bosomed Cari person all the gentlemen were in such alt over three years ago when we were here. And he can't say that *they* stayed only on sofas, either, now I come to think of it, for while I am not certain about Miss Wilson, I do know that the notorious Cari was used to ride out hunting on occasion, just like Letty Lade, for Wakefield said something about it and laughed, saying the men could not keep their eyes on their hounds whilst her mounds were bouncing about amongst them. A very good joke he thought it, too, as I recall."

"Philippa, really," Mis Pellerin said, frowning at her, "you cannot believe Rochford numbers you amongst such persons. Moreover, you ought not to repeat Wakefield's jests to Jessalyn, nor yet even to introduce those dreadful women's names in front of her."

Philippa looked wildly at her stepdaughter, who was now listening avidly to their conversation. "Oh, to be sure, Jessalyn, you are not to repeat anything I have said. Goodness, I have said too much, but I am so angry there is no bearing it. I should have liked to—" But here, realizing that it would really be going beyond the line to say she would have liked nothing better than to have hit Rochford, she broke off and turned to her cousin. "I beg your pardon, ma'am. I have let my tongue run away with me. 'Tis most unseemly."

"To be sure, my dear, I had thought you must have outgrown the lamentable tendency you displayed as a child to act rashly and without proper consideration whenever your emotions outran your good sense, but I see you have not. Moreover, I believe you have paid a great deal too much heed to Wakefield's advice."

Bristling, Philippa said stoutly, "He gave me very good advice."

"With regard to matters of business, perhaps," Miss Pellerin agreed, "but did you not say Rochford had proposed marriage?"

Philippa nodded, but she was not really attending. She was annoyed with herself for allowing her tongue to run on like a fiddlestick in Jessalyn's hearing, but for all that, her temper had been fanned too many times of late to be easily brought under rein.

She wanted nothing so much as to teach the viscount a lesson. Had she been a man and he not injured, she would have liked to knock him down for treating her feelings and wishes so lightly. Yes, and it was another offense of nature that ladies were not allowed to fight duels, for surely there were times such as this in any woman's life when she must wish for the chance to take sword in hand to right her wrongs. Men had life well in hand, did they not? A man could lose his temper and have little fear of being made to suffer for it, but a lady must always contain her emotions. That rule of conduct was as contemptible as the one which sought to deny ladies the pleasures of the hunting field.

She was still lost in thought some moments later when they entered the stone hall and Miss Pellerin dismissed Jessalyn to her bedchamber to prepare for dinner. "You are very angry still, are you not, Philippa?"

Philippa regarded the older woman blankly for a moment before the words penetrated, bringing a hard glint to her eyes. "Angry? Indeed, I am, ma'am. Rochford deserves to be boiled in oil."

"But, mercy me, you cannot be angry with a man for wishing to marry you, and Mr. Assheton-Smith said the same thing about sofas and saddles. You were annoyed, to be sure, but you were not ready to order him boiled in oil."

"Truly, ma'am," Philippa said, drawing herself up grandly, "I cannot think why the words should sound so much more offensive on Rochford's lips, but that is the case. And Mr. Assheton-Smith had no reason to think himself beholden to me, what's more," she added as though putting in the clincher.

Miss Pellerin stared at her in no little dismay. "Why, I do believe you offered to help Lucinda merely to put Rochford under an obligation to you, and you did flirt with him—you know you did—and for the selfsame reason, I make no doubt."

"Nonsense," Philippa said, but she could not make the word sound convincing even to her own ears. Oddly, this failure served only to make her want to cry one moment and to exacerbate her temper the next, and the fact that she could not explain all her wrongs with perfect clarity to her cousin made matters that much worse. Thus it was that, pleading an incipient headache, she soon excused herself to her room, denying all interest in dinner.

The wish to be revenged upon the viscount continued to grow, but rack her brain as she would, she could think of no suitable way to bring him to a clear recognition of his misdeeds. Indeed, the more she thought and the more she attempted to paint him a villain, the more her imagination tended to present her with a mental picture of the viscount laughing or recounting an amusing tale of his adventures on the Continent as he had been wont to do from time to time when he visited them in the afternoon. She next found herself remembering her encounter with him on the parapeted terrace at Belvoir Castle, remembering the feelings that had swept through her as she stood near him, the happy little humming that had filled her mind when he smiled at her that day. From that thought others followed, until it was with truly affectionate amusement that she recalled the exasperated way he had shaken his head at Lord Robert Manners's description of the feud between the duke and Sir William Manners. It was at this point in her reflection, however, that Philippa suddenly sat up straighter and smiled. It was not a friendly smile. Her thoughts had become clear at last, and before she fell asleep that night, she knew precisely how she would punish the viscount.

Accordingly, the next morning she sent for her bailiff to present himself to her in the common parlor at his earliest convenience. Since Mr. Weems was astute enough to recognize a royal command when he heard one, he came at once and found his mistress, attired in a becoming sprigged-muslin morning gown, standing at the window in rapt contemplation of the front drive. She turned to face him, but she did not speak immediately. Indeed, she looked as though she were still lost in thought.

"What is it, my lady? I had not believed you would wish to see the accounts before Monday morning."

"Never mind the accounts now," Philippa responded tersely, giving herself a little shake to clear her mind. "I have more important business for you to attend to. I want signs clearly posted all around our land, tenant farms included, barring anyone from trespassing without permission from me."

The plump little man stared at her uncomprehendingly. "No-trespassing signs, my lady? Surely you can't mean that."

"I do mean it, Mr. Weems. I have never in my life been more serious about anything. This property is no longer open to any hunter who chooses to ride his horse across it without regard for crop or garden. Why, I heard that only last year one of Mr. Assheton-Smith's hunts ended in a front garden in Leicestershire, so I suppose we must be grateful that they have not ridden straight up our drive or even into the stone hall."

"My lady, at the risk of speaking above my place, I must venture to say that there is little risk of such a thing occurring. I believe, moreover, that you are being precipitate in ordering this land posted against trespassers. You will achieve little but to bring the wrath of your neighbors and tenants down upon your head. Why, a man of Tom Giles's temperament, for example, won't thank you for protecting his fields from the hunters."

"Well, he should thank me," said Philippa flatly, "for now he can go about his business, which should be to get a good crop of winter wheat out of that north field, for one. Yes, and now I come to think of it, there is no reason why our dairy cattle must be kept in the barn eating expensive hay and grain when they might benefit from the excellent pasturing hereabouts. There can be no objection now, I expect, to putting them out to graze."

"But the hunters," protested poor Mr. Weems, mopping his brow with a handkerchief yanked from his coat pocket for the purpose. "My lady, you cannot have thought of what this will mean. Every hunt in the shires crosses this land upon occasion."

"They must hunt in other directions," said Philippa with a dismissive shrug. "There is sufficient open land in Leicestershire to make it unnecessary that they should wish always to cross the Whissendine, you know." She drew herself up haughtily. "In any event, Mr. Weems, I have given you your orders. I hope I shall not find it necessary to repeat them."

"No, my lady," said the bailiff morosely. "I'll see to it, right enough. Not that it won't be as much as my life is worth to speak to Giles or Sam Cudlipp," he added, muttering.

Philippa chose not to hear him, merely nodding dismissal, and when he had gone she sat back in her chair, pleased with her morning's work. Now let Rochford prate of women and sofas. Let him still pretend that what she wanted was marriage with its resulting loss of independence. Whatever she had said to Weems about the hunts having all of Leicestershire in which to indulge their sport, the Wyvern must lose six foxes out of ten if they could not hunt across the Raynard-Wakefield estate. Thus would Rochford be punished, for he would be quickly brought to realize that he had underestimated her strength, and that although she might not wish to wed, her determination to ride with the hunt was as strong as ever.

Later that afternoon, having had her fill of Jessalyn's complaints of boredom, she invited that young lady to ride out with her, and having crossed several fields, soon came to the first posted notice.

"Goodness," said Jessalyn, "whatever is that, ma'am?"

"That is to keep the hunters from trampling over our crops," her stepmother replied matter-of-factly.

Not being Leicestershire born and bred, Jessalyn accepted the explanation without comment, but at the supper table that evening, when she mentioned seeing the sign, Miss Pellerin was not so naive.

"Mercy me, Philippa, tell me you have not done such an outlandish thing."

"Well, I have done it," Philippa replied defensively. "I hope you will not say I had no right."

"As to that, I know only what you do yourself, that there was a court case in London and nearly another between Rutland and his cousin, but having the right is not the same as doing the right thing. There can be no good reason to make an enemy of Rochford, nor yet of any of your other neighbors."

"Well, I do not care for what Rochford or anyone else might think. They care only for their stupid prejudices and nothing at all for what is fair, so 'tis no more than they deserve, to be sure."

Such opposition served to make her wish the inevitable confrontation with his lordship would come quickly. But it was not Rochford whom Bickerstaff announced while Philippa was still in the breakfast parlor the next morning, but Mr. Thomas Assheton-Smith.

"Goodness to mercy!" Philippa exclaimed.

"He cannot know how little advanced is the hour," said Miss Pellerin in a bemused tone, "for no gentleman would call before a lady has had proper time in which to break her fast."

"Well, I daresay he is not thinking of my well-being, but of his own," Philippa said with a tight smile. "To be sure, I had not thought to see him here, but I do recall that the Quorn hunts this side of the county on Fridays."

With this vague utterance, she gathered the skirts of her jonquil linen frock and preceded Bickerstaff from the room. "Where have you put him?" she asked over her shoulder.

"In the saloon, my lady. If I might venture to say so, ma'am, the gentleman is in a rare taking. You ought not, perhaps, to see him alone."

"No, indeed, that she shall not," declared Miss Pellerin, bustling up behind them. "The very idea. He scarcely behaved in a polite fashion when we called at Quorndon Hall. I should not care to think what he may say now if you have vexed him, Philippa."

That she had indeed vexed Mr. Assheton-Smith was perfectly apparent the moment they laid eyes on the gentleman, for he was pacing back and forth across the elegant Aubusson carpet in the huge saloon, his large hands jammed into his coat pockets. At their entrance he whirled to face them, anger clearly etched on his thin face.

"There you are!" he bellowed, jerking his right hand from its pocket in order to point an angry finger at Philippa. "By God, madam, if you were my wife, I should know how to deal with your treachery, damme if I wouldn't."

"Treachery, sir?" Philippa widened her eyes. "There has been no treachery."

"Has there not, by God? Let me tell you, madam, that if there were but one fox in this county, that fox would learn by dawn tomorrow that your land has a safe earth to hide him, and then where should we be? I'll tell you, damme if I won't. We should be in the briars, madam, in the briars. Of all human pursuits, hunting is the best, and of all living things, a fox is the most valuable, but not if he is allowed to run wild and proliferate the countryside. Not then, madam, but that is what you will see here if you are permitted your foolishness. You've no right to post your damned signs, and we are under no obligation to acknowledge them, and so I have come to tell you to your face. A hunter has every right to chase the fox, wherever he runs, in order to keep him from making a pest of himself, and so I tell you and so I'll tell anyone who asks me. Damme if I won't."

"You must know that simply is not so," Philippa said calmly. She had thought she would be afraid of him, but he was too loud, too blustering, too much out of control. She looked him straight in the eye without difficulty. "As Master of the Quorn, sir, it is your duty to be aware of changes in the laws that affect your hunt; therefore, you must know that the London court has, more than once, upheld the right of the landowner over the right of the hunt. If you cross my land, I shall prosecute. Do not think I won't."

"Damme if I'll let a chit dictate to me, madam. If you were a man, I should know how to bring you to your senses."

"Well, I am not a man, nor, I am most thankful to say, am I your wife, so you will have to give in as graciously as you can, Mr. Assheton-Smith. There are many acres in Leicestershire besides those under my control, so I daresay your hunt will not be much disrupted. You are merely annoyed that I have dared to oppose you. That was not my intent when I posted my land, but I cannot say I am sorry for it, so if you have nothing more to say to the purpose, my butler will show you the door."

Assheton-Smith glared at her impotently for some seconds before, with a sound perilously near a growl, he allowed Bickerstaff to show him out.

Philippa expelled a sigh of relief. "How I dislike that man!"

"No doubt he is a very good master of hounds," Miss Pellerin said temperately, "and you must admit, Philippa, you have given him cause for annoyance."

"Yes, but that is all, ma'am, for the Quorn truly don't hunt over this land but maybe once or twice in a month. 'Tis unfortunate they rode here yesterday, for their normal run is to the west of Melton, you know. I daresay we shall hear from Lord Lonsdale next. The Cottesmore does ride this way rather often."

"Indeed, though they have all of Rutlandshire at their disposal, do they not?"

Philippa grinned at her. "I shall remember that, ma'am."

She did receive a visit from Lord Lonsdale, and although he was more polite than Mr. Assheton-Smith, the visit was still an ordeal, for he was much annoyed with her. She was rid of him at last, however, and decided to escape any other confrontations, for the moment at least, by going for a ride.

"May I go with you, ma'am?" Jessalyn called after her from the gallery railing when she saw Philippa crossing the stone hall and realized from her habit where she was going.

Philippa hesitated on the brink of giving her permission, but she really wanted time to think, and Jessalyn's unceasing prattle would make thought of any kind impossible. "Not today, my pet, but perhaps tomorrow after church you may ride to Wyvern Towers with Jake Pottersby to pay your respects to the Lady Lucinda."

Jessalyn agreed enthusiastically, well pleased by the compromise, and Philippa went on her way, determined to find solitude in the park behind the house. When she reached the stable, however, she was quickly brought to realize that she would find no peace in the immediate future. There seemed to be some sort of confrontation taking place between Jake Pottersby and a younger, brawnier man whom she recognized as one of her tenants.

"Here now, what's this?" Philippa demanded, striding up to the two as the younger man gave Pottersby a push.

"Nay, lass," said the groom hastily, " 'tis naught of importance."

"Aye, ye'd say that, ye old puffguts," snapped the younger man. He was built heavily in the torso, with thick shoulders and hamlike thighs, and he was dressed in homespun and a heavy woolen jacket that stretched tightly across his huge shoulders. "Yer fine mistress don't know what she be a-doin', but ye'll defend 'er and tell 'er that whatsoever she wants be the goods, 'n all."

"Who are you?" asked Philippa, speaking more calmly. "I collect that something I've done has aroused your anger."

"Aye, wrap it up any ways ye want, me lady. Ye've beggared me and mine, is what ye've done."

"I've done what?"

"How am I t' feed my bairns wi'out an income, if ye please?"

"Without an income? I thought you to be one of my tenants."

"Name of Thomas Giles, not that the same'll be of interest t' ye."

"But it is, Mr. Giles. You are indeed one of my tenants, then, are you not?"

"One o' Lord Wakefield's tenants, I be, and the old baron were awake ter the time o' day, which ye be not, I'm thinkin'."

"What on earth do you mean, Mr. Giles?" She looked helplessly at Pottersby. "Do you understand him, Jake?"

"Eh, lass, but yon caper-wit be fidgetin' hisself over nobbut t' gelt, choose how. Happen it'll be better nor like wi' a tidy few o' yer other folk. This'un just be a mite more shutful wi' 'is gab."

Noting Giles's bewilderment, Philippa explained, "He says you are concerned only with the money—the damages you collect, I suppose—and that others may feel the same way, but that you are more outspoken. You would do better to have brought your concerns calmly to me, Mr. Giles, so that we might discuss them."

'Calmly, is it? Discuss? I'll show you *discuss*." Giles moved toward Philippa with enough menace in his expression to cause her to step quickly away from him.

"Here, we'll have nowt o' that!" exclaimed Pottersby, leaping forward to clutch at one of Giles's muscular arms. Knowing he was no match for the other, he took the precaution of shouting at the same time, "To me, lads, to me!"

Instantly a number of stableboys and grooms appeared as though out of the woodwork, and Giles, seeing himself outnumbered, let his hands fall to his sides and glared at

Philippa. "I'm not daft, m'lady. But never think I'll keep me gab shut o'er this piece o' work. I mean t' speak t' all the tenants, and we'll see how ye like havin' 'em all beatin' their chests over yer foolishness."

"Mr. Giles," Philippa said pacifically, "I am certain that you will make plenty of money if you will but put your effort into farming the land. This is excellent, fertile soil, you know, capable of producing many crops."

"Aye, and in the spring we'll see to it proper," he growled. "But ye be denyin' us our best crop, 'n we won't be a-standin' fer it, ye'll see."

He stepped forward again, and Philippa had all she could do not to scurry out of his way, but he passed her without moving his clenched hands from his sides and strode angrily from the stableyard.

Jake Pottersby let out a long breath, and she turned to him with a twisted little smile on her face. "I've done it this time, haven't I, Jake?"

"Aye, choose how, lass. That Giles be fatched, 'e is and all, and what he mun be framin' t' do don't bear thinkin' on."

Philippa bit her lower lip. "Perhaps I did act hastily, Jake. I didn't understand how much the tenants depend upon their damage suits, and though I cannot approve of such a practice, I see it has become a tradition with them."

"Aye, mistress, it has, 'n all."

Deciding not to ride out after all, she left him and returned slowly to the house, entering by the park front terrace and the saloon. Perhaps, she told herself, she had let her temper run away with her in her wish to punish the viscount. What had seemed an excellent idea at first now seemed to have taken on ramifications she had never anticipated.

As she crossed the baroque saloon to the tall, pedimented doorway leading into the stone hall, there came a thunderous knocking on the front door and she saw Bickerstaff step across the hall to open it with more speed and less dignity than was his wont. Scarcely had he unlatched the door than it was thrust open from the outside and Viscount Rochford erupted into the hall.

His entrance was less than graceful, for he was forced to

make use of the cane he carried in order to limp into the hall, but once inside, he straightened, and when he saw Philippa in the doorway opposite, he raised the cane and pointed it at her at though he would pin her where she stood.

"So there you are," he said grimly. "Well, I've come to put a stop to this foolishness, so just you come here to me, madam."

—11—

PHILIPPA'S FIRST EMOTION upon seeing Rochford was distress that he might have reinjured himself by riding the five miles between Wyvern Towers and Chase Charley, but his angry words and curt command put distress to flight. She stood where she was, having all she could do to control her own rising temper.

Rochford shot a look at the hovering Bickerstaff. "Take yourself off, man. You're not wanted here."

"How dare you?" demanded Philippa, finding her tongue at last and adding sharply, "Bickerstaff, you are to go nowhere. His lordship mistakes the matter. I am not at home to callers."

Bickerstaff glanced from her to the angry viscount, clearly undecided as to his proper course. No doubt he ought to obey his mistress and put the unwelcome visitor out the door. On the other hand, even with his injured ankle and what bruises might remain about his person, the viscount was a force clearly to be reckoned with. At the moment he looked particularly formidable. Still, Bickerstaff did his best. Spreading his hands appealingly, he said, "My lord, perhaps it would be best—"

Rochford turned slightly and flicked the butler a glance that halted the words in his throat and froze his hands in their movement through space. The flintlike gaze then shifted back to rest upon Philippa. "Tell him to leave," he said, gritting the words through his teeth.

His anger, having first chilled her to the marrow, now sent sparks shooting through her veins. She straightened her shoulders and lifted her chin, meeting his look eye to eye with an icy one of her own.

"You are behaving like a brigand, my lord," she said tartly. "You have no right to roar your way into my house, waving your cane like a madman and bellowing orders at my servants. If you have something to say to me, be sure I will listen to you, but not here in the hall where you will be making a gift of your words to every passing servant. Come into the library, if you please. You may say what you like to me there." She looked briefly at the butler. "Bring refreshment in fifteen minutes, Bickerstaff. His lordship will no doubt need something to cool his throat by then."

Having said her piece, she swept past the viscount, carrying the train of her riding habit over her arm It was not until she was halfway through the common parlor that it occurred to her that he might have difficulty walking so far as the library. But when she paused to look over her shoulder, he was directly behind her, and although he was limping, he did not lean as heavily on the cane as he had when he entered the hall. She found herself wishing suddenly that he had left that cane in the hall, and the thought sent a small shiver of fear up her back.

In the library, she turned to face him, her color high, her hands pressed tightly into the folds of her skirt.

Rochford pushed the door shut with the head of his cane. That he was still angry was evident from his expression, but she saw lines of pain in his brow, as well, and felt immediate contrition at having brought him to such a pass.

"Perhaps you ought to sit down, Rochford."

"What, before I fall down? I am not such a weakling as that, madam. Nor was there any reason to repair to this room, for I have only one thing to say to you. You are to order those signs removed at once."

Philippa stiffened. "I beg your pardon?"

"It is not my pardon you must beg, but that of the men whose hunting you have disrupted with your childish whim. Your quarrel—whatever it was—was with me. You had no business to act so precipitately, and you must put matters right at once."

"I see," Philippa said, wondering how it was that this man

could turn her softer feelings to blazing anger with so little effort. "Because you order it, I am to submit to your wishes. Is that the case, my lord?"

"The case is that you don't realize what you have done, and I do. For once in your life, dear Philippa, you will attend to wiser counsel than your own. This is no time to allow you to indulge in a temper tantrum, though from what I have come to know of you, I do not doubt that you have been allowed to indulge yourself far too often in the past."

"Dear me, you sound very like Mr. Assheton-Smith," she retorted sarcastically. "He left me in no doubt as to what method he would like to use upon me."

"He has my sympathy." Rochford was clearly having difficulty keeping rein on his temper. "If I were in better trim, I'd at least give you the thorough shaking you deserve for this piece of work. But I did not come here for discussion. If you like, I will convey your instructions to your bailiff before leaving here." He turned back toward the door.

"Mr. Weems already has my instructions," said Philippa hotly, "and I daresay he knows better than to take any from you, sir. If you have said all you mean to say, I wish you will go away, for I have nothing further to say to you."

He took an unwary step toward her, wincing as he came down on his left foot. "Do you mean to tell me you refuse to do as I bid you?"

"Indeed, sir, for I do not recognize your authority. A proposal of marriage—which, I might remind you, I refused—scarcely gives you the right to dictate to me."

He let out a long breath of exasperation. "Though, as always, I cannot wish to contradict you, madam, no offer of marriage was made. If you will but recall the moment in question, I am persuaded you will agree."

She knew he was right. She had never allowed him to say the words he had begun to say, and oddly, now that memory irritated her. She shrugged. "What you said or didn't say does not signify. I recognize no one's authority save my own."

"Philippa," he said gently, "I should dislike being put to the trouble of applying to your trustees in such a matter as this, but do not think I will not."

"You cannot," she retorted, triumph gleaming in her eyes, "for there are no such persons. I am the principal trustee for my own estate as well as for—"

"Good Lord, do you mean Wakefield was such a flat as to put full control of your entire inheritance into your own hands?"

Philippa's chin rose sharply. "And why should he not, sir? Wakefield was not so gothic as to think women cannot decide things for themselves. Besides," she added, "he taught me everything I need to know, so he could scarcely declare me unfit and give my affairs into some one else's hands."

"But your father! Surely Wakefield must have named him—"

"I am sorry to distress you further, my lord, but you have only me to contend with, and I have no intention of taking orders from you or any other man. I have every right to do what I have done, and some good may even come from it if your precious Melton men learn a lesson in civility. It cannot hurt them, certainly, to learn that a love of hunting does not endow them with the right to crash through property without the owner's leave to do so. And now I must ask you to take your departure, sir. There is no more you can possibly have to say to the purpose."

He hesitated for a moment, regarding her narrowly, and she thought she saw dawning respect in his eyes. But then he turned on his heel without another word and she watched with a sudden tightness in her throat as he limped across the common parlor to the hall. For no reason that she could call to mind, she had a wish to burst into tears, and when the front door had shut behind him, she slumped down into one of the library chairs in a way that would have promptly called maternal censure down upon her, and shut her eyes as tightly as she could, as if by doing so she might stop her tears from flowing.

It was impossible to maintain this position for long, of course. First her eyes began to ache and then the muscles in her back began to protest. When she heard footsteps approaching the library from the direction of the hall, she straightened quickly, putting a hand up to smooth her hair as Bickerstaff entered the room carrying a silver tray. He glanced around in bewilderment.

"Oh," Philippa said, attempting to sound casual, "his lordship has gone, Bickerstaff. I am surprised you did not hear the door shut behind him."

"But you ordered refreshment, my lady."

"So I did. Well, you may leave the tray, in any event. I am parched, myself, and can do with a restorative."

The butler looked her over with an experienced eye, but he said nothing, taking his dismissal without protest. That he believed she ought not to be left to her solitude, however, was brought home to Philippa some minutes later when Miss Pellerin entered the library.

"Mercy me!" that lady exclaimed, throwing up her hands as though she were startled to discover Philippa in the room.

"Doing it much too brown, as Edward would say, Cousin." But Philippa smiled at her. "I collect that Bickerstaff advised you to seek me out, believing I was in need of solace or some such thing."

"Well, dearest," Miss Pellerin said, taking a seat and feeling the teapot for warmth before pouring herself a cupful, "he did say that Viscount Rochford had called."

"And he no doubt also said his lordship was blustering like bull-beef when he descended upon us. Well, he was, but as you see, I have routed him, foot and guns, and have come through the ordeal unscathed."

"Oh, Philippa, what did he say?"

"Why, he was angry that I have posted our land, of course, and he had the unmitigated gall to order me to take the signs down. To tell you the truth, Cousin," she added with a rueful sigh, "I was well along to a decision to do just that before he came roaring in, shouting his orders."

"Oh, dear, he ought to have known a demanding attitude would merely serve to set up your back."

Philippa grinned at her, more relaxed now. "Well, yes, I think he ought. But the poor man clearly thinks he is still on the Continent leading a squadron or whatever it was he led, with subalterns who salute and say 'Yes sir' to his every command. But I am no subaltern, and he ought not to bark his commands at me."

Miss Pellerin regarded her speculatively. "He did not behave well, certainly, my dear, but must you continue at odds with him this way? You did say you had intended to have the signs removed."

"I didn't say that, precisely," Philippa corrected her. "I confess I had had some thought of doing so, for I met one of our tenants, a perfectly horrid man who would have liked nothing better than to string me to the nearest tree, I think, and he has threatened to arouse the other tenants. Then, of course, Mr. Assheton-Smith and Lord Lonsdale are put out, and I never meant for anyone to be affected but Rochford."

"You did not think the matter through carefully, Philippa. That has always been one of your worst faults, you know."

"Yes," Philippa replied candidly, "I do know, and since this was by way of being a decision about a business matter, I cannot think why I did not consider it in the methodical way Wakefield taught me. I daresay, however, that left to myself I would have had the stupid signs removed when I discovered what a row they had stirred. But you must see that I cannot do such a thing now, or Rochford would believe I have bowed to his will. That, ma'am, I could not tolerate for an instant."

"No, I don't suppose you could," her companion said with a sigh, "but perhaps you ought to consider the wisdom of returning to London."

"What? Run from the storm? I promise you, I am not such a rabbit as that. I daresay things may become a trifle difficult, but we shall muddle through."

"Difficult" proved to be a mild word to describe the events of the next week. Indeed, at Saint Mary's church in Melton Mowbray the very next morning, Philippa saw that word had passed to everyone about her dreadful deed. A good many glares were shot her way, and after the service she received the cut direct from no fewer than three gentlemen. Mr. Brummell shook his head at her, but she was certain she could detect a glint of amusement in his eyes. In Lord Alvanley's, when they met on the flagway afterward, there was none.

"Harden your heart and tighten your girth, ith that the way of it, my lady?" he asked with a carefully blank expression.

"Oh, sir, are you at outs with me too? I promise I never meant to make so many people angry."

"Mutht have meant to," he said. "Certainly did a proper job of it. Daresay you intended only to play off a trick against

Rochford, but your game affecth many more people than that. Hunting's therious business in Melton, ma'am."

She tried to explain that it was no game to her, but she could not feel that she had succeeded, and as the week progressed she came to see just how seriously the Melton men took their hunting. On Wednesday Weems informed her that he would have to send to Grantham for feed for their horses.

"Good gracious, I thought you attended to all that in Melton Mowbray," Philippa protested.

"To be sure, ma'am, we have done in the past, but there seems to be no feed available at present." He gazed steadily at a point beyond her left shoulder as he spoke.

"I see," she said, seeing very clearly. "Very well, do what you must."

Her tenants reacted just as Giles had predicted they would, but she instructed Mr. Weems to explain matters to the most assertive of these, which the poor man did as best he could. Her gamekeeper presented yet another problem, for Jake Pottersby had informed her that Sam Cudlipp was as annoyed with her as Tom Giles was. By far the greatest portion of Sam's income came from his earth-stopping fees, which were considerable. Still, she could not see what was to be done about that and determined to avoid the gamekeeper altogether for the present, if she could manage to do so.

In order to avoid any incident that might jeopardize Jessalyn's or Lucinda's safety, Philippa was forced to forbid their afternoon riding, causing Jessalyn to express her annoyance in such inconsiderate terms that the scene between them ended with Philippa's ordering her to bed without supper. Fortunately, however, although his own frequent visits had ceased, Rochford did not choose to forbid his sister's daily visits to Chase Charley—probably, Philippa told herself acidly, because he would then have had to look after her himself. Nonetheless, she was grateful to him, for she was convinced that without Lucinda's visits to keep Jessalyn's boredom at bay, her stepdaughter must have driven her mad. As it was, by Friday she was exhausted and sick to death of the whole business. When she entered the drawing room that afternoon in time to see Miss Pellerin whisk a sheet of crude paper out of sight beneath her gray woolen skirt, it was nearly the final straw.

"What, pray, is that, Cousin?" she asked coolly.

"That?" Miss Pellerin removed her silver pince-nez and gazed up with limpid innocence. "Why, 'tis nothing at all, the merest trifle."

"Then you will not object to showing it to me, my dear ma'am." Philippa held out her hand, looking down at the older lady in such a way as to make it clear that she would not be denied.

Frowning a little and shaking her head as much in annoyance with herself for having been caught out as for any other reason, Miss Pellerin extracted the sheet of paper and handed it over.

Philippa scanned the clumsily penciled note quickly, her indignation rising with every word. "Who dared to give this to you, ma'am?"

"Why, Bickerstaff did, of course, but you must not be angry with him, for he only did as I asked. That is not the first such missive we have received, you know, but when the first arrived, you were out somewhere, so he brought it to me, and I could not think that showing it to you would serve any good purpose. I made no doubt, in point of fact, that it would infuriate you, just as this one seems to have done. In any event, I instructed Bickerstaff to bring any future things of this sort to me."

"How many have there been, Cousin Adeliza?"

"Oh, merely two or three," that lady replied airily.

"I see. Did they each threaten harm to me and mine if I did not see reason, as this one does?"

"Oh, to be sure, none was precisely conciliating, my dear, but wild threats, you know, must not be taken too seriously. I am persuaded no one would truly wish harm to any of us."

"Well, I cannot like it. Has Bickerstaff any notion who is sending them?"

"No, and they do not come through the post, as you can see. He merely finds them stuck in the door, and there was one in the grain wagon when they came back from Grantham with supplies for the stables. No one can think how it got there. I did ask Mr. Drake if he had any suggestion, you know, but he agreed with me that the least said, the soonest mended."

"Mr. Drake? Was he here?"

"Well, you know he was, Philippa, for you spoke to him yourself."

"Oh, yesterday. I had thought you meant today."

"No, no, and I must say I take it very kindly in him that he has not aligned himself with Rochford over this business. He says there is plenty of hunting and that the affair is no concern of his. And he comes to visit as often as he did before, which when no one else does must be considered a point in his favor, you know."

"Yes, of course," Philippa said vaguely. "Do you know, ma'am, I had thought this nonsense would blow over rather more quickly than this."

"Well, it hasn't. Mr. Drake says poor Rochford has felt the force of it, too."

"Rochford? How can that be?"

"Well, you see, my dear, the Melton Men seem to have come to the conclusion that he is somehow at fault for your behavior. I dare say you may thank Mr. Brummell or that rattle Alvanley for putting the notion in their heads. Mr. Drake says that however strongly they might pretend in public that his lordship is merely a victim like themselves, privately they are pressing him most urgently to do whatever he must to bring you to a more conciliating frame of mind. Some, Mr. Drake says, have even gone so far as to badger Rochford to organize a ladies' hunt."

Her words gave Philippa food for thought, but she had barely had time to consider whether either the Melton men or Rochford believed that a tame ladies' hunt would satisfy her, before she had other matters to occupy her mind, for they had no sooner sat down at the dining-room table that evening than there was a clatter of wheels and horses' hooves on the drive outside the window, and the sound of several masculine voices upraised in cheerful shouting.

"Mercy me!" exclaimed Miss Pellerin, exchanging a startled glance with Philippa. "Has there been an invasion?"

Jessalyn, forgetting her manners in the excitement of the moment, leapt from her chair and scurried to the tall, heavily draped window. That neither of the older ladies censured this unladylike conduct spoke volumes for their own curiosity. For her part, Philippa held her breath, watching the child as she pulled the heavy blue velvet curtains aside and peeped out the window.

Jessalyn let out a shriek of joy. "It is Edward! Edward is come. Oh, ma'am, may I go to him? Please."

"You will do no such thing," said Miss Pellerin firmly. "The very notion. You will sit down at the table and eat your dinner like a Christian, young lady, and we will hear no more about running out to meet what sounds like a whole cavalcade of gentlemen."

"Well, there were at least four of them," acknowledged Jessalyn, returning to her place with patent reluctance. "I daresay he has brought friends from school for hunting, and maybe to spend Christmas with us. 'Tis only a fortnight off, after all."

Philippa had not said anything, but to say that she was delighted by her stepson's arrival would have been to exaggerate the matter. Rather, she was dismayed. Whether Edward had come for the hunting, which was all too likely, or merely to spend Christmas in what was left of the bosom of his family, he could not be counted upon to take cheerfully the information that his stepmother had set herself against the whole of Leicestershire.

Nor did he. It was apparent before ever he opened his mouth upon entering the dining room that he had seen at least one of the signs. Young Lord Wakefield was in his eighteenth year and had been raised by an affectionate father and a succession of doting nannies to think himself quite a fellow. Even his years at Eton had done little to lower his opinion of himself, for he had had the good fortune to be very good at games and thus was able to escape most of the trials of being a less-than-brilliant scholar. He was of medium height, with curly blond hair, an athletic build, and a generally sunny temper; however, at the moment, his blue eyes were narrowed ominously, and his lips were pressed firmly together, bespeaking his displeasure.

Philippa spoke quickly. "How do you do, Edward? You ought to have sent word ahead, apprising us of your intended arrival. However, if you and your friends do not object to taking potluck, I daresay we can contrive to feed you. And pray, do not think you must change," she went on hurriedly when he opened his mouth to speak. "We are quite *en famille* tonight and will not mind you all in your dirt. Will you not introduce your friends to us? You do remember my cousin Adeliza Pellerin, do you not?"

"Well, of course I do," the young man said abruptly, but her rapid burst of words had served her purpose, for he had evidently recognized the unsuitability of speaking his mind before such an audience. He grimaced, shot her a look of intent, then turned to usher in the three gentlemen who had accompanied him. "That's Winky—Lord Winkburn, that is," he said, indicating the first of these, a young man whose neckcloth was rather taller than allowed for comfort and whose body one might have thought a trifle too chubby for the tight yellow pantaloons and bright green jacket he affected.

"How d'ye do?" he said, bowing stiffly, his cheeks reddening from the exertion.

Smiling at him, Philippa found herself wondering how on earth he had managed to ride a horse into Leicestershire from Oxford, but then she recalled the rattle of carriage wheels and deduced the Lord Winkburn had either driven himself or been driven. The others were introduced as Peter Dauntry, a slender young man whose eyes fairly popped out of his head at sight of his hostess, and Lord Reginald Partridge, a rakish gentleman with a blue-and-white Belcher handkerchief knotted casually around his throat.

"Son of old Walmsey, you know," Edward added to the latter introduction.

"The Marquess of Walmsey, I collect." Miss Pellerin nodded to the rakish gentleman, whose twinkling eyes and twitching lips gave Philippa to recognize a kindred spirit. The older lady added placidly, "I've known your papa and your dearest mama for years, young man, but I daresay you were always away at school when I chanced to visit Walmsey Hall."

"Or locked in my bedchamber, more like," replied Lord Reginald with an impudent grin. "Dashed if I didn't spend most of my formative years on bread and water, ma'am."

"But it was white bread and the purest spring water," quipped Lord Winkburn dryly.

"Well, I can't see that the diet did you any harm," said Miss Pellerin. "Do sit down, gentlemen. Here is Bickerstaff, right behind you, to take your orders."

"Something to wet our whistles, first off, man," said Mr.

Dauntry with an air of having dealt with the most important matter before he returned his admiring gaze to his hostess.

"Dash it, Pippa," Edward said in an undertone as he drew near her chair, "I wish to speak to you. I cannot think—"

"Yes, Edward," she replied quietly, "but not until after supper, if you please."

He nodded curtly, moving to take his place at the head of the table, but she could not be astonished when he joined her not ten minutes after the ladies had left the gentlemen to enjoy their port. She had instructed Bickerstaff to direct him to her in the library, Miss Pellerin having kindly agreed to keep Jessalyn occupied in the drawing room until the other gentlemen arose from the table, at which time the child was to be sent off to bed.

"What sort of bumble-broth have you created, for God's sake?" Edward demanded before he had even shut the door.

"Lower your voice, sir, and come into the room like a gentleman."

"Dash it, Pippa, don't try coming the stepmother over me. I won't stand for it. Not when you're less than eight years my senior."

"Since I am also your principal trustee, Edward, it would behoove you to tread courteously when dealing with me," she warned.

He pushed a hand through already tousled blond curls. "Dash it, how do you expect me to behave when I come into Leicestershire to find you've turned Chase Charley into a battlefield? You've embarrassed me before my friends and made me a dashed laughingstock. I came to hunt, but now I daresay Assheton-Smith and Lonsdale won't let me within sight of their hounds."

"Don't be absurd, Edward. They will not blame you for my doings. They know only too well that I am their opponent in this matter."

"Well, dash it, you've got to take those signs down at once, Pippa."

She refused to yield, but she could not say, when she finally took leave of him, that she had succeeded in explaining her reasons or in mitigating his wrath with her.

In the week that followed, tempers at Chase Charley became more frayed than ever, and although Edward and his friends got in several days of hunting, they were given to understand that their company was suffered by the other hunters rather than enjoyed by them, making it clear that the ill feeling in the neighborhood was growing, not diminishing with time. By the end of the week Philippa would have liked nothing better than to rip down every one of her no-trespassing signs. The only thing that stopped her was that she could not do so without seeming to give in to Rochford. Even that, as a reason, now seemed insufficient.

He had not come with his uncle to collect Lucinda after lessons in nearly two weeks, and she missed his company. She even missed having a chance to argue with him, and it occurred to her that she had come to look upon his friendship as a necessity to her comfort. When his eyes had glowed with warmth, she had felt that warmth spread all through her body. And, she realized uneasily, when the gray eyes had turned chilly, she had felt the chill, as well. Until she had allowed her temper to set her against him, until she had taken offense at what everyone else considered to be a trifle exploded out of all proportion, she had enjoyed only the warm feelings. Now, on the other hand, since it had become clear that he had no intention of allowing her to force his hand, it seemed the chill was all that was left. The thought was scarcely a comforting one, but it haunted her through the week.

Thursday afternoon, Edward and his friends returned early from their hunting, bringing with them Lord Alvanley and two of the gentlemen Philippa had seen the day of Rochford's accident. They entered the stone hall as she was passing through on her way to the saloon.

"No sport today, gentlemen?" she asked, smiling at them.

"We have," said Alvanley with a grimace, "been up Tilton Wood and down Tilton Wood and *through* Tilton Wood, and they'll very likely *finish* at Tilton Wood. We grew bored with Tilton Wood."

Several of the others chuckled, but Edward said rather sharply, "There was no sport in it today, a parcel of thrusters and crammers, heading the fox this way and that. There was no bearing it, so we came home. If we could have hunted over this country, it dashed well would have been different."

As a final straw it was sufficient. Philippa turned on her heel and without so much as a polite farewell to any of them walked through the saloon, out the terrace door, and down the steps. Giving no thought to purpose or direction, she strode angrily across the lawn to the gravel pathway leading into the park, wanting only to put as much distance as possible between herself and her stepson. Not until she heard the gurgling of the stream ahead did she realize she was drawing near to the keeper's cottage. The thought of encountering Sam Cudlipp was enough to cause her to turn back toward the house, congratulating herself upon a narrow escape from an undesirable confrontation. It was only by the greatest bad luck that she found herself, five minutes later, face-to-face with Tom Giles.

The burly tenant farmer stopped in his tracks, but when she would have passed by with no more than a polite greeting, he barred her way.

"What hurry, m'lady? 'Tis time 'n all we had some chat."

"I've nothing further to say to you, Mr. Giles."

"Seems like I got a deal to say to you, howsomever, and this be a good place to talk, I'm thinkin'." He moved a step nearer, and Philippa became aware of a growing fear that he might hurt her.

She stood very still. "You must let me pass. Lord Wakefield will soon come to look for me, you know, for I walked out only for a breath of air."

"Let 'im come. I've a deal t' say to 'is lordship, as well. Seems 'e oughta take a hand hereabouts."

"You must know that he cannot, that he is underage."

"He's a man, ain't 'e? T'ain't fittin' fer a woman t' be dealin' wi' what don't concern 'er. Woman bends t' man, m'lady. That be the way of it."

"Well, I shan't bend to you, for heaven's sake," Philippa said, stepping back, then crying out in alarm as his thick fingers closed around her arm. "Here, let go of me! Who do you think you are? Oh, thank goodness!"

A strong hand grabbed Giles by the shoulder from behind and swung him around. A second hand, balled into a fist, connected sharply with the point of his jaw, and Mr. Giles went down like a felled oak tree at Rochford's feet.

—12—

RUBBING HIS BRUISED knuckles, the viscount eyed Philippa sternly. "Goodness had nothing to do with this, my girl. I've been wanting to smash something for days." He reached down to help the groggy Giles to his feet.

The farmer glared at him sullenly but measuringly as well.

"Yes, I know you'd like nothing better than to plant me a leveler," Rochford said grimly, "but I wouldn't advise you to try it. Though you may not believe me, I am on your side in this business, and you may thank heaven for it, since that is the only reason you are getting out of this with no more than a sore chin. If you're wise, you'll take yourself off before I change my mind."

Philippa said nothing until, with no comment beyond a surly shrug, Giles had gone. Despite the rush of relief she had experienced upon seeing her rescuer, she wasn't by any means certain that she was safer with him than she had been with Tom Giles. Her first inclination had been to fling herself onto Rochford's broad chest and allow him to hold her very tightly, but the glitter of anger in his eyes when he looked at her stopped her cold. Now she wanted only to get back to the house with a whole skin, and by the look of him, that might not be an easy task.

She lifted her chin. "I must thank you for your timely arrival, my lord, but I collect that you have come to escort your sister back to Wyvern Towers. She will be wondering what has become of you."

As she moved to pass him, Rochford caught her arm. His grip was light at first, but when Philippa attempted to free herself, he shook his head, grasping her much more firmly.

"Oh, no, you don't, my girl, not until I have said a few things to you."

"Let me go, Rochford," she said, trying to sound dignified and succeeding in sounding apprehensive instead. She tugged again, but this time, somehow, he caught hold of her other shoulder.

"Little idiot," he muttered through clenched teeth as he shook her, "you *will* listen to me." He stopped shaking her almost at once, but while she attempted to catch her breath, he went on harshly, "I suppose you meant just to walk off alone again into God knows what sort of trouble. To leave the house unescorted, knowing as you must how distressed your people are, was the height of folly. Did you *want* someone to serve you a mischief?"

"No, of course not," she retorted, nettled. "I didn't think at all, of course. I merely wanted to get out of the house."

"Ructions again, I suppose," he said, releasing her. And then, when her head came up and she looked at him in surprise, he smiled grimly. "Oh, yes, I have heard all about Wakefield's displeasure. Uncle Archie hears a good deal from Miss Pellerin, and of course Lucinda prattles constantly of what she learns whilst she is under your roof. Bad manners, of course, but I have an interest, so I don't scold her." He was quiet for a moment. Then he said evenly, "You can scarcely blame your stepson for his attitude, ma'am. Your actions have made life for him amongst the sporting set well nigh insupportable."

"He is bearing up well enough," Philippa said, attempting to match the calmness of his tone. "He has hunted three days out of the four, and if he has not had so many invitations to dine afterward as he had anticipated, I am sure I am the one who suffers for it, not he, and not his friends. They have plenty to eat and drink at Chase Charley, and I've noticed that when he invites guests, they come."

"Come to see you in your den, most like," said the viscount flatly. "Curiosity accomplishes much in social enterprise. Do you dine with your stepson and his guests?"

"Yes," she replied slowly, "for Cousin Adeliza enjoys their company. I do not allow Jessalyn to do so, of course, but I could not deny my cousin her pleasure." She grimaced.

"They may come to see what I am like, sir, but at least Bickerstaff has not had to turn any gentlemen callers from the door of late, and I have not received a proposal of marriage in nearly a fortnight. That must be accounted to the good."

His mouth tightened briefly. "If you should receive an offer, I strongly advise you to refuse it," he said, "for you may rest assured that any suitor in these parts who offered marriage to you now would be doing so in order to achieve the right to beat you soundly. Every man jack of them wishes you had a husband or father at hand to bring you to your senses."

With a gasp of indignation, she pushed past him then and strode furiously toward the house, but Rochford had no intention of letting her escape so easily and, keeping pace with her stride for stride, he described for her conversationally, but in no uncertain terms, her stubbornness, her foolish pride, her childish desire for revenge—paltry revenge, he called it—and her foolhardiness in not properly looking after her own safety. Before they emerged from the park, Philippa was gritting her teeth and wishing she could take wing like the finch that shot out of a hedge ahead of them.

"Considering that you have done all you can do," he said as they moved briskly up the terrace steps to the house, "to make enemies of every man in Leicestershire, one might expect you to show at least the good sense to avoid a face-to-face confrontation with any of them. But no, you have to go out looking for trouble— Good day, Wakefield," he said with only the slightest change of tone when Edward stepped onto the terrace from the saloon as they approached the door. "Were you looking for her ladyship?"

Edward flushed uncomfortably as he looked from Philippa's angry face to the viscount's calm one, but he strove for a tone of casual unconcern. "As . . . as a matter of fact," he said, "I was just thinking of going round to the stables to look in on those new nags of mine. Prime bits of blood and bone. Would you like to take a look at them?"

"If they are the two you sent on ahead of you, I've seen them, thanks," Rochford said evenly. He did not offer further comment, and Philippa, who had already heard his opinion of both young hunters and knew it to match Jake

Pottersby's, believed Edward had reason, whether he realized it or not, to be grateful for the viscount's reticence.

Edward glanced at her just then, and she knew from his anxious look that he had indeed been coming to look for her. She managed to smile at him.

Relief sounded in his voice, but the words he spoke—to Rochford—were scarcely calculated to please her. "I say, my lord, won't you join us for supper? We've a number of good sorts here already, and I daresay it will make for just the sort of gathering you particularly like. Alvanley's here, you know, though Mr. Brummell's returned to London. And there's Reg Partridge and Winkburn, and . . . oh, a host of fine fellows. Do say you will."

Rochford glanced at Philippa, but she avoided his eye. She could hardly be so rude as to say outright that she did not wish him to stay, but surely he would refuse Edward's invitation if she made no move to second it. Apparently, however, he was not so conciliating as she had hoped.

"I should like very much to stay," the viscount said smoothly. "I believe my uncle is in the library with your cousin, and of course my sister is also here. I could send her home in the carriage, but as I have been given to understand that Miss Raynard-Wakefield does not dine in company, perhaps you will not mind if Lucinda remains to bear her company."

"Devil a bit. Shouldn't be surprised but what Jess will be glad to have her," replied Edward, clearly gratified at being applied to in such a case. He glanced from Philippa to the viscount, then added diffidently, "I say, I hope I didn't interrupt anything, bursting out upon you in such a way. I'll leave you to finish your discussion, and when you've done, Rochford, perhaps you'd like to join the rest of us in the billiards room. Alvanley has challenged all comers to a tournament. Should be some good sport."

Rochford nodded, and when Edward ducked back inside, he turned to Philippa with a wry smile. "Seems to have forgotten he was to look in on those nags of his."

She shrugged. "I daresay you were right, and he was coming to look for me. He does not like to be at outs with people, but he has a nasty tongue and I left him abruptly. No doubt, after a time, his conscience began to trouble him, and he wished to apologize." The door had swung to behind Edward, and she reached to push it open again. "You will be wanting to join the others, sir. The billiards room is through the dining room, at the northwest corner of the house. It was used to be a picture cabinet, and you will see some fine examples of Mr. Ferneley's and Mr. Charles Lorraine Smith's work hanging there."

When she would have turned away from him, Rochford stopped her just as he had done earlier, with a hand on her arm. This time, however, his touch was light. She made no attempt to pull away, but neither did she look at him. His touch was warm, and in that moment she found herself wishing with all her heart that she could simply put things back the way they had been. He spoke quietly. "I cannot let you go just yet, Philippa, not until I have attempted to make amends for my own hasty tongue. I fear I have been guilty of the same fault I deplored in you, and have let my temper carry me beyond the line."

"You are apologizing to me for what you said?" Skepticism sounded clearly in her tone, for except at the very beginning, he had not sounded as though his temper had run beyond its leash.

Rochford shook his head, amused. "Not for all I said. Merely for allowing my tongue to run on like a fiddlestick. I've no doubt I said much more than it was necessary to say. Seeing Giles go for you like that frightened me witless."

She turned then, unimpressed, intending to tell him to his face that, temper or no temper, he had said more than he had had any right to say, but the look in his eyes diverted her. Instead of putting him firmly in his place, she found herself gazing into those light gray eyes as though she might read his thoughts there. And, indeed, he seemed to be sending her a message that had nothing to do with hunting or arguments or no-trespassing signs. There was warmth in the message, and something more, something that after a bare second or two made her wrench her gaze from his to look with a sense of profound relief at the top button of his coffee-colored waistcoat. It was a pearl button, and by concentrating very carefully upon the luminescence of the pearl, she was able to bring her suddenly disordered senses under some control. She was still deeply conscious of his hand on her arm. Her skin tingled where he touched her, and oddly, she found herself remembering the strength of that same hand when he had shaken her. A little thrill coursed through her at the realization that she had unleashed such power in this man, that she could unleash that power again simply by arousing his anger or, perhaps, his passion.

"Philippa." His voice sounded ragged, and she realized he must be feeling some of the same emotions she was experiencing. She could not meet his eyes again, however—not just yet—so although she straightened her shoulders, she continued to look at the pearl button.

"I must change my dress before dinner," she said breathlessly.

With a sigh Rochford held the door for her, and she hurried past him, crossing the saloon to the stone hall, then nearly running up the grand stair. Lucinda and Jessalyn were in the morning room, their heads together over a romantic novel, but Philippa merely smiled at them in passing. A moment later, she was safe in her own bedchamber, with their giggles behind her and the door shut firmly.

There was still some time before she might expect Bickerstaff to announce dinner, for since Edward's coming the hour had been set back to accommodate him and his friends. Though she would wish to look her best, she did not ring for her maid at once but stood for some moments, her back against the door, as though she had need to catch her breath.

She had suspected for some time that her relationship with Rochford was not the usual flirtatious matching of wits that she customarily enjoyed with gentlemen friends—when they were not pressing her to marry them, in any event—but she had not thought any man could shake her so, merely by looking into her eyes. It had not been flirtation she had missed when he ceased his frequent visits, but simply his company. He could make her laugh, and she had felt a kinship with him that she could not remember having felt toward any man before, including the late baron. Or perhaps especially the late baron. Wakefield had been, after all, old enough to be her father, and in many ways his attitude toward her had been paternal rather than husbandly. He had been gentle and loving, but he had treated her as though she had been something fragile, albeit intelligent, except of course during the hunting season, when he had scarcely chanced to think of her at all. He had given her many lovely things, and he had taught her to manage her own affairs, but perhaps that was because he had not liked to think of a day when another man might control her. Cousin Adeliza had said once that the baron had carried his teaching too far. Was it possible that she had had the right of it?

Looking back now, Philippa was quite certain that Wakefield, in preparing her for the day when he would be gone, had prepared her for a solitary life, not for life with another man. Even his attitude toward her here in Leicestershire, she could see now, had been aimed at teaching her that she could get on with only herself or another woman for company. And now that she came to think of it, she realized that many of the faults she had discerned in the men who had courted her in London and Brighton had been faults Wakefield had disparaged in his fellowman, not necessarily faults that would have disturbed her before his having so assiduously pointed them out to her. But he had not known Rochford.

She smiled a little as she moved at last to ring for her maid. Rochford was surely as stubborn as Wakefield had been. He was nearly as stubborn, for that matter, as Philippa herself. And he had other faults as well. Surely she could list a number of them without half-thinking about it. But one thing Wakefield had never warned her about—that she might meet a man whose faults were as nothing to her. From the outset there had been that little humming in her mind whenever she chanced to be in the same room with him. Even when he was angry, the humming went on. And when she had contrived to make him laugh at something she said, the result was much like that moment in Mr. Haydn's Surprise Symphony when he had meant to startle the emperor's select audience from their dozing.

Her maid entered then, and Philippa tore herself away from her thoughts long enough to instruct the woman as to which dress and shoes she would wear that evening. "And I'll have my hair up in a top knot, Alice, *à la chinoise*, I think, with just a few ringlets to soften the neckline. You know the way."

"Aye, mum," replied Alice, setting to work to assist her mistress out of her frock and into a bronze velvet evening gown with tiny puffed sleeves, a high waist and slim skirt, and a daringly low-cut bodice. The sleeves and waist were trimmed with knots of silk mistake ribbons, shaded from coffee to gold, and Philippa wore a gold chain with a yellow topaz pendant that rested at the top of her cleavage, and matching earbobs rested waiting on her dressing table to be donned once Alice had arranged her hair.

Relaxing as the maid stroked the silver-backed brush through her dark golden tresses, Philippa found her thoughts turning once more to the viscount and to a wish that she could be at peace with him again. If only, she thought, it were not necessary for her to appear to give in to his wishes or to the pressures of such men as Assheton-Smith and Lord Lonsdale in order to attain that peace. The disorder arising from her decision to post her land appalled her. She wanted nothing so much as to be able to rip every sign down, to allow the hunters to ride wherever they wished to ride, to put men like Tom Giles in the way of making their fortunes from the damages paid them, and to allow Sam Cudlipp to go back to stopping earths for the various hunts. But to give in to them all unconditionally was more than her pride would allow. Her independence was too important to her, and she knew full well that the entire countryside would be of the opinion that Rochford had talked her round if she ordered the signs removed.

That thought brought another on its heels. Though he had certainly torn a strip off her that afternoon, though he had ranted and raved about her foolhardiness in exposing herself to danger, and her stubbornness in general, he had not once repeated his earlier demand that she take down her signs. She could not doubt that he still wanted her to do so. That went without saying, perhaps. Nonetheless, he had not said it. He had said many other things, to be sure, but he had apologized for the worst of them. And he had looked at her in *such* a way.

"Here is your glass, my lady," said Alice in her quiet way. "You'll be wanting to look at the back now."

Startled, Philippa took the silver hand mirror and turned

this way and that, paying little heed to her hair but using the opportunity to quiet her thoughts. "That will do, Alice," she said after a hasty glance. She reached for her earbobs. "You may go to your dinner now. I'll ring when I want you later."

"Yes, mum. I'll just be waiting until I've seen your skirt straight."

Philippa smiled at her, stood up obediently, and turned as Alice twitched the velvet slightly here and there until the total effect met with her approval. Then, handing her mistress a gold net shawl and helping her to drape it properly from elbow to elbow, Alice dropped a brief curtsy and took her leave.

Philippa followed a moment later, pausing only to pinch more color into her cheeks. Downstairs, she found her cousin and Mr. Drake already in the yellow drawing room, engaged in a spirited exchange of opinion.

"My dear Mr. Drake," Miss Pellerin was saying indignantly, "I cannot believe I am hearing such fustian with my own ears." Looking up, she spied Philippa entering the room and at once demanded that she attend to "this nonsense" with her own ears. "Would you believe, my love, that Mr. Drake is of the opinion that young ladies are capable of learning no more than deportment and sketching? He avers that even botany is beyond them, that their brains are not capable of attending to such detail as must be demanded of a scholar."

"Goodness, Mr. Drake," Philippa said, smiling at that discomfited gentleman, "surely you must agree that Cousin Adeliza, at least, has proved you wrong on all counts. I am sure she is much better educated than most men of my acquaintance."

Mr. Drake coughed gently behind his hand. "Indeed, my lady, your cousin has been most oddly raised by a doting sire, and she appears to have been blessed by a rare ability to understand what she reads, but I cannot agree with her that any young woman must possess that same ability. One knows from vast experience that teaching the fair sex to read is a most difficult process. Their heads being so full, as they are, of matters of fashion and gossip, there simply is no room left for sensible learning. And men will have it no other way, I fear, for the dear creatures are quite fascinating as they are. A woman raised as your charming cousin has been raised can only confuse those gentlemen whom she chances to meet who have not had the benefit of her broad education and thus cannot know what to say to her."

"They are frightened," said Miss Pellerin ominously, "of revealing their own lack of understanding."

"Pish tush, dear lady, I daresay that no gentleman would fall prey to such a nonsensical fear. To be sure, a man of the working classes must inevitably be dismayed by coming upon a lady versed in only the simplest matters of education, but he need not fret that it will happen to him more than once in a lifetime, thank goodness."

"Sir, you may think yourself fortunate that I do not have a bucket of cold water at hand, for I declare I should know precisely where to empty it," said Miss Pellerin awfully, getting to her feet with an angry swish of her peach satin skirts. The other gentlemen entered *en masse* just then, and she was able to turn her attention to them, demanding to know if Edward had rung for preprandial refreshment.

"Bickerstaff is just bringing it, ma'am," said that young man, eyeing his angry relative with dismay. "What has occurred to put you out, Cousin?"

" 'Tis nothing at all, Edward," Philippa said quickly, forseeing that the discussion would inevitably become a general one if it were so allowed. "Do you all mean to ride into Melton after dinner tonight?"

As a diversion it proved to be an excellent choice, for it seemed that the gentlemen did indeed mean to ride into town to attend a horse auction, after which they would join friends at the George for cards and drinking.

"Well, if you mean to hunt in the morning, you will be sorry for it if you waken with sore heads," she told them teasingly.

The conversation followed the normal course of such conversations then, and remained general throughout dinner. Although Mr. Drake was clearly trying to soothe his dinner partner's ruffled feathers, Philippa noted that Miss Pellerin paid him no heed, confining her conversation to Edward when she was not attending to the general discussion.

Rochford sat at Philippa's left hand, and at first she had been disconcerted to find him there, but his manner was adroit, and he soon had her chatting easily about all manner of things under cover of the general noise around the table.

"That gown seems to be a trifle lacking if you wear the velvet for warmth," he said at one point, his appreciative grin making it clear that he did not mean to suggest the slightest disapproval.

She smiled at him. "I am quite warm, sir, except when I must traverse the stone hall. I declare, that room, even with both fireplaces roaring, is always like ice."

"The heat goes up, you see," he said, "so your fireplaces are doing their possible to warm the gallery, not the hall."

She nodded, and suddenly there came one of those odd moments when nearly everyone in a group falls silent at the same time. Only one lone voice sounded, that of Lord Reginald Partridge, speaking to his neighbor, Mr. Dauntry.

"One must wonder, dash it, how the late baron came to leave such a fine little hunting box to a woman instead of to Wakefield as he should have done."

Recognizing the *faux pas* immediately, both Lord Reginald and Dauntry turned in dismay to look at Philippa. Lord Reginald said hastily, "Oh, I say, ma'am, I meant nothing at all by it, you know. Can't think how I came to make such a cake of myself." He looked round at the others frantically. "Not at all the thing. Must apologize to all. Spoke out of turn. That is, thought it was a private conversation, you know."

Dauntry observed morosely, "Should have known they'd all go quiet soon as you said anything out of turn."

Philippa couldn't help herself. She chuckled. And when Lord Reginald turned back to face her, bewilderment clear upon his youthful face, she shook her head at him. "You needn't apologize, sir. If my late husband had indeed done such a thing as that, there is no one who would not wonder at it."

"But he did, dash it!" exclaimed Lord Winkburn from the other end of the table. Then, as he realized he was slipping into deep waters with the others, he muttered defensively, "Surely that is how the matter was explained to me."

"Well, I cannot think who might have explained it so," Philippa told him frankly, "for although Wakefield left me the major portion of his unentailed property, that does not include Chase Charley, which was merely left to my use for my lifetime. I may stay here anytime I wish, but the estate belongs to Edward."

A stunned silence followed this innocent announcement, and as Philippa glanced at each astonished face in turn, she discovered that even Rochford was gaping at her. Just as she opened her mouth to ask what ailed them all, her stepson gave a shout of triumphant laughter.

"By God, she's right. I never paid the least heed to all the dashed nonsense my papa's man of business babbled at me, and there's so dashed much property I daresay I never had the straight of what was entailed and what was not. What with everything being in the hands of my trustees until I'm twenty-five, I paid little heed to any of it, but Chase Charley must be mine."

"Then she ith not the owner and cannot post the property," declared Alvanley, regarding Philippa challengingly, as though he hoped she might wish to debate the issue.

Her first inclination was to do just that, to point out to Edward—indeed, to all of them—that she had every right to do what she had done, but the others had already joined noisily in his triumph and were encouraging him in his declaration that every no-trespassing sign would be gone by morning.

"Dash it, we'll make a night of it. No reason we can't see to the business before we go into town. I'll roust my people out the minute we get up from table, and I'll wager Giles, Cudlipp, and the rest will see to the business before morning."

No one said anything further to her, and a moment later, under cover of the general din of victory and shouts for claret and brandy, she signaled to her cousin and got up from the table, ignoring the questioning look in the viscount's eye.

In the drawing room, Miss Pellerin demanded, "Ought you not to have explained the matter to him, my dear? I could not feel that it was my place to say anything, of course, but I do believe you might have informed them that you had done nothing wrong."

Philippa shook her head. "Can you imagine, ma'am, what

must have been the result had I even tried to make myself heard amongst all that noise and revelry? And what a witch I should have looked to dampen their enthusiasm, as I must have done, had I informed them that as Edward's principal trustee I do control his property."

"But, my dear, Edward did mention that his property is managed by his trustees."

Philippa shrugged. "It will occur to none of them that I am one, however, for women are rarely named to such a position. Edward has been told, again and again, but he has little awareness yet of what my position entails. Since he has not yet outrun the constable, I doubt he even realizes he must apply to me if he needs more generous funding. Such an event must certainly have brought home to him what power I wield. If he has thought about the matter, he no doubt assumes his uncle to be in charge of his affairs, though why he should think that, I cannot imagine, for he must know that his papa held Mr. Raynard-Wakefield in the greatest contempt and named him associate trustee merely as a sop to those who would rant and rave at his putting a woman in control. But Wakefield's will was clear. I need no one else's consent to act on Edward's behalf."

"But you ought to explain that much to Rochford, at least. He was not cheering with the others, you know. He was watching you."

"To speak the truth, ma'am, I am heartily sick of the business and can see no good reason to explain anything to anyone. I acted in haste, and I have realized for some time that my actions were unwise. Until tonight, however, I could see no way out of the quagmire that would not make it appear that I had succumbed to wiser counsel—specifically, Rochford's counsel. That, my pride would not allow. 'Tis foolish, you'll say—"

"Nonsense, I shall say no such thing," replied Miss Pellerin tartly. "After this evening I have seen precisely just how ridiculously high men hold themselves in their own esteem. I can certainly admire your desire to avoid puffing any one of them any higher than he puffs himself." And having relieved herself of this opinion, Miss Pellerin retrieved her fancywork basket from behind a claw-footed sofa, placed her silver pince-nez on her little button nose, and settled herself down to an unexceptionably ladylike pastime. Philippa paced the floor for some moments, attempting to convince herself that matters had now settled themselves admirably, but by the time Rochford and Mr. Drake came to take punctilious leave of them, she had flung herself into a chair and was engaged in knotting and unknotting one of the ribbons at the waist. She straightened quickly.

"The others have taken themselves off, I fear," Rochford said to her, smiling, "and we must collect Lucinda and be on our way."

"We could not go, however," said Mr. Drake with his usual formality, "without taking proper leave."

"How kind," said Miss Pellerin dryly before turning to Rochford. "Have you heard from your father and sisters, dear boy? Do you anticipate their arrival before Christmas?"

"Indeed, ma'am. My sister Margaret writes that we may expect the party from Leamington Spa by the first of the week if my father's health permits."

A moment later the two gentlemen had departed, and Philippa breathed a sigh of relief, giving devout thanks that Rochford had not chosen to demand an explanation for her seemingly outrageous behavior in giving orders that were not hers to give.

—13—

THE WEEK BEFORE Christmas passed quickly, for those married hunters who had previously been enjoying the life of the merry bachelor were, in the main, joined by loving wives and children looking forward to spending the holiday with Papa. Fortunately for conjugal relations in these abodes, as well as for the numerous social activities planned by the wives, the weather took a turn for the worse—from a hunter's viewpoint—and a hard frost succeeded by heavy fog and several days of light snow made sport impossible. To a man the hunters declared themselves dedicated family men and aided and abetted their womenfolk in planning entertainments to pass away the long hours before hunting would be possible again.

Philippa and Miss Pellerin found themselves the gratified recipients of nearly as many invitations as they might have received during the Season in London, and spent their time each morning cheerfully discussing how they would use their day and in making plans for their own rout party to be held on Christmas Eve. To their astonishment, on Tuesday they received a personal invitation from Margaret, Lady Kegworth, to take Christmas dinner at Wyvern Towers with the Drake family. Lady Kegworth, paying a morning call with her little sister, took the opportunity to thank Philippa and Miss Pellerin for all their kind offices on that young lady's behalf.

"For I am sure she has never thought to thank you properly herself," said Margaret, smiling down at Lucinda, who had clearly taken her good looks from the same source as her eldest sister.

Lucy flushed and bowed her head, "Oh, Margaret, I did, often and often."

"To be sure, ma'am, she did," Philippa said, laughing. She had liked Margaret at once, finding her a merry, cheerful person. Though in her late thirties, or even her forties, she had made no effort to retain the beauty of her extreme youth. The glossy darkness of her hair had been tempered by numerous strands of white, giving it a salt-and-pepper look that was vastly becoming to her fair skin and rosy cheeks. If she had exerted herself in any way at all to retain her former beauty, the effort had been expended on her elegant figure. She wore her red carriage dress with an air that spoke of much use in earlier years of the backboard, but there was also willowy grace to her movements, a grace that Philippa would have given much to be able to imitate.

The ladies from Wyvern stayed no longer than the requisite twenty minutes, but during that time Margaret made it quite clear that Jessalyn, Lord Wakefield, and any guests that might remain at Chase Charley were included in her invitation. "For I am persuaded that we should miss them all if they did not come with you," she said, laughing and patting her sister's shoulder. Lucinda blushed deeply, and when they had taken their leave, Philippa chuckled.

"Do you suppose poor Lucy has developed a *tendre* for Edward or one of his friends?"

Miss Pellerin smiled. "Stranger things have happened, my love. She is at an age when young ladies are easily smitten, and her friend's older brother must always be of interest, I suppose."

"Well, I hope Edward has better sense than to marry such a goose," Philippa said, "for he hasn't much sense himself."

"It would be a good match," Miss Pellerin said thoughtfully. "Wyvern would put no rub in the way. Edward will be a wealthy young man, after all."

Feeling a strong need to divert her cousin's thoughts at this point, Philippa asked her opinion as to which of several invitations for that evening they ought to accept. The result was that they found themselves at a dinner party that was followed by an evening of childish games in a hunting box on the north side of Melton Mowbray. The cheerful company included Lord Alvanley, Viscount Rochford, and a number of their other acquaintances, as well as Lady Kegworth, her distinguished-looking spouse, and the Earl of Wyvern, a thin, graying man whose pale complexion revealed his lack of good health.

"I trust your father does not overtax his strength by coming out like this," Philippa said to Rochford when they chanced to meet near the roaring fire shortly after the gentlemen had abandoned their postprandial port in order to join the ladies.

Her hostess was laughingly handing out counters for the Royal Game of Goose, and Rochford accepted his allotment before he replied, "On the contrary, ma'am, I believe that good company bucks the old gentleman up considerably."

"Mine alwayth enjoyed a good row," put in Alvanley over his shoulder as he accepted his counters, making no secret of the fact that he had overheard their exchange. "Put him in fine fettle for dayth on end. My uncle lackth his spirit, however. Keep hoping someone'll put him in a temper that will bring on an apoplectic fit and take the old man off."

"My lord," Philippa protested, "surely you cannot mean such a thing!"

"Of a certainty, he does," Rochford told her, chuckling. "Been living on his expectations of that old man for years now. He'll be fairly sent to grass if old Arden don't die and save his groats."

"True," Alvanley admitted glumly. "M' corn factor's turned awkward now, so I've put my man onto fetchin' biscuits for the horseth instead, but I darethay the confectioner will next wish to be paid."

Rochford chuckled, exchanging an intimate glance with Philippa that sent warmth coursing through her body. "What's the word on that latest harebrained scheme you and Brummell have going?" he asked Alvanley as the three of them moved away from the fire toward the table where the spiral gameboard had been set up.

"Not in it yet, myself, but it ain't harebrained at all," declared the younger man indignantly. "Have you know Charles and Robert Mannerth are going partnerth with Brummell. That ought to tell you!"

"Tells me Rutland hasn't got wind of it, is all," retorted the viscount incorrigibly. Holding Philippa's chair, he grinned down at her. "They've been contracting to pay annuities in return for single cash payments. The interest and possibly even a portion of the principal, if I know them, is used to cover their gaming debts."

"A risky business, my lord," said Philippa, cocking her head a little to one side to look up at him.

"Well, I don't thuppose you really know much about it, ma'am," Alvanley said kindly, taking his own seat and glancing round the table to assess the competition, "but when I tell you the interest alone amounth to fifteen percent, I darethay that will make you thtare."

"What will make me stare, sir, is what will happen to you all when the annuities must be paid, and you have spent the money," she retorted, goaded.

"Here, now, tighten your girth, ma'am. Mean to thay, no intent to give offenth."

"Then you ought not to have assumed that her ladyship knows nothing of business matters," Rochford told him, bestowing a keen glance upon Philippa as he took his seat beside her and laid his counters before him.

She smiled blandly at him and received a warm grin in return. Neither of them noticed when their hostess called for the first cast of the dice, but a moment afterward Lord Alvanley said cheerfully, "Lay you five to one in guineath, Rochford, that I overtake you three timeth at least before you reach thirty-three."

"Done," said the viscount amiably, turning his attention at last to the game. Not that night nor yet the next when Philippa met him at a caroling party at Oakham Castle did he say a word about the posting and subsequent unposting of the Raynard-Wakefield land. That the news of her downfall had spread all over Leicestershire was clear, for she encountered a number of gentlemen who looked down their noses at her in a smug, superior sort of way, and she noted also, to her chagrin, that Rochford received more than one hearty, congratulatory clap on the shoulders that told her better than words might have done that the complete tale had not yet made all the rounds. Rochford was quick to deny any part in the business, however, and one way or another Edward came in for his full share of the congratulations. She had all she could do, more than once, to stifle angry words of reproach or bitter explanation when her stepson repeated for the umpteenth time that he could not think how she had ever believed she had the right to do anything so corkbrained as what she had done.

By Christmas Eve, most of the uproar seemed to have died away, and Philippa looked forward to the evening with pleasure. Nearly everyone she had invited to her rout party had accepted, including Mr. Drake, Rochford, the viscount's two sisters, and their husbands, all of whom came early to dine; for, besides the usual conversation that attended such parties, there was to be dancing in the stone hall after dinner when the other guests arrived.

Jessalyn had been quite cast down by the information that she was not old enough yet to make one of the party, and clearly would have indulged herself in a mild tantrum at least, had Philippa not had the fortunate thought to remind her that Father Christmas was like to look askance at such behavior. Although Jessalyn thought herself above a childish display of excitement at the notion of Father Christmas bearing gifts to well-behaved children, she was nonetheless not so foolish as to chance bringing the displeasure of her stepmother down upon herself before she had received her Christmas gift. As a reward for her smiles, she was allowed to sit in Philippa's bedchamber to watch her prepare for the evening ahead, and when Philippa was dressed, a nod to Alice produced from the wardrobe an exquisite, brightly embroidered round gown of creamy Denmark satin trimmed with blue silk ribbons. Jessalyn sat up in amazement.

"Good gracious, is that for me?"

"It is, my dear," Philippa said, grinning at her. "I thought you would want something to make the gentlemen stare at Wyvern Towers tomorrow and again when you attend the christening of the young Marquess of Granby at Belvoir next month."

Jessalyn's eyes widened still further when Miss Pellerin rushed in, still in her dressing gown, to present her with an embroidered silk reticule to carry when she wore her lovely gown, and to deliver Edward's present, which proved to be a string of matched pearls, quite the most grown-up present

Jessalyn had ever received. It was a very pleased young lady that Philippa left behind when she went downstairs to greet her guests.

Edward, quite puffed up in his own esteem, for this would be the first such party at which he would play host, joined her in the saloon some moments before their first guests were expected to arrive.

"I say, Pippa," he said grandly, "I'd never have contrived all this off my own bat, you know. Dashed good idea it was. Hope it don't come on to snow, though, or we shall have them all here through Christmas as well."

She smiled at him. "If we get no more than the dusting we've been getting, you need have no fear of that."

"Aye, just enough to put a stop to the hunting, but not enough to make the weather interesting," he grunted. "Just when we might finally have seen some good sport near to home, at that."

"Edward—" she began warningly.

"Oh, aye, not another word," he said, shooting her a rueful grin. "Daresay I've said more than you want to hear on the subject."

"You have," she agreed. Then, as voices were heard from the hall, she hastily smoothed her pale blue satin skirts, adjusted the coral silk bow at her décolletage, and smiled as Miss Pellerin hurried into the saloon from the green drawing room, adjoining it to the west.

Miss Pellerin was out of breath. "My abigail couldn't seem to get all the hooks on this gown fastened," she puffed. "I thought I should never be ready in time, and I fairly ran down the west stair. Fortunately, there is an entrance to that drawing room from the stair hall, for since you, Wakefield, are inhabiting the green velvet bedchamber, I could scarce take a course through there. And guests arriving already. Philippa, dearest, is my hair tidy?"

Philippa reassured her, and they turned to greet their guests. Dinner was a success, and the small chamber orchestra that Philippa had hired from Leicester played from the gallery afterward for dancing. Philippa, having danced twice with Rochford and discovered him to be an accomplished partner who made her feel quite as though she were floating, was wondering whether she might dare to stand up with him for a third dance if he were to ask her to do so, when another gentleman trod upon her satin train, tearing nearly three inches of the material from its moorings at her waistline.

"Oh, dear!" she exclaimed when she heard the telltale rip.

The gentleman apologized profusely, and she did her best to reassure him that the damage was not irreparable, but she breathed a sigh of relief when Miss Pellerin came hurrying up to her.

"Mercy me, I saw what that clumsy oaf did. Do you come with me into Wakefield's dressing room, for he will not be wanting it at present, and no one will disturb us while I stitch that up again, which I can do in a trice, for I carry the wherewithal right here in my reticule."

Thanking her, Philippa followed Miss Pellerin through the west stair hall and an anteroom, to Edward's dressing room. As expected, the room was empty, and Miss Pellerin effected the repairs with admirable speed. While she worked, she chattered happily on the success of their party, and from sundry observations Philippa was able to deduce that Mr. Drake was in favor again. She commented appropriately when her companion chanced to pause for breath, but when the mending was completed and Miss Pellerin announced brightly that they might now return to the others, Philippa shook her head.

"You go along, ma'am. I mean to take advantage of Edward's looking glass to be sure my hair is not all falling down about my neck. I shall be along directly."

With a chuckle for the vanity of the younger generation, Miss Pellerin took her leave. Philippa spent a number of moments smoothing strands of hair back into her topknot, then twisting loose ringlets carefully round her fingers before she decided she was ready to return to the party. At last, gathering up her skirts, she left the dressing room, carefully shutting the door behind her, only to discover upon turning around again that she was face-to-face with young Mr. Dauntry, who had just stepped out of the small bedchamber across the way.

Startled by the encounter, she realized that that was indeed the room he occupied, and managed a polite greeting before turning to continue on her way.

To her surprise, Mr. Dauntry caught her arm and said anxiously, "Pray, ma'am, don't go. I should like to . . . indeed, I must speak with you!"

"Certainly, Mr. Dauntry, but this is scarcely the place for a proper conversation. Do you give me your arm back to the hall, if you please."

"No, please, Lady Philippa, I have been silent too long already."

She looked at him then and realized that he was laboring under deep emotion. Recognizing the familiar symptoms, she resigned herself to the inevitable. "What is it, Mr. Dauntry?"

"You are so beautiful," he said, catching both her hands in his and squeezing them eloquently. "I have sat at the dining table these past days drinking in your beauty. I want to have that privilege all the days of my life."

"Very prettily said, sir, and it should give you good practice for that day when you will offer your hand to a suitable young lady."

"But I am offering it to you," he said in surprise. "Surely you must know that, ma'am. I wish nothing more than to have you for my wife."

"How old are you, sir?"

"What can that signify, dash it? I am old enough to know what I want."

"It signifies a great deal, however. A pretty figure you would have me cut. I must be all of eight years your senior."

"Well, you are out there," he said, not without a touch of triumph, "for Wakefield told me you are but six-and-twenty. I am only *six* years younger."

"Oh, well, that must make a great deal of difference," she said wryly.

"Well, of course it does. When you are fifty and I am merely forty-four, I daresay it won't occur to either of us to dwell on the matter at all."

Ruthlessly Philippa stifled the laughter that threatened to overcome her. She liked young Dauntry, and not for worlds would she humiliate him with her laughter. She tried, instead, to administer a gentle damper. "I am Edward's stepmama, you know, and I could not reconcile it with my conscience to take advantage of one of his friends,'' she said.

''But 'tis I who would be taking advantage, assure you,'' he protested, pulling her closer and attempting to put his arms around her. ''I shall be run off my heels if I don't make reparations soon, and my father refuses to frank my excesses any longer. Begging your pardon, ma'am, but you should be doing me the greatest service to accept my offer of marriage. Pockets to let, assure you. Can't even come up with the rhino for a new hunter, and my black lamed himself on a shard of ice not two days ago. Must marry. Nothing else will serve the purpose.''

''Your notions of romance overwhelm me, sir,'' Philippa said coolly, attempting to extricate herself. They stood now in the doorway leading from the anteroom into the west stair hall, and Dauntry had backed her against the doorjamb. ''Please, Mr. Dauntry, you must let me go.''

''Can't. Love you.'' He leaned closer, and she realized he had had more than his share of port after dinner. ''Prove how much I care for you, Philippa dearest.'' He planted a damp kiss on her cheek and murmured, ''Wakefield said twenty thousand a year. Can't think why I didn't fall in love with you when first we met.''

''Because you were sober, for the most part,'' she said sourly, ducking to avoid his seeking lips. ''Let go, you odious boy, or I shall kick you.''

''You like me, I've seen that you do,'' he protested. ''You even winked last evening when Wakefield was telling tales from school.''

''Why, I never did anything so improper. Perhaps I had got something in my eye, but it can have been no more than that. Now, Peter, do leave go.''

The sound of music from the stone hall increased momentarily in volume, giving her a notion that the door into the stair hall had opened briefly and shut again, but her view of that door was blocked by her suitor's head, and she was, moreover, fully occupied in attempting to effect her own release. Dauntry had now managed to get his arms fully around her and was plastering his wet kisses around and about her right ear. She tried to kick him but realized after the first effort that satin dancing slippers were poorly constructed for such a purpose.

"Darling Philippa," he murmured against her ear.

"Good God, Mr. Dauntry, do give over. You are mussing my dress and my hair, and I promise you I should never agree to marry anyone capable of making such a cake of himself."

"No, indeed," said a quiet, amused voice by her right shoulder, "I shouldn't advise any lady to contemplate matrimony with such an idiotish cub."

Dauntry went rigidly still at the first sound of that voice. When he pulled his head away from Philippa's ear—to her profound relief, for she was in danger of succumbing to the alcoholic vapors that wafted beneath her nostrils whenever he sighed—she had a good view of Rochford, standing close beside them but making no effort to separate them. The viscount merely looked on with arms folded across his broad chest, as though he found their antics interesting.

"Rochford, do something," Philippa demanded.

At that Mr. Dauntry fairly flung himself away from her. "No need, ma'am, assure you. Just going. Your servant, my lord." And he scuttled away, opening the door into the stone hall and shutting it quickly again behind himself.

Philippa was left to face Rochford alone. "If you must make a practice of rescuing me from embarrassing situations," she said, glaring at him, "I do think you might have interfered earlier."

"He was no match for you, my dear," the viscount said, taking a handkerchief from his inner pocket and employing it to remove some smut from her chin. "It wasn't until I realized you stood in danger of injuring your dainty foot upon his shin that I decided to take a hand."

"I must look a sight," she said with a small sigh.

"You look charmingly," he said, pinching up one of her puffed sleeves and smoothing a lock of dark blond hair off her cheek.

His voice was low and contained a note in it that brought a flush to that same cheek. Extraordinarily conscious of his nearness and of the fact that they were quite alone, Philippa experienced a dizzying sense of danger that had been altogether lacking in her confrontation with young Dauntry. In an attempt to break this strange mood, she said, "That idiotish boy said he needs to recoup his losses, that his father refuses to frank him any longer. Would you believe, sir, he actually seemed to believe such a reason would entice me to accept his hand?"

"Sheer foolishness," said the viscount in that same caressing tone of voice. "Altogether unromantic and shortsighted. That's what comes of dallying with younger men, my dear."

"But I wasn't dallying. Oh, you are being ridiculous, my lord, and I wish you will take me back to the dancing. I cannot think how you came upon us, anyway," she ended a trifle lamely.

"Why, I missed your charming presence, of course, and I had seen young Dauntry follow you and your cousin from the hall. Having been nauseated from the outset by the damned sheep's eyes he persists in casting your way, I suspected he might choose such a moment to waylay you."

"Did you, indeed?" She looked at him then, and her eyes narrowed. "Since Cousin Adeliza and I left the hall some fifteen minutes ago, my lord, and Mr. Dauntry, if he did indeed follow us, must have done so immediately, you certainly did take your own time in coming to my rescue."

"Did I say I came to rescue you?" He grinned at her. "That was not my intent. I waited until Miss Pellerin had returned without you, and then I waited a moment longer, so as to ensure that my arrival would be welcomed by you, and then—"

"I hope," Philippa said awfully, "that you will not take it amiss, sir, if I tell you to your face that you are a . . . a . . ."

He lifted his eyebrows. "Well, what am I, sweet Philippa?"

"Words fail me."

"I thought they might." He was still quite close to her, and now he took her hands in his in exactly the same way that Dauntry had done. Somehow, though, her hands felt much more comfortable in his. She looked up at him questioningly, and he smiled. "The problem is, I think, that the lad is inexperienced. He ought to have known better than to thrust his attentions upon a lady. A younger lady would be frightened by such precipitate action, and a lady with experience greater than his own must certainly be seriously annoyed. He would have done better to have approached you gently, to have taken your hands in his, thusly. Then, when you looked up at him, as you must''—Philippa looked up almost shyly to find his gaze warmer than ever, his eyes twinkling with affectionate amusement—''then, and only then, should he have kissed you. Like this,'' he added, bending his head slowly, mesmerizingly, toward hers, and suiting action to words.

His lips were warm against hers, and soft, at first. Then, as she moved responsively, he let go of her hands and pulled her gently into his arms, his mouth moving more possessively against hers as he did so. She was aware of his hands on her back, but she scarcely noticed when her arms went around him, urging him to hold her more tightly. When his fingers caressed her, it was as though the silk of her gown didn't exist, as though he touched bare skin. There was a warm, tingling sensation wherever his body touched hers. And when the moving fingers of his right hand drifted lower to her hips, then up again along the curve of her waist to her breast, the distant sound of music in the stone hall faded away altogether as the humming in her mind swelled to a thunderous crescendo worthy of Mr. Handel at his finest hour.

A moment later he set her back upon her heels, and Philippa stared up at him breathlessly. When she could speak, she said, ''Rochford, why?''

He grinned at her. ''I shouldn't like you to think I've retired from the lists, my dear, though I've certainly better sense than to press my suit upon you at such a time as this.''

''Well!'' she said, her sharp tone covering a wave of disappointment that she would not have cared to attempt to explain to anyone. ''I cannot conceive of why you should think tonight a worse time than any other, when I am scarcely flattered by such attention as Mr. Dauntry's at any time. I fear Wakefield was right when he said I should be happiest to remain a single lady. No one cares a jot for anything but my fortune.''

The expression in the light gray eyes hardened suddenly. ''If I did not care prodigiously, my girl, you would precious soon come to understand that I won't tolerate having that accusation flung at me more than once. I do apologize, however, if my levity was offensive. I had forgotten for a moment how distressing this time of year must be to you."

Having listened to his first words with skepticism, she eyed him now in bewilderment. "Distressing, sir?"

"Do not feel you must be on your guard with me," he said gently. "My mother has been gone these eight years and more; yet, at Christmastide, the good memories flood my mind, and it seems like the event occurred only yesterday. So I know well that even when one believes one's period of bereavement to be over and done, the holiday season can be trying. And this past two weeks or so have been more than ordinarily difficult for you." He paused, regarding her closely, then added more gently than ever, "Perhaps it will relieve your mind a little to know that I've no intention of saying anything further about that no-trespassing business."

"Your silence has already made that clear," she said, relieved not by his words so much as by the fact that he had got onto another subject. Though she had felt a wave of compassion when he spoke of his mother, she was not by any means certain she was ready to attempt to explain her feelings for the late baron to him, for the disappointment she had experienced upon his saying he would not press his suit had been replaced by a small sense of relief that she could not explain even to herself. She went on now, quietly, "I should not have expected you to crow over me, in any event, sir. You have always shown yourself a gentleman."

"Not always, my pet, but in this particular instance your instincts are not at fault. Nothing would be accomplished by pointing out your errors again to you, and I have never thought you did not believe you had the right to act as you did. To discover that you had not must have come as a bitter blow."

She looked up swiftly from under her eyebrows, for she thought she detected a quizzing note in his voice, but he was regarding her blandly. Drawing a deep breath, she said, "I have no quarrel with what has come to pass, sir, but I do think that if we are to avoid undue comment, we must return to the dancing."

He bowed, and if she was disappointed that he did not solicit her hand for another dance, she managed to keep that disappointment from showing; however, it was hours after her last guest had departed before she fell asleep that night, so jumbled were her thoughts.

Christmas morning was peaceful for the simple reason that, except for the servants, everyone slept through most of it. At eleven, when they gathered in the breakfast parlor, Philippa, Miss Pellerin, and Edward received the small gifts Jessalyn had made for each of them and exchanged gifts with one another. Later, gifts were handed out to the servants before the four attended services at Saint Mary's Church in Melton. They had no sooner returned to the house, however, than it was time to dress for the journey to Wyvern Towers.

Both Miss Pellerin and Jessalyn were ready long before Philippa was, for she had wanted her appearance to be perfect, and both of them came to her bedchamber to urge her to greater speed and to confer over her choice of attire. She looked her stepdaughter over critically, and the child shifted from foot to foot anxiously, awaiting her verdict.

"I knew that dress would become you, Jess," Philippa said, smiling her approval. "The ribbons match your eyes, and that Denmark satin will be a deal warmer than muslin, I believe."

"I have never," Miss Pellerin said, "understood this passion to dress all young girls in pure white muslin until they catch a husband. She will have to wear such stuff for her come-out in a few years, of course, but there is nothing to insist upon her wearing it now, particularly in the country and to a family dinner."

"But it is not our family," Jessalyn objected, "and I daresay Lucy will wear white muslin, for she fairly dotes upon it, you know."

"Yes, and the purity of the color is excellent for her, because her own coloring is so vivid," Philippa said, watching now as Alice swept her golden tresses high on her head in the style she liked best. The gown she had finally chosen was one of emerald-green velvet with a skirt that hung in soft folds from a high waistline. The sleeves were three-quarter-length with deep lace ruffles, and there was a wide edging of lace at her hemline as well. She wore several gold chains wrapped around her lovely throat, and there were emerald pendants for her ears. Alice threaded a gold cord through her curls, twitched two ringlets into place behind each ear and, once the earbobs were in place, pronounced her ready.

Philippa stood up, turning so the others might enjoy the full effect of her gown. "Have you your cloaks?" she asked.

"Indeed we have," Jessalyn answered. "We have been ready this age, ma'am." The child was fairly dancing in her eagerness to be off, and Philippa decided the enthusiasm must be contagious, for she felt much the same way herself.

—14—

DUSK HAD FALLEN by four o'clock when the Raynard-Wakefield party reached Wyvern Towers, but inside the magnificent marble entry hall, every candle had been lighted to welcome them. Having never been inside the house before, Philippa stood transfixed upon the threshold, staring at the wondrous marble hall. Designed by William Kent in the Palladian style, the chamber was of a stupendous height, fully as tall as the building itself, and was surrounded by fluted Ionic columns. The ceiling was richly coffered and ornamented, and the marble was not ordinary marble at all, but pink alabaster, glowing vividly now in the light of a hundred or more candles.

Their party was guided up a broad staircase in an apse at the inner end, to the state rooms, which were hung with Genoa velvet and Brussels and Mortlake tapestries with both classical and hunting motifs. Passing through these rooms, the guests were led into a drawing room with walls of plain ivory and gold, which was distinguished by a collection of antique sculptures gathered over the years by succeeding Drakes in the course of their grand tours. It was here that they found their host, his relations, and a number of other persons.

Lady Lucinda Drake, who had been sitting demurely beside her eldest sister upon one of several red Kent-designed settees with gilt claw feet, leapt up and crossed the blue-and-red Axminster carpet with more haste than grace to greet her friend, chattering as she moved.

"Oh, Jessalyn, what a lovely gown! Was that a gift from your stepmama? Is this not exciting, to be permitted to dine in company?"

"Lucy, darling, where have your manners gone begging?"

inquired Lady Kegworth as she rose gracefully to her feet. "Philippa, Miss Pellerin, how delightful that you all were able to come to us tonight." Her gesture included the group of young gentlemen following behind, and she nodded to her butler to begin offering wine to those who wished to take a glass before dinner.

Rochford, who had been standing beside the marble fireplace, stepped forward then to extend his greetings to the newcomers, and Philippa was astonished when he approached her, took her suddenly in his arms, and kissed her soundly.

"Rochford!" she exclaimed, when she could catch her breath.

Twinkling, he pointed upward, and she discovered that a sprig of mistletoe had been secured to one arm of the chandelier overhead. "Happy Christmas," he said to her in a low tone.

"Oh, is it not famous!" exclaimed his youngest sister, dancing at his side. "Seldon caught Margaret there and Kegworth caught Catherine, but neither has caught his own wife. Jess, you must stand underneath and see who will kiss you, too. I certainly mean to do so."

No one rebuked her for her enthusiasm, but Rochford did lay a calming hand upon her shoulder, and Philippa noted that Jessalyn was blushing furiously. Edward noticed too.

"A lady should certainly be kissed under the mistletoe at her first grown-up party," he said calmly, taking his sister gently by the elbow and nodding to Rochford and Philippa to stand out of the way. They did so willingly, and smiled when Jessalyn accepted her kiss with a good deal more shyness than was her wont.

Lucinda had fallen suddenly silent and was watching her friend with wistful eyes. When Edward straightened again, he glanced first at her and then at Rochford, quizzingly. The viscount grinned at him.

"Will you do me the honor, Lady Lucinda?" Edward said then quietly, smiling at her.

Silently, as though she were in a trance, Lucinda moved toward him, and when she was properly under the sprig of mistletoe, Edward bent and gently kissed her on the lips.

Immediately there was an uproar as Lord Reginald Partridge, a proper neckcloth around his neck for once instead of his customary Belcher kerchief, stepped forward saying, "Dashed if I know why you should have all the fun, Wakefield. Here, Lady Lucinda, if you mean to stand under that stuff like that, I'd like my turn as well. Dashed pretty little thing, your sister, Rochford. Yours, too, Wakefield. Must share and share alike."

Lucinda stared at the rake wide-eyed, but Jessalyn looked only too willing now to comply with his demand, and Philippa looked urgently at Edward, warning him to stop his friends before they became carried away. It was Rochford who came to the rescue, however, when the other gentlemen laughingly agreed that the younger ladies' favors must be shared. Gray eyes twinkling, the viscount said, "Enough, my friends. You will turn the little ones' heads till there will be no living with them. These chits, pretty as they unquestionably are, won't properly be out for another three years. Moreover, you have not yet made your manners to my esteemed father."

Thus gently reminded of their duty, the young gentlemen stifled their groans and stepped forward to make their legs to the earl, who sat near the cheerful fire in a comfortable chair that matched the red settees, his feet propped up on a velvet-covered stool. He had nodded to his guests but had said nothing, and Rochford said quietly to Philippa as he drew her forward to follow the others, "He is nearly burnt to the socket, I fear, but he insisted upon being present for the festivities tonight."

"Dear me, I hope he won't become quite ill," she said.

"Devil a bit, he's enjoying the attention. 'Tis merely that he has allowed himself to become overtired. A few days' rest will see him right again, I promise you. He's a number of years left in him yet."

She could see that he truly was not concerned about his father's health and so she was able to greet the earl with her customary poise. He looked up at her, grimacing.

"Hope you'll forgive an old man, my lady. Promised my overconcerned family I'd slow the pace tonight. I am even to permit my butler to do the carving."

"And rightly so, sir," she said, daring to tease him a little. "Why, in days gone by you should have had a proper carver at your side, wielding a half-dozen knives, you know."

"Surely not all at once, Philippa," said Rochford in the same bantering tone.

"Well"—she wrinkled her nose—"I do not know precisely how the business was achieved. I believe he had some sort of carver's apron in which he kept his knives. We must ask my cousin or your uncle to set us straight on the matter."

"Good God, Rochford," protested the earl in crusty tones, "don't let her set Archibald off on some dashed historical point. He'll keep us up all night with his prating."

Philippa joined the general laughter, but Mr. Drake, entering the drawing room just at that moment and demanding to know what was the jest, found nothing particularly humorous in it when it was explained to him.

"Nothing wrong with knowledge," he said almost as testily as his brother had spoken earlier. "Wouldn't have done you a mite of harm, Wyvern, to have attended to your books as a lad."

"Bosh," retorted the earl. "Learned more by my travels than I'd ever have learned from books."

"No doubt," said Mr. Drake, but his tone was such that no one made the mistake of believing that he was agreeing with his brother.

When the earl turned his head to address a comment to his son, Philippa moved a little away with Mr. Drake, and said quietly, "I was perfectly serious when I suggested appealing to you to set us straight about the matter of the carving, sir."

His expression softened somewhat. "Don't doubt that, ma'am, but 'tis a subject that would indeed take long to explain. And don't," he added hastily as he noted Miss Pellerin approaching them, "think for a moment that I doubt your ability to comprehend the matter. 'Tis merely that carving was an art, with specific instructions laid down for each sort of bird or beast. Quite fascinating, some of the methods are."

Having come up to them in time to catch the meaning of his words, Miss Pellerin inquired gently, "Do you by chance have in your possession any of those books of instruction, sir?"

"Indeed," Mr. Drake replied, his expression gentling even more as his gaze came to rest upon her soft pink face.

"Perhaps you would care to join me in a glass of Madeira, Miss Pellerin, while I tell you about them." And without so much as another glance at Philippa or Rochford, again beside her, he guided Miss Pellerin to a sofa at some distance from the others, where he kept her engaged in conversation until the butler announced that dinner had been served.

Philippa found herself seated at the long, highly polished table, between the earl and the viscount, across from Miss Pellerin and Mr. Drake. The dinner was a magnificent one, worthy of the occasion, and included several courses and a vast number of removes and side dishes. The first course began with a soup santé removed with fish, which was in turn removed with a roasted turkey and a haunch of venison. The side dishes that accompanied these included semels and poivrade sauce, three sweetbreads, larded and glazed, asparagus and peas, glazed neat's tongue, a souties of mutton and cucumber, grenadines and endive, and beef collops *à la tortue* with truffles, as well as numerous other dishes. Chief over all, however, was the boar's head, that splendid dish of pagan ancestry, which was borne to the table with immense ceremony, upon a magnificent platter of gold, by four liveried, bewigged footmen.

As she stared at the spectacular platter, then looked around at the splendid dining room, Philippa remembered the even greater splendor of the marble entry hall and decided, not without a touch of chagrin, that whatever she might think of Rochford, she must certainly acquit him of desiring her merely for her fortune. With a glance she discovered that he was watching her rather than the procession. Blushing to think he might read her thoughts, she returned her attention to the ceremony.

The boar's head had been a traditional Christmas dish since the late fourteenth century, and this one, like its ancestors, was decorated with rosemary, bay, and holly, and had an orange thrust between its teeth. No singing or trumpeting accompanied its progress, however, so it was not long before it was set down before the earl, who removed the orange from its mouth and presented it to his butler in lieu of a chief singer. The golden platter was then removed to one of the side tables, where the meat might be cut into narrow slices for serving.

Philippa had enjoyed the ritual, but when the dish was offered to her, she shook her head.

"You don't fancy boar's head," Rochford murmured, shaking his head at the footman in turn.

"I prefer the chicken in celery sauce that I see coming after it," she told him with a smile, "and if I don't mistake the matter, there is yet another course to come."

"And plum pudding," he told her. "Margaret and Catherine, like my mama before them, believe in doing things properly."

"Well, if I attempt to eat even a single bite from every one of these delicious dishes, I shall burst a seam before I rise from the table," she confided.

"In other words, you don't like boar's head."

Philippa grinned at him, and he nodded, satisfied.

The second course was as complete with removes and side dishes as the first, and Philippa made her way through it cautiously, accepting only the narrowest slice of game pie and but a taste of her caramel pastry basket, refusing the chantilly cream altogether. A bite of spinach with croutons, a smattering of broccoli in brown sauce, one small Jerusalem artichoke in white sauce, and the merest slice of pheasant, and she thought herself replete until a footman presented cheesecakes as yet another suggested a mince pie.

"Oh, Rochford, I cannot," she protested, turning a laughing face toward him. "Send them away, do, for I have not the willpower to do so myself, and I shall surely disgrace myself if I eat another bite."

The viscount waved the footmen past, chuckling. Then he said with a perfectly straight face, "How disappointed Margaret and Catherine will be that you do not like their dinner."

Philippa sat straighter, dismayed. "Oh, I would not give offense for the world." She heard a harsh chuckle to her left and turned quickly to discover that the earl, who had ignored everyone while he attended to his dinner, was looking at her now with very nearly the same charming twinkle in his eyes as she had often seen in his son's.

"The girls don't expect anyone to eat everything that is

offered, my lady. Indeed, I believe they would stare at anyone who could. You must not allow my detestable son to roast you in such a fashion."

Philippa smiled at him and turned an accusing grimace on the viscount. "So, sir, you choose to make game of me, do you?"

"Easy game, as it transpired," he agreed, still smiling. "You rise most eagerly to the bait, ma'am, as always."

"Well, now I am forewarned and shan't do so again."

"As you say," he replied, bowing slightly. "Ah, here is the pudding."

The others had noted the arrival of the pudding too, and Lady Lucinda's voice could be heard above the others, announcing that the members of the Drake household had all helped to stir the batter, so as to have good luck through the coming year.

"Even Papa," she added in her chirping voice. "But we cannot say what is in it, you know, for that must not be revealed to anyone or the wishes we made whilst stirring will not come true."

Her sister Catherine, a willowy, light-haired young woman, uttered a trill of musical laughter. "Oh, Lucy, you goose, 'tis not the nature of the pudding that must not be revealed, but the nature of the wish."

"Oh," said Lucy naively, "but I had always thought, 'twas the recipe. Why, I always tell about my wishes. That must be why they have none of them ever come true."

General laughter followed her remark, causing her to color up to her eyebrows and look down into her plate, but the arrival of the pudding, crowned with a sprig of scarlet-berried holly and flamed with brandy, took the focus of attention from her small self, and she was soon able to regain her composure and to laugh as heartily as anyone else when the earl was served with the slice containing the thimble, prophesying a single life.

"Dear me," said that gentleman, "the charm comes after the need."

"Why, Papa," exclaimed Catherine, "what an odious thing to say!"

"No, was it, my dear?" he inquired innocently.

Peter Dauntry, discovering the silver coin in his portion, promptly announced that his father must have had a change of heart and meant to increase his allowance in the coming year. "Dashed if I don't think I ought to go visit the old gentleman if this curst weather holds," he said generously.

Philippa, breaking into her piece of pudding, noted the gleam of gold and quickly attempted to push the slice back together again, but Rochford, seeing her movement, shook his head and covered her hand with his.

"No, no, sweet Philippa, you must not hide your fortune from the rest of us. Look here, everyone, Lady Philippa has got the ring."

"Oh, ma'am, that means you are next to marry, don't you know?" Jessalyn exclaimed. "I have got a gold charm fashioned like a book, which Mr. Drake says means my studies will prosper."

"Well, he's got the wrong end of the stick there," said Edward with a laugh. "No doubt 'tis a romantic novel, and you will be soundly thrashed and ordered to your bedchamber on a diet of bread and water when Miss Blandamore discovers it in your possession."

Mr. Drake had opened his mouth to speak before Edward's interruption, but he graciously gave way to the indignant lady to his right by shutting it again as Miss Pellerin said militantly, "I daresay there is no reason that dearest Jessalyn might not become a very good scholar if she would but put her mind to it. I may say that I have been pleasantly surprised by the progress made by both young ladies these past weeks."

Mr. Drake hesitated no longer. "Any progress they have made," he said clearly, "must certainly be due to your excellent instruction, ma'am, for I am persuaded that you turn even the stalest of historical tales into perfectly fascinating drama."

"Oh, she tells wonderful stories," Lucy said enthusiastically, as Miss Pellerin turned astonished eyes toward Mr. Drake.

"Here now," protested Mr. Dauntry, his mouth full of plum pudding, "some of the history I've read at Oxford is dashed improper stuff. Not at all the thing for feminine ears, you know."

"Nonsense, young man," said Miss Pellerin.

"I am quite certain," said Lady Kegworth with gentle amusement, "that Miss Pellerin has never acquainted the girls with any but the most improving of historical tales."

Rochford chuckled and leaned a little toward Philippa to say in an undertone, "I cannot say I ever expected Christmas dinner to be enlivened by an argument over the propriety of educating females, but it has served you well enough, my girl. I had hoped to encourage you to confess that you have come to recognize certain advantages to the married state and soon mean to announce which of your suitors you have decided to accept."

"I intend to marry none of them, sir," she retorted, keeping her voice low with difficulty. For some reason quite unknown to her, she experienced a strong desire to snap the viscount's nose off.

"What, none of them? But you must, ma'am. The pudding never lies, so you must surely choose one amongst the multitude."

"You are impertinent, sir."

"No, am I?" His eyes twinkled wickedly, and Philippa found herself one moment wishing she had nerve enough to box his ears in front of them all and the next wishing that when he looked at her in just that way it wouldn't cause such a stirring in her midsection. She felt warmth creeping into her cheeks and forced herself to look away from him. His chuckle served only to increase her blushes.

Fortunately, everyone else seemed still to be engaged in light argument, although the topic had changed from feminine education to the weather and the possibility of a hunt the following day.

"Why, surely, you will not think of hunting on a Sunday," protested Lady Kegworth over the other voices. " 'Twould be most unseemly."

The younger gentlemen looked at one another in consternation, and it was Lord Reginald who spoke for them all, saying simply, "Forgot tomorrow was Sunday. Daresay the weather will have cleared again by Monday."

"If it does, will you have your pack out?" Philippa asked the viscount in an attempt to regain her composure.

His grin was not helpful. "I daresay I will, ma'am. Are you remembering my promise of a family hunt?"

She nodded.

"Well, I don't say there won't be one, but the weather will have to cooperate, for I know that Catherine and Seldon intend to depart for Sussex a day or so before the rest of us go to Belvoir for the christening, and Margaret don't like to be conspicuous, as she would be were she the only lady besides yourself to ride with us."

"There are other ladies in the neighborhood, sir, who would welcome an invitation to join you. I have spoken to several, myself."

He grunted but did not commit himself either way, and as fortune would have it, he had no need to do so, for although Sunday morning dawned brisk and clear, the ground softening in such a way that all the young gentlemen at Chase Charley fairly chafed to be out and about, by early evening a fog had rolled in, which became so dense by Monday morning that one could not see the terrace stairs from the breakfast-parlor window.

"I must say," said Edward, turning from the window in displeasure, " 'tis most unfair. Why, yesterday was perfect for hunting. Whoever laid down such a dashed silly rule, I should like to know."

Miss Pellerin looked up at him from her place at the table. There was understanding in her expression, but she could not let such sacrilege pass without comment. "Dear boy, surely you would not begrudge the Lord one day of the week?"

Edward shrugged and moved without comment to load his plate at the sideboard. Winkburn, who had been the first of the gentlemen to present himself in the breakfast parlor, exchanged a look with Philippa. "Not himself before breakfast, ma'am," he said apologetically. "Must beg you will forgive his bad manners."

She grinned at him, but then turned toward her stepson. "Edward, don't be surly. Cousin Adeliza spoke to you. You owe her the courtesy of a reply."

Looking somewhat taken aback by Philippa's sudden leap into stepmotherhood, Edward glanced at her and then, more sheepishly, at Miss Pellerin. "Expect I owe you an apology, ma'am. Like Winky says, not my best before breakfast."

"Oh, I understand," said Miss Pellerin, smiling at him. "'Tis most unfortunate that the weather should have taken such a turn just when you must be wishing so heartily for a good day's hunting."

"It is a curst misfortune, is what it is," he agreed tartly.

"You know," put in Lord Reginald, who had not taken his attention from his breakfast during this exchange, "I shouldn't be surprised if this doesn't turn into one of those four-day fogs. You know, the sort that just settles in and don't dissipate—grows thicker, if anything."

Groans from his compatriots greeted this morose view of the matter, but as it happened, his lordship was in the right of it. Only his prediction of the number of days was off, for the fog was one that would in later days be noted by historians as one of the longest, densest fogs ever to cover England. It lasted a full eight days, and although by Wednesday there was sufficient visibility in Mr. Assheton-Smith's estimation to encourage him to lead the Quorn, by the end of the afternoon the gentlemen returned dispirited, damp, and very tired, giving it as their opinion that they might as well all go with Dauntry to visit his father before returning to school.

Word came that same day from Viscount Rochford that he had suggested organizing a family hunt, only to be overruled by both his sisters. Lady Seldon and her husband, he wrote, were still at Wyvern because the weather was thought too unpredictable for travel, but Catherine had no wish for sport unless the sun should present itself, and Margaret agreed with her.

Therefore, when a missive arrived on Thursday morning from the Duchess of Rutland, begging her to put forward her visit to Belvoir by two days, Philippa harried her cousin, her stepdaughter, and the maidservants in such a fashion that by noon she was ready to depart. The journey, by virtue of the fog, was a slow one, but they managed to arrive before dark and were welcomed by the duchess and her mother-in-law with expressions of great relief.

"For I cannot tell you, Philippa," the Duchess Elizabeth said breathlessly upon greeting her in the pink-and-gilt drawing room, "how dull it has been these four days without any gentlemen about. Rutland took them all with him when he departed for Althorp to meet Prinny and his party. They expected to reach Cottesmore this morning, but whether they did, I do not know, and with this wretched weather, Rutland positively forbade us to attempt to meet them there. Not that I should have done, in any event, for of course I must be here when they arrive on Saturday, but Mama Isabella might very well have done so, only but for Rutland saying she must not."

"This dreadful fog," put in the dowager, cocking her head a little to one side to look at Jessalyn as she waved Philippa and Miss Pellerin to nearby seats. "You, girl—I daresay you'll be wanting to go to young Elizabeth. You can have no wish to be sitting here doing the pretty. Not if I know anything about it."

Casting a glance at her stepmother and receiving a smile in return, Jessalyn replied with commendable aplomb, "Yes, ma'am, I should like very much to see Beth, if you please."

The dowager nodded approvingly. "Well, so you shall. Here, Frederick," she added, turning to the footman who had accompanied them through the corridors, "do you take Miss Raynard-Wakefield upstairs to the schoolroom, where she will find the Lady Elizabeth. And tell Douglas to order tea. Even this room reeks of fog. I must have something hot to drink."

The footman bowed and held the door for Jessalyn. Once they had gone and the dowager had smoothed her purple Denmark satin skirts, she said, "Poor Prinny, this is all very disrupting for him, I daresay, and he does so like his plans to go smoothly."

"Have things not gone smoothly, then?" Philippa inquired.

"Oh, dear me, no," said the duchess quickly. " 'Tis all most dreadful. I had a letter from Rutland only this morning, you know, and the messenger who brought it also brought us the *Times*, for you must know that we have had no mail out of London in days, and therefore no news at all, of course, for the newspapers are delivered by the mail coaches just as the mail is, don't you know."

"Yes, I had realized that," said Philippa, smiling at her.

"Oh, I know, my tongue runs on," said the duchess with a shake of her head.

"It does," agreed the dowager, reaching for the newspaper which rested at her side on the pink settee. "Here, this is Tuesday's paper. I shall read you what it says. The great news, of course, and that for which everyone has been waiting these past weeks and more, is that that despicable Bonaparte has agreed to peace again. Not that it will signify in the end, of course," she muttered, turning pages. "Ah, here it is. Listen to this. 'The Prince Regent, having condescendingly agreed to stand sponsor to the heir of the Duke of Rutland, left town yesterday for Belvoir Castle, where the ceremony is to be performed with much splendor,' and so on and so on. Here is the part about the fog. 'The Prince Regent left Carlton House about seven P.M. yesterday, in two carriages'—a peculiar way of traveling, I should think," the dowager interjected. "Oh, I see, 'accompanied in two carriages.' Well, that is a trifle better, is it not?"

"Do go on, ma'am," said the duchess, "for Rutland's letter has it that the Regent didn't leave Monday at all, so I should think there must be more."

"Indeed," replied her mama-in-law, twinkling, "but as I told you, this is Tuesday's paper. We also, thanks to the fact that the mail coach did get through today, have Wednesday's as well. On Tuesday, he was said to have proceeded to Hatfield, where he slept with the Marquess of Salisbury."

Miss Pellerin jerked her head up in astonishment. "Isabella!"

The dowager was unrepentant. "Very well, it says Hatfield is the seat of the Marquess and that Prinny slept there. Only, of course, he did no such thing, for on Wednesday, it says . . . Just one moment, whilst I search it out. They always put the interesting news on the third page. Ah, here it is. 'The Prince Regent, who was supposed to have proceeded on his tour last evening, got no further than a mile from Tottenham Court Road, when one of the outriders was thrown into a ditch. They could not see the road, for the lamps were of no use, and the flambeaux were insufficient. The Prince Regent got out of the carriage and was knee-deep in mud for some minutes. By taking off the leaders, the carriage was turned, and proceeding slowly with flambeaux before the horses, reached Carlton House at nine-thirty. They left again yesterday' —that would be Tuesday—'at half past twelve.' " The dowager looked up. "So there you are, and there is poor Rutland, kicking his heels for two days at Althorp, although according to his message this morning, Prinny arrived there all right and tight on Wednesday, only a day late, by not going first to Burghley House as he had planned to do."

"So they ought to have gone on to the Earl of Lonsdale today, don't you think?" Elizabeth asked her guests, arching her eyebrows.

"I should think they would," opined Miss Pellerin, "if that was their intention. The Regent's other visits must take second place to his visit here. I should think you may continue to expect their arrival on Saturday unless this dreadful weather should become even worse."

"At least we shall not be entirely devoid of masculine company until then," said the dowager. "You were wise, Elizabeth, to think of inviting Wyvern to join us a day before the others."

"Well," said the duchess, smiling, "I knew he would not wish to ride about the countryside with the other gentlemen when they escort the Regent, and his health must excuse him from being thought lacking in courtesy. Moreover, Margaret suggested it would be better for him to have a day to recuperate from the journey before the others arrived. Of course," she added with an arch look at Philippa that threw that lady into some confusion, "I am persuaded Wyvern will suffer little discomfort with Rochford at his side to see to everything."

—15—

FRIDAY MORNING PHILIPPA awoke with a sense of anticipation much like that experienced by a child at Christmas. But Christmas was over and done, and she was not a child, so for some moments after awakening, she could not think why on earth she should feel as she did. Surely it could not be that she looked forward to more of the same entertainment she had enjoyed the previous evening. To be sure, it had been a most pleasant, most relaxing time. The duchess and the dowager were both delightful hostesses, and dinner had been excellent despite the fact that the duchess had apologized more than once for the disorder reigning in kitchens that anticipated the imminent arrival of the royal party.

Conversation after dinner had been lively, too, for the dowager could never be otherwise. Of that Philippa was certain. Duchess Isabella and Miss Pellerin, having been acquainted for many years, stood on no ceremony with one another, and Philippa had quickly come to feel, the first time she had met both the dowager and the duchess, that it would be difficult for anyone to feel uncomfortable in such company. Still, there had been something lacking in the evening's entertainment, something that would not—if her feeling now was anything to go by—be lacking this coming evening.

Because of the odd, arch look the duchess had shot her way the previous day, she tried to convince herself that she had merely become spoiled through having so much company around her these past weeks, that she missed having a host of young gentlemen gathered in her dining room enjoying too much port and claret after their dinner. But she knew in her heart that there was a better explanation than that for the fact that she so looked forward to the forthcoming arrival of the party from Wyvern.

The door opened and Alice entered carrying a painted wooden tray containing Philippa's morning chocolate and a copy of *La Belle Assemblée*.

"Good morning, ma'am. Her grace sent up the magazine. Said it arrived yesterday by the post and is the new issue, that you might wish to look it over with your chocolate."

"Good gracious, is her grace already up and about, then?" Philippa demanded. "It is scarcely nine o'clock."

Alice laughed, setting down the tray and moving to open the curtains. "She's up with the birds, that one, her people say. Shrewd as she can hold together. It's her as runs this house, ma'am, and no mistake, and the duke's other properties as well. They say the Duchess Elizabeth knows at Cheveley if a sheet has been ripped at Haddon Hall or if a hound's gone missing at Belvoir, and that she knows it before ever a message could be sent to her, as if anyone *would* send a message on such an account."

"Well, perhaps if she is as good a manager as she sounds to be, they do send such messages to her, you know." Firmly repressing all thought of what sort of rumors the duchess might also have gathered by such means, Philippa picked up the magazine, smiling at the extraordinarily elongated lady gracing its cover, and shaking her head a little at a morning dress decked all over with large pink beads. "Sitting down in a gown like this one must be vastly uncomfortable, don't you think, Alice?"

Alice glanced obligingly at the cover and gave it as her opinion that a woman as tall as that one wouldn't fit in anyone's furniture so the point would never arise. Then she sighed, glancing at the window again. "I don't expect you'll be wanting your riding habit, ma'am. 'Tis still as gloomy as an Irish bog out there, and no mistake." Shaking her head, she moved to the fireplace, where a fire had already been laid and lighted by an earlier-rising servant who had managed the business without disturbing Philippa in the slightest. The fire had chilled, but Alice, wielding the poker deftly, stirred the logs, causing smoke to billow forth briefly before the flames leapt with renewed energy.

Philippa wrinkled her nose a little at the smell of the smoke but turned back to her magazine and, after a moment, said absently, "Just fetch out that light green allapeen morning gown you packed for me. Belvoir Castle may be well-appointed and as elegant a country house as one might find anywhere, but its corridors are drafty. I brought the gold-and-green Norwich shawl, too." She turned a page before continuing, "When you have laid out my things, you needn't wait, for I shan't get up just yet. Go instead, if you will, to look in on Miss Jessalyn. One of the maidservants has been asked to wait upon her, but I should like her to know that she is not entirely unsupervised by her nearest and dearest." She looked up then, smiling.

Alice returned the smile with a knowing one of her own. "I'll do that, my lady. 'Twouldn't do for that young limb o' Satan to be getting up to any of her tricks while we are guests in this house."

"No, certainly not, although to do her justice, she has behaved very well, and I expect she will continue to do so for the present. She rather likes playing at being grown up, you know, and I don't believe she will take any risk of being denied permission to attend the christening ceremonies on Tuesday."

"No, indeed," Alice agreed, much struck. As she moved toward the door, she looked back over her shoulder. "They say the Archbishop of Canterbury himself is to do the business, ma'am."

Philippa smiled at her. "Yes, so her grace explained last night. Of course, the young Marquess of Granby will succeed to one of the greatest titles in the land, you know, so one ought not to be amazed by the archbishop's condescension, I daresay."

When Alice had gone, Philippa leafed absently through the magazine for some moments longer before she realized that she was paying little heed to its content and that, furthermore, she was restlessly twitching her toes beneath the bedcovers. Stilling them did no good. They stirred of their own accord.

"Ridiculous," she said aloud in a scolding tone as she pushed the covers aside and stepped out onto the carpet beside her bed. She shivered in the chilly air and reached quickly for the woolen dressing gown left at the foot of the bed the night before. Slipping into it, she shoved her feet into lambskin slippers and moved nearer the fire.

As she stared into the flames, she knew she was as excited as a young girl by the prospect of being at close quarters with the viscount again. That was the long and the short of the matter. Much though she might wish to retain the independence that had been hers since her late husband's death, she knew she could no longer pretend to herself that Rochford was at all like any of her other suitors. Would she be able to continue to deny her feelings for him once he came to decide that she no longer pined for Wakefield? And if she could not, would she lose her independence entirely?

How, she wondered, could a man who spoke easily, as he had once done, of the sensibility of proper education for women maintain a foolish masculine prejudice against allowing them in the hunting field? And if she bowed to his decision on her behalf in that regard, what other decisions would he insist upon making for her? Truly, the matter of her hunting, having been reduced to a trifle, now loomed large again.

Fortunately for her peace of mind, the duchess was able to provide her with a number of little tasks to make the day pass quickly after she and Miss Pellerin had broken their fast, for the party from Wyvern, having begun their journey at noon, did not reach the castle until shortly before dinner. Philippa was dressing when they arrived, so she did not see Rochford until they met in the pink-and-gilt drawing room just before the meal.

The Lady Lucinda having been sent to dine with Jessalyn and Lady Elizabeth Manners, only the earl, Lord and Lady Kegworth, Mr. Drake, and Rochford were with the duchess and the dowager when Philippa and Miss Pellerin entered the room.

"I see your sister Catherine and Seldon did not accompany you, sir," Miss Pellerin said to Rochford when they had taken their seats. "I had thought with the fog to keep them in Leicestershire, they might have done so."

"No, ma'am," he replied, smiling at her. "Seldon seems

to have contracted a head cold over the holiday and had no wish to make a gift of it to everyone here.''

''No, good gracious!'' exclaimed the dowager, who was seated on her customary pink claw-footed settee. ''Only think what his highness's reaction must be to being sneezed upon.''

''Prinny quacks himself, if you ask me,'' said Mr. Drake austerely.

''Very true,'' agreed the duchess. ''Why, Mama Isabella, you was used to say yourself that he has himself bled for the least little reason and takes to his bed if only his footman chances to cough behind him.''

''Well, I may have said so, but I should never be so daft as to say such things to his head, Elizabeth, and you ought not to repeat them in company.''

The duchess did not appear to be at all cast down by this rebuke, but looked up, smiling, when Douglas entered just then to announce that dinner was served. ''Shall we go in?'' she asked, adding flirtatiously to the earl, ''You shall give me your arm, my lord.''

Rochford offered his arm, by virtue of her rank, to the dowager, whereupon Mr. Drake turned a compelling eye upon his niece's husband. ''I daresay, Kegworth, that you will not object to escorting two such lovely ladies as your wife and Lady Philippa,'' he said suavely, ''while I lend my arm to this charming lady.'' He bowed to an astonished Miss Pellerin, who must have expected to escort herself, since there were no other gentlemen present and since both Philippa and Margaret must take precedence over her. Indeed, only after Lady Margaret laughingly insisted that she did not object in the slightest to sharing her husband's escort with Philippa, did the older lady place the fingers of her right hand on Mr. Drake's forearm and allow him to take her into the dining room.

Philippa smiled at Margaret. ''Really, I am guilty of the most regrettable lack of forethought. I ought to have insisted that Wakefield and his cronies put off their visit to Mr. Dauntry's father, in order that they might even her grace's numbers at table.''

Her good mood lasted through dinner, for her gaze encountered Rochford's more than once, and when the duchess arose to indicate that the ladies should leave the gentlemen to their port, she was unsurprised when he shook his head and said that he, for one, had no wish for port that evening.

"Indeed, ma'am, I had thought that perhaps if Lady Philippa has not seen your picture gallery, I might have the pleasure of introducing her to Holbein's King Henry the Eighth."

The duchess assured him that she believed Lady Philippa would adore to see the Holbein, ruthlessly stopped the dowager from saying whatever appeared to be on the tip of her tongue, and ushered the other ladies from the room.

Philippa stared at Rochford, but he merely gestured toward the door at the end of the room opposite that through which the others had departed. "The gallery is the next room to this one, you know. Will you come?"

"Yes, thank you," she said, aware of the odd humming in her mind again.

The picture gallery, another ivory-and-gilt room, was long and narrow with a decorated barrel-vaulted ceiling. The carpet and furnishings were simple so as not to detract from the lovely paintings, which ranged in style from Holbein's huge portrait of Henry to smaller, less magnificent, but entirely admirable renderings of the hunt by John Ferneley. Neither Philippa nor Rochford commented upon the pictures, however.

"I have missed seeing you these past days," he said quietly.

"Have you, sir?"

"Indeed, I was sorry to be obliged to deny you your hunt."

"You need not apologize, sir," she said, smiling at him. "I am persuaded it would have been a tame affair at best."

"Well, in this weather, of course—"

"Oh, Rochford, give over, do." She chuckled. "The weather has nothing to do with it, and you know it. Will you dare to tell me to my face that the hunt you had planned for your sisters, Jessalyn, and me would have been anything like the hunt I joined in progress some weeks ago?"

"Well, no, of course not," he said, frowning. "I have already expressed my views with regard to ladies attempting the fast-paced hunting that true sportsmen demand, my dear."

"So you had planned a nice, quiet day of riding after foxes

in the old style, had you not? No grand runs at a full gallop, just a nice dignified trot after the huntsman and his hounds, the latter still coupled and on leashes, I daresay."

"Philippa, for the love of heaven, why must you insist upon putting your lovely neck at risk? You are not, I thank the fates to say it, a man with a man's strength and stamina. Surely you must realize that your limitations are greater."

"That may be so, my lord," she said calmly, willing him to listen and to understand, "but I should like to be given the opportunity to discover my limits for myself, not to have limits imposed upon me by others."

His jaw tightened, and she could see that he was becoming angry, but she refused to unsay the words. Though she had come to realize that she cared greatly for this man, even perhaps loved him, it was impossible to believe that she would continue for long to love a man who insisted upon wrapping her in cotton wool. Until he agreed to allow her to hunt in her own style—to make such decisions for herself, in fact—they would have little upon which to build the sort of relationship she would wish to establish with a husband.

The simplicity with which the last thought followed upon the others caught her by surprise, but fortunately Rochford had decided that a change of topic was in order. Having taken a deep breath, he said, "I hope you will ride out with me to meet the royal party tomorrow, ma'am."

"I daresay we shall all ride out, sir," she replied matter-of-factly. "In point of fact, I shall be astonished if the whole of Leicestershire does not do so."

If not the whole county, then certainly a large portion of it did indeed ride to meet the Regent, the Duke of York, and the others in their party, who were riding from Cottesmore and intended to stop only once on the way at Oakham Castle, where tradition required that a peer of the realm pay tribute to the lord of the manor in the form of a shoe from his horse. According to the dowager, who had had one of her frequent letters from him, the regent intended to present a horseshoe of great size and magnificence, made of bronze and ormolu and carved with his name and the date of presentation. It would be nailed outside the castle gate beside all the others which had been presented by reigning monarchs since the days of Henry the Second.

The group from Belvoir Castle met the royal party near Denton, where they discovered that some two or three hundred horsemen—the gentry and the yeomanry of the county, as well as many of their wives and daughters—had assembled to escort his highness to Belvoir. With the arrival of the Prince Regent on the scene, the air was rent with a burst of loyal enthusiasm, and there was much jockeying, cavorting, and wild galloping as each one attempted to ride as near as possible to his traveling carriage.

"Like lunatics," said the dowager, shaking her head. "Look at them."

Rochford, riding between the dowager and Philippa, obliged her, then said, raising his voice a little over the din, " 'Tis enough to reassure him as to his popularity, is it not, ma'am?"

The dowager chuckled, and the noise increased after that, making further conversation impossible, so there was nothing to be done but to let the crowd sweep them back toward Belvoir Castle. There, as the Regent descended from his carriage, a royal salute of twenty-one guns was fired from the castle ramparts, with a second volley following in honor of the Duke of York.

Only with great difficulty and much persuasion were the Rutland servants able to dissuade the cheering, shouting throng from removing the Regent's matched bays from their traces and transforming themselves into carriage horses. The Duke of Rutland, having managed to ride on ahead, was at the door with his duchess to greet the visitors, and after the Regent had been ceremoniously presented with a gold key to Staunton Tower, Belvoir's chief stronghold, the party entered the castle.

Philippa scarcely saw Rochford except in passing for the next three days, because with the arrival of the Regent and some two hundred invited guests, the entertainment began in earnest, and it rapidly became clear to all that the Duchess of Rutland had outdone herself. There was not a moment unfilled. For the invited guests, every waking moment had been arranged, including a shooting party for the gentlemen and an al-fresco luncheon for the ladies, who enjoyed nearly a half-hour of pale sunlight on a hillside near Grantham.

In the park and on the grounds, sounds of the tenants' revelry continued long into the first night and the next two nights as well, for a bonfire had been organized for Sunday night and the tenants' annual ball in honor of the duke's birthday fell on the Monday. None of this festivity, however, was anything to compare with the merrymaking that took place on Tuesday, the day of the christening and, incidentally, the Duke of Rutland's thirty-sixth birthday.

The christening ceremony was relatively private, with only those two hundred noble guests who had been specifically invited to attend. The Regent was at his most condescending, and both he and his brother the Duke of York played their part in the performance with practiced ease. Her grace, the dowager Duchess of Rutland, representing Queen Charlotte as the little marquess's godmother, behaved with noble aplomb, and the Archbishop of Canterbury performed the baptism with solemnity and grace. But although the ceremony was soon over, the festivities had just begun.

Open house and lavish hospitality were the order of the day, and the citizenry availed themselves of all of it. It seemed to Philippa that wherever she turned that day, she was continually tripping over some stranger, and it was as likely to be a common peasant as an earl. The Duchess of Rutland had opened the castle from top to bottom, even arranging that anyone who wished to do so might pay his respects to the young marquess, and Rutland's butler had had the happy notion to provide a huge oval cistern containing fifty gallons of strong punch in the servants' hall. Many times over, the members of the household as well as the tenants drank to the heir, wished many happy returns to the duke, and called for God to preserve their noble Prince Regent.

At one point, the Regent, attired in the Belvoir uniform of scarlet and buff in honor to his host, appeared smiling and nodding before the enthusiastic throng to reply to the toast to himself with his customary eloquence. "Damme, Rutland," he said at the end, "so long as we live, we shall never forget the manner in which we have been received at Belvoir Castle."

The toasting began all over again then. Everything and

everyone was toasted, right down to the duchess's sparkling eyes, until, despite Mr. Douglas' careful management, the cistern of punch had laid many a brave fellow prostrate. The passages of the house, Rochford observed on one of those rare occasions that afternoon when he chanced to meet Philippa in passing, reminded him of nothing so much as a castle taken by storm.

"If the toasting goes on much longer," he added wryly, "articulation will cease altogether."

By the time the guests assembled for dinner that evening, it was plain to see that many of them had been toasting quite as freely as the tenantry. Even the dowager duchess appeared to be tipsy, though she was by no means castaway and was clearly enjoying the festivities. Philippa had had several cups of punch herself, and was looking forward to the dancing that was to take place after dinner.

Her dinner partner was a young lord whom she had not had the pleasure of meeting before, but he had had a great deal of punch and did not let a little thing like a lack of long acquaintance stop him from promptly—once he realized who she was—offering his hand to her in marriage.

"I beg your pardon, sir," she said, "but was I not earlier introduced to your wife?"

"Wife?" He peered at her blearily, then gaped unsteadily up and down the long table. "By God, ma'am, so you were. Forgot I had a wife. Thought of your fortune put thought of her sharp tongue straight out of my head."

Shaking her head in exasperated amusement, Philippa went back to her dinner, but despite the fact that there remained a certain amount of stiffness yet between herself and Rochford, she quite looked forward to recounting the conversation to him. Not until the musicians had struck up for the second waltz, just before the midnight supper was to be served, was she able to enjoy a dance with him, however. He stepped up then just as she was about to bestow her hand elsewhere, and neatly cut the gentleman out by saying with cool aplomb, "My dance, I fear. Her ladyship must have misread her card."

"Rochford, you are unscrupulous," Philippa told him as he swept her onto the floor, leaving her erstwhile partner staring. "You know perfectly well you did not put your name down for this dance."

"Couldn't find you to put my name down at all," he admitted frankly. "Why didn't you put me in my place, sweetheart, if you wished to dance with that fop instead?"

She twinkled at him and said in a saintly tone, "Because I have learned not to contradict you, my lord." Then she added in her normal, forthright way, "And because I wished to talk with you, of course." When she regaled him with the tale of her latest proposal, he enjoyed it quite as much as she had hoped he would.

"I was cornered over the port," he said, grimacing, "by two gents who wished to discuss Bonaparte's latest nonsense. Since they were in alt, I had all I could do to be civil to them."

"Why, what did they say?"

"Oh, the usual. You've heard, of course, that Boney has announced himself ready for peace."

"Yes, of course. The dowager told us, and I read the article in the *Times* myself—the bit about how he has accepted our preliminaries for the sake of his empress and the fathers and children of the French empire. A lot of hogwash, the dowager called it."

"She's a right one, is Was-a-Bella," he said, smiling toward the lady in question, who was dancing energetically with a determined-looking young man. "If Boney's not gulling us again like he did with the Peace of Amiens, you may call me a Dutchman. The only use he ever makes of a cessation of hostilities is to prepare for further conquests. He is now at our mercy, damn him, with his own people against him. I just hope we will not leave him in a condition to disturb the peace of the world any more than he has done already."

"You are severe, sir," she said, dimpling up at him.

He smiled ruefully. "I am, am I not? 'Tis my fight, you see, but I ought not to bring it into a ballroom, sweetheart, and for that I do apologize."

"You need not, sir." She realized that he had twice called her sweetheart and that she had not reproved him. No doubt it was because she needed to concentrate upon her steps.

At that moment, Rochford's arm was jostled and he looked around to discover his uncle and Miss Pellerin dancing beside him.

"You may wish me happy, nevvy," said Mr. Drake with a broad smile.

"Good Lord, sir, have you been making inroads in the punch, too?"

"Devil a bit. Adeliza has consented to be my bride."

Both Philippa and Rochford nearly came to a standstill, but fortunately the viscount came to his senses in time to avoid collision with any other dancers. "I do wish you happy, sir, but, Miss Pellerin, are you quite convinced that you are being wise to do such a thing as to tie yourself to this old curmudgeon?"

Miss Pellerin merely nodded, casting an uncertain glance at Philippa, then looking quickly away again.

"For shame, sir," scolded Philippa, as the movement of the dance parted the two couples again, "to tease her so. I think you must have bewildered her, too, for she looked uncommonly unsure of herself."

"Well, I do think she must be demented to wish to live with that old scoundrel," said Rochford roundly. Then he looked down at her and smiled confidently. "That is not why she looked the way she did, however. She was my dinner partner, you know, and I think she believes she may have betrayed you."

The music stopped just then, but when Philippa, having barely heard his last words and not really taken in their meaning, turned away, Rochford moved quickly beside her. "Will you go down to supper with me?"

"No, thank you, sir. The duke means to hunt tomorrow if the good weather holds, and he has asked me to join him. I have had very little sleep these past nights, with all the noise, and I confess I should not like to disgrace myself by dozing off midway through the first field and falling off my horse. 'Tis midnight, after all. I am going to bed."

"Not alone, you aren't," the viscount said almost harshly.

She did stop then, turning to look up at him in indignation. "I beg your pardon, Rochford."

At first he did not seem to realize what he had said, but

after a moment spent gazing at her in bewilderment, his brow cleared and he chuckled. "That didn't come out the way I meant it to, not that it isn't a splendid idea. No, no, my dear, don't poker up again. I have no intention of pressing my company on you overnight. If I had, I promise you I should never have been so clumsy in my approach. But if the halls of this place are not alive with drunken men intent upon mischief of any sort, then I shall be surprised. You are not to attempt the journey from here to your bedchamber alone."

"You make it sound like a pilgrimage, sir," she said, relaxing and rewarding him with a smile, for once not minding at all that he was making her decisions for her. "I confess, though, that there was so much activity in the corridor while I dressed for dinner that I expected to be interrupted at any moment. Alice practically barricaded the door."

"Good for Alice. I hope she had the good sense to remain after you left, but I'll not be amazed if she has joined the festivities in the servants' hall instead. I'll accompany you upstairs."

"But what of Cousin Adeliza? I should not go away without telling her."

"Uncle Archibald will look after her, and if it will make you feel better, I'll see that someone informs her that you have gone to bed. Here, Alvanley," he added, reaching out to grab a passing arm.

The young baron looked around indignantly. "Thee here, Rochford, that's my best arm."

"Yes, indeed, 'tis the one you cast the bones with, is it not? I would not for worlds do anything to render it more adept. Look here," he added hastily when Alvanley looked eager to engage in repartee with him, "be a good fellow and find Miss Pellerin, who is with my uncle, I believe. You may tell her that Lady Philippa has retired."

"Oh, I thay, ma'am, my pleasure," said Alvanley, bowing. With a knowing wink at Rochford, he took himself off.

"Silly ass," said the viscount without rancor. "Shall we go?"

As he had predicted, there were numerous overmerry gentlemen littering the corridors, but with Rochford as her escort, Philippa reached her own bedchamber without incident.

There was no one inside, and she was a little dismayed when the viscount followed her in and shut the door, locking it behind himself.

"Rochford, what are you about?" she asked curiously. The humming in her mind had reached a high pitch again, and she experienced the odd sense of danger that she had felt before in his presence. The sensation increased when he smiled at her.

"I want to assure myself that this room is empty," he said evenly, moving across the room to look behind the window curtains. No intruder lurked there, so he went to the bed and peered under it.

Philippa laughed. "Really, sir, do you expect to find a lover or a felon?"

"This is no laughing matter, madam," he said seriously, straightening to look at her sternly. "You have seen what those fellows are like. Neither your rank nor your position will protect you from one who is sufficiently intoxicated. Perhaps you do not know that the duke saw fit to put guards on the stairs to the upper floors in order to prevent anyone from harassing the children. If he felt it necessary to protect them from the rabble out there, can you blame me for wishing to protect you?"

He took a step nearer, then seemed to think better of the notion and turned away to continue his search. When he was thoroughly satisfied that they were alone, he turned back to face her.

Philippa had not moved. She regarded him speculatively, thinking he looked uncertain, which in her experience was most unlike him. "What is it, my lord?" she asked when he continued silent.

His lips tightened briefly, and for a moment it was as though he could not meet her steady gaze. Then he visibly gathered himself together and shot her a straight look from under his brows. "Did you truly wish to leave the dancing because you are overtired, or have I vexed you again in some way?"

"Vexed me?" She wrinkled her brow.

"Perhaps I ought not to have pursued the matter with Miss

Pellerin when it was clear she hadn't meant to say anything about it, but I—"

"Pursued what matter? Oh, you mean your conversation with her at dinner about her marriage proposal and her supposed betrayal. I didn't quite catch your words at first, what with the music stopping and people talking and moving about, but you know how it is, Rochford. The echo of words comes back to one. I cannot think why she should think of her impending marriage in such a light, for I have no contract with her, so her own interests must come before mine. I shall no doubt find another companion, though perhaps not one so congenial."

"I first learned of her impending marriage to my scholarly relative when you did, sweetheart." His eyes were gleaming now with amusement and renewed confidence. When Philippa stared at him, more confused than ever, he said lightly, "Her betrayal was in letting slip the fact that you did indeed have every right to post Wakefield's land. Why, after so much stubborn struggle, did you yield without even a challenge? I believe I know the answer," he added, moving toward her with the clear intent of taking her in his arms, "but I should like to hear the words from your own sweet lips."

—16—

PHILIPPA EYED THE viscount coldly. "Is this an attempted seduction, after all, then, sir? Because I can think of no other reason for your odd behavior tonight."

Rochford stopped short. "Seduction? Good God, Philippa, why would you think such a thing as that?"

"Because your confidence—nay, your arrogance—this evening makes it clear that you believe I yielded, as you put it, through a desire to please you. You should know, sir, that I believed silence at that point provided the simplest way out of what had become an intolerable situation. It was a decision I made based upon many factors, not an impulse based upon emotion."

He was silent for a moment, digesting her words, but then a smile began to tug at his lips, and he took another step toward her.

Knowing she could not trust herself to hold to her principles if he were to touch her, Philippa stepped hastily back. "Please go, Rochford," she said in an expressionless voice. "There is nothing more to say."

For a moment he looked as though he would argue with her, but then his hands fell to his sides, and he turned away. With the door open, he turned back long enough to say harshly, "Lock this behind me," and then he was gone.

Having obeyed his instructions to lock the door, she moved to survey herself in the cheval glass near her dressing table. She looked much as she usually did, and the first thought that was allowed to gain purchase in the chaos of her mind was a hope that she would be able to get out of her silken ball gown unaided, since it was clearly not sensible to ring for Alice.

Even if the abigail were within hearing of the bell, the chance that she might reach Philippa's bedchamber unmolested was a slim one.

Without giving thought to her movements, she began automatically to divest herself of her clothing and to prepare herself for bed. Not until she was safely tucked under the eiderdown did the thoughts so carefully held at bay come flooding in upon her mind. Was she being unpardonably foolish to keep him at arm's length when her love for him was growing stronger by the day? Had the late baron done her a disservice by giving her such a taste for her own independence of spirit and decision? Philippa wriggled beneath the covers, thinking of the look on Rochford's face as he had begun to approach her. She could think of nothing more pleasurable than to be held in his arms, and she had no doubt that she would enjoy his certain expertise in matters of the flesh.

Really, she thought, considering that she had been married five full years, she knew little of such matters. That had been one area Wakefield had not explored with her beyond assuaging his own needs. Of course, during the last two years of his life, his health had not permitted any such activity, but before that there had been a time or two when she had suspected that there might be a great deal of pleasure to be found in carnal pursuits. No doubt that was wicked of her. Still, by virtue of the fact that Rochford stirred her blood by his very presence, and in a way that Wakefield had never stirred her at all, she rather thought she would like to discover just how much pleasure might be enjoyed under the viscount's guidance.

Nevertheless, she could not bring herself to accept his guidance in everything else, and if he would not allow her to discover her own limits in the hunting field, how could she believe he would allow her to discover those limits anywhere else? Though her thoughts always seemed to come back to that same point, the course they took seemed to grow more and more complicated until there was nothing more than a jumble of words in her brain, but at last she slept, and when she awoke there was little on her mind other than the thumping on her door.

Sitting bolt upright, she called, "Who's there?"

" 'Tis Alice, my lady. The door be locked."

Remembering, Philippa jumped from the bed and snatched

up her dressing gown, flinging it around herself as she moved to unlock the door. Alice stood in the corridor, holding the chocolate tray and looking rather sheepish.

" 'Tis sorry I am, ma'am, that I didn't be here to help when you came to bed."

"Never mind that now, I know how it must have been," Philippa said, "and I came up quite early, you know."

"Well, I know the dancing went into the wee hours, ma'am. They say the dowager was the last to give it up and that the poor musicians was ready to throttle her by the time she did."

"Oh, dear, I hope that does not mean she will not hunt today!" Philippa exclaimed. Then, ruefully, as she realized how selfish she must sound, she added, "I would not wish her to overtire herself, of course."

"No chance o' that," said Alice, setting the tray down upon a table when she saw that her mistress did not intend to get back into bed. "Her grace left orders to be awakened for the hunt breakfast. Said she means to be in at the kill. She's a grand one, she is, right enough."

Glancing at her clock, Philippa was dismayed to see that it was already ten o'clock. "What time is breakfast, then? I should have thought they would be finished by now."

"Oh, no, ma'am. They will begin serving at half-past, but the meet ain't till half after eleven, so you've plenty of time."

Nonetheless, Philippa hurried, with the result that she, like Cupid, whom she had chosen as her first mount, was fairly champing at the bit before the huntsman had organized his hounds to draw the first covert. At last, however, the horns were sounded, the hounds were loosed, and it was not long after that before the "View Halloo" was heard and the field was off in a burst across the Vale of Belvoir. The dowager was there among them, just as she had promised, wearing an emerald-green habit and a matching hat with a startlingly bright red plume and a veil that she could pull over her face to protect her if she had to push through a bullfinch.

Philippa's hat also boasted a veil, but her habit was not nearly so dashing, being of dark brown velvet with gold trim and barrel snaps down the front. She guided Cupid in the dowager's wake, settling well into her saddle, feeling delight swell within her at the exhilaration of the hunt.

There were nearly one hundred riders in the field, and it soon became obvious that the duke had not planned a tame ladies' hunt but one that would test the mettle of every hunter. The fox made a long point, and the scent was breast-high. Across the pleasantly undulating country of alternate grass and plow they rode until they came to a wood, where it seemed at first that the fox must go to ground. But the wood was cut in both directions by rides, broad corridors made to accommodate an even bigger hunt than this, and the earths had been efficiently stopped. After disappearing momentarily into the underbrush, the fox was sighted first across one of the rides and again as he broke covert at the end of the wood.

"Gone away!" shouted the huntsman, and the cry was taken up by hounds and men as the long sound of the hunting horn echoed through the wood. Glancing to her right, Philippa saw Rochford beside her on his big black. She grinned, feeling nothing but pleasure in the sport and wanting nothing more than to be in charity with everyone. To her relief, he smiled back at her, and when the suspicion crossed her mind that he was riding near in order to keep a sharp lookout for her safety, there was no resentment in the thought, only a deepening of her love for him.

A part of the pack, in high feather, had struck the line of a fresh fox, and the hunters thundered past, leaving it to the whippers-in to clear the hounds from the wood. Fortunately for them and for some of the hunters, as well, there was a check a few moments later, the huntsman having to make a wide cast, and before he hit the line again most of the stragglers had caught up.

By the time they neared Bottesford, Cupid was beginning to sink, but the dowager had warned Philippa to have a second horse ready, so she was able to change to Black Nestor after the second exciting run. More than half the field, including Lord Robert Manners, Lord Alvanley, Kegworth, and nearly all of the ladies, fell out at Bottesford or before for lack of a second mount or merely because they were exhausted. Philippa was not tired at all, and she and the dowager were at the head of the field after the change. Glancing over her shoulder, she saw that Rochford and the Duke of Rutland were close behind them.

There was another check ten minutes later, and the huntsman was forced to cast again, but the hounds soon hit the scent, giving the hunters scarcely time to draw breath before they were off again in full cry, sterns feathering merrily. The second run was well over eleven miles long, through bullfinches and over blackthorn hedges, timber fences, water-filled ditches, and oxers, before the fox went at last to ground. By then they had crossed into South Nottinghamshire, so by rule the fox could not be dug out nor the covert be drawn for another fox—not without risk of bringing the wrath of Squire Osbaldeston, master of the South Nottinghamshire hunt, down upon all their heads. The horn was blown, calling the halt.

While the huntsman and his whippers-in stopped the hounds, several of the gentlemen could be heard cursing their bad luck, but most of the hunters, like Philippa, cared more for the hard riding and the challenge of the obstacles than for the kill and were perfectly contented with the day's sport. At first the twenty or so riders who remained stayed together, but as they passed one inn and then another, the numbers dwindled accordingly until by the time they were within three miles of the castle, Philippa found herself riding in a much smaller group with the dowager, another lady whom she did not know, two gentlemen who seemed to be with the lady, the duke, and Rochford. A few moments later, the two gentlemen and the lady turned off together when one of the gentlemen mentioned knowing an excellent posting house less than a mile to the east.

When they had gone, the dowager chuckled. "I confess I should have liked to go with them but for the stir it would cause," she said. "Haven't had a chase like that in weeks. The exercise does bring on a thirst."

The duke smiled at her. "You never cease to amaze me, ma'am. At your age, you ought to be thinking of a nap, not a mug of stout ale."

Philippa looked at the dowager duchess, wondering for the first time just how old she was, and catching her look, the dowager winked. "Fifty-seven my last birthday," she said, "though 'tis the fashion to keep such stuff a deep dark secret.

Born in August like my illustrious, long-awaited grandson, and they say those of us born under August stars are like to be stubborn and cling to the things we enjoy, even when good sense tells us to leave well enough be."

"I, too, am August-born," admitted Philippa.

"And stubborn," muttered Rochford at her side.

She shot him a speaking look, but the dowager laughed and said, "No need to swallow your words like that, Rochford. Say it or don't say it. To my mind, there is nothing wrong with a lady's having a bit of spirit."

Philippa looked at Rochford again, grinning saucily, but he said nothing further. In fact, now that she came to think about it, he had been strangely silent most of the way back.

They had been riding at an easy, distance-eating canter across an open plowed field flanked by a thicket of stout oaks on one side and a field of stubble on the other. Ahead of them rose a long, low, neatly trimmed blackthorn hedge. Philippa, thinking about Rochford's odd silence, was no longer concentrating or she might have chanced to remember Black Nestor's contrariness with regard to hedges, but by the time she realized he had not gathered himself for the jump as he ought to have done, he had refused it altogether and she had flown right off the saddle. Twisting frantically to avoid landing on her head or shoulder, she landed flat on her backside instead, the wind whooshing out of her in a sharp cry of dismay.

The duke and dowager, riding far enough ahead that they were already committed, made the jump, but Rochford, slightly behind her, wheeled his mount at the last moment and slid quickly down from his saddle to rush to her side.

"Philippa, are you hurt? What a ridiculous fall! My good child, one must pay heed when one is in the field. Here, can you get up?"

Angrily shaking his arm away, she said, "Leave me be, Rochford. Of course I am not hurt, and you need not say anything more about how heedless I was. I know that without your pointing it out to me, but I daresay that you will throw this up to me if I am ever so cork-brained as to ask you to let me hunt again. This fall proves, does it not, that there is no place for ladies in the hunting field. Though you know perfectly well that I merely suffered a momentary lapse of attention, such as might happen to anyone after a long day's hunting when one's concentration has been intense, but you will no doubt continue to be the greatest beast in nature and will—''

''I say, Lady Philippa, are you all right?'' It was the duke, peering at them from the other side of the thorn hedge.

Recalled to her surroundings, Philippa reluctantly allowed Rochford to help her to her feet, and forced a smile for the duke. ''I am indeed quite unharmed, sir, since this field has so fortunately been recently plowed.''

''Not recently,'' he corrected her. ''Before the freeze, actually. And the fog, of course. But like as not, when it thawed again, only the outer crust was hardened—fortunately, as it happens.''

''Please, sir,'' Philippa said dryly, drawing the reins through her fingers and congratulating herself on not having released them as she fell, ''don't you begin to scold me for my inattention. I assure you that Rochford has already said all that is necessary.''

''Oh, not by any means everything that is necessary,'' corrected Rochford in a low tone, sterner than any she had heard him use before. Raising his voice, he said, ''I hope, Rutland, that you will not take it amiss if I tell you that your presence has become infinitely *de trop*.''

Philippa looked at the viscount and saw that he was regarding the duke with a challenging look in his eye.

The duke responded with an amused grin, ''You will understand, I hope, that I shall more willingly take my congé from her ladyship, Rochford. She is a guest in my house, after all, and therefore entitled to demand my protection.''

''Rutland, take a damper,'' recommended his mother outrageously, bringing her mount to his side. Straightening her hat, she regarded the two on the ground with a sympathetic eye, and added dryly, ''You must forgive him, my dears. He has an unceasing sense of the ridiculous, which is why he so much enjoys making it clear to disbelievers that he gives his duchess her head in all things. He is roasting you, Rochford, but I cannot say you have done nothing to deserve it. You have been a fool, my lord.''

''Indeed, I am grateful for your grace's generous reading

of my character," began Rochford with gathering wrath, "but I should—"

"You would think me more generous if I would but take my precious offspring and disappear with him as quickly as possible," the dowager finished for him, still twinkling.

Reluctantly he returned her smile. "Indeed, your grace. That's the nut with no bark on it."

"Well, I shall do so, then, but you will displease me, sir, an you return to Belvoir without having settled your affairs in a suitable fashion."

"Wait, your grace," Philippa called. "You cannot truly mean to leave me here. I assure you I have no wish to be alone with him. I *do* demand your protection!"

Rutland looked hesitant, but his mother put an end to further discussion by snatching the reins of his hunter into her own hand and wheeling her mount toward the castle, thus forcing the mighty duke to follow.

"I say, ma'am!" was all they heard of Rutland's protests before the hoofbeats faded into the distance, leaving the field wrapped in silence.

True silence was only momentary, for Philippa was quickly aware of the sound of her own breathing. Then came the noisy screech of a magpie, followed by a black-and-white flash of movement as the bird, or another like it, took wing from the nearby thicket. A moment later, a trilling chirp heralded the appearance of a small goldfinch, recognizable by the gold and red markings on its black head and wings as it shot from the hedge a little way from where she and Rochford stood. For a long moment Philippa focused her attention on the hedge, noting dried brown stems and heads of cow parsley among the thorny green branches and, below, a soldier beetle struggling to climb a plowed ridge of earth at the foot of the hedge. Even as she watched these fascinating things, however, Philippa was entirely too conscious of the tall, silent man beside her. In an effort to break the gathering tension between them, she looped her reins in the hedge, shook her skirts, and began to brush dirt from her hips.

"Here, let me help you," said Rochford dryly, and before she knew what he was about, one of his strong hands had clamped itself to her upper arm and the other was brushing energetically at her backside.

"Rochford, stop that!" She wriggled, trying to pull away from him, but all she got for her trouble was a harder smack on the area he was attempting to dust for her. "Ouch, you beast, that hurt!"

Without having the slightest understanding of how it came to pass, she suddenly found herself wrapped in his arms, her face pressed against his broad shoulder. She could smell the masculine scent of him, mixed with the warm-wool odor of his dark jacket, and she could feel his breath soft against her cheek. Then one of his hands moved to her hat, pulling it loose, and when she looked up at him in protest, he said, "It's most damnably in my way, you know, though I fear I've mussed your hair badly."

"In the way, sir?" she repeated, clinging to important matters.

"Yes, for I mean to kiss you before we have our little talk, sweetheart."

"Do you? I thought you were angry."

He spent the next moments proving to her that he was nothing of the sort, and not much to her own surprise, she could discover no wish to stop him. Instead, as warmth spread rapidly through her body, she discovered she had a great desire to urge him on. When one of her hands found its way inside his jacket to the softness of his shirt, Rochford drew a long, ragged breath and reluctantly set her back on her heels. He regarded her ruefully.

"Perhaps I should not have done that," he said. "I keep telling myself I ought not to press you—"

"It is not thought of Wakefield which keeps me from encouraging your suit," Philippa murmured, looking now at Rochford's patient horse, still standing where he had been left.

"Then what?" the viscount demanded. "Does this hunting business mean so much to you? Because if it does, I can tell you—"

"It isn't that," she said quickly. "Not the hunting alone, although at one point I did think that was it. But the dowager came nearer the mark, sir, when she described herself as one who clings to independence. 'Tis my own independence I guard, my need to make decisions for myself, even if they prove to be the wrong decisions. 'Twas my greatest gift from the baron, you see, and I cannot give it up so freely, even for love of you, my lord." She would have gone on then to attempt to explain her relationship with Wakefield, but Rochford stopped her with a gentle finger to her lips.

"I do wish you would learn not to interrupt, sweetheart. Someday I hope you will come to understand that my opposition to ladies in the hunting field stems not from mere male arrogance but from my care for their safety."

"But, Rochford—"

"No," he said, giving her a shake, "you will listen to me, if you please. I was wrong to let my concern for you keep me from hearing the things you were saying to me. The one time I actually saw your prowess in the field, I let my anger keep me from realizing that I was becoming as stubborn as you over what was essentially a petty argument. No, no, you will listen until I have quite finished." He glared at her, waiting to see if she would again attempt to speak. When she remained meekly silent, she was rewarded with a smile of approval. "You were right to be angry with me, sweetheart, but you also made a few mistakes. I need not point them out to you. Indeed, I have said I will say nothing further on that head, but there is one thing I must say, for it covers a broader range. You made it clear enough when we discussed annuities with Alvanley that you have a good head for matters of business. You do not, however, approach more emotional matters with that same clear head."

"No," she said forlornly, "you are right. Cousin Adeliza says I don't think matters through. Wakefield said the same on occasion, but I thought I had learned better, and the business of the hunt was important to me. It still is, for all that."

"Then let me say at once that I should have to be the greatest of nodcocks not to admit that if a lady of the dowager's years can hold her own in the field, you can do as well if not better. You are a bruising rider, sweetheart, and even if you were not, I have indeed come to recognize your need to discover that fact for yourself."

"You have?" Her eyes widened.

He smiled at her. "I have. I was trained to a habit of command, Philippa, so seeing myself as you do has not been easy for me. I went from a household where my father made all the decisions, to the army, where I had only to give an order to see it obeyed. But I have seen changes, even in my home, where my sisters now make decisions of which my father is not even aware, out of concern for his health. They deferred to me, of course, and to their husbands, so I was not quick to see the change, but I did note that they are not nearly so dependent on masculine authority as my mother was. Then I saw how Rutland is with his amazing duchess. If ever a lady gave the appearance of being a sad shatterbrain, that one does, but she is nothing of the sort, for the duke is no namby-pamby dandy, but a man as sound as a roast who was raised knowing he would wield great power. And although his mother is a demanding lady who knows her own mind, she would never have made the mistake of raising a duke who could not make decisions. Therefore, 'tis plain as a pikestaff that the duke gives his duchess full rein only because he wishes to do so."

"The dowager said it amused him to do so," Philippa reminded him.

"How amused do you suppose he would be if she made a mull of it?" he asked.

"But she doesn't. She was trained to her position, too, sir."

"Certainly she was, but so were you. The more I learn of your late husband, the more I realize that he prepared you very well for life without him. I wouldn't trust Lucy to make a decision, I can tell you that, nor would I have trusted Margaret or Catherine before now. I knew how they were raised, you see, and I judged you by what I knew of them. It was unfair, Philippa. Perhaps you will find it difficult to believe that I have learned so much, but I should like to have the opportunity to prove myself to you. Then, when you have got far enough beyond your bereavement to see what others have seen—that we love each other and that you are not so averse as you think to the married state—perhaps you will be willing to agree when I ask you to be my wife."

The humming had begun in her head again the moment he

said what he did about Wakefield preparing her for life as a widow, and now she had all she could do not to grin at him. She had never expected to find him capable of such understanding. Had it not taken years before she had reached that understanding for herself? Yet, here he was, putting into words things she had only begun to think out fully. He was right, too, about others having seen what she had not. Even Mr. Brummell and Lord Alvanley had seen from the outset that it was a case between them. Next there had been the duchess with those arch little looks whenever she mentioned Rochford. And finally, today, the dowager had ruthlessly drawn the duke off and ordered Rochford to settle his affairs *suitably*.

Taking herself firmly in hand, Philippa looked up at the viscount from under her long lashes and asked demurely, "Tell me, my lord, after all this roundaboutation, if I marry you, will you allow me to hunt regularly with the Wyvern?"

His eyes widened and he regarded her much as though she had changed shape under his very gaze. "Hunt with the Wyvern?"

She nodded, lowering her lashes before he could see the twinkle in her eyes.

The viscount's eyes narrowed in suspicion. "I thought I had spoken to that point already. It is palpably clear that you are not meek enough to agree to remain placidly behind with your knitting while your husband and sons go hunting—"

"And daughters."

"While the rest of your family goes hunting," he amended obligingly, beginning to smile. "Therefore, since it has likewise become obvious that I should be wise to keep you where I can watch over you, lest you begin a crusade against the Quorn or the Cottesmore, thus bringing the wrath of every sporting man down about my ears, I suppose I must give my consent."

"Sensible of you, sir," she said, "but I have not agreed to become your wife, you know, so this talk of sons and daughters, let alone of hunting, is rather premature."

He folded his arms across his chest. "I am a patient man, sweetheart, as you have seen."

"Have I?"

He grinned. "I didn't wring your pretty neck over those damned no-trespassing signs, did I?"

"No, sir."

"And," he added, his voice growing gentle, "I truly have tried not to press you, sweetheart. I know that from time to time you must still miss Wakefield."

"I don't miss him," she said simply, watching him carefully the while. With pleasure she observed growing awareness in the viscount's eyes and felt a responding warmth invade her body. The humming in her mind grew louder than ever before, and when Rochford opened his arms, she cast herself into them.

"Are you quite certain?" he muttered near her ear.

"Quite," she replied. "I will always remember him fondly, Andrew, for he taught me much and was kind to me, but I no longer feel an obligation to his memory."

His arms folded around her crushingly, and it was several moments before she made any attempt to free herself. Then, pushing hard against his chest, she looked him straight in the eye and said, "Don't think for a moment that I have merely given way to your stronger will, sir. I made up my mind to marry you weeks ago. I just didn't think to do it right away."

"Little fool," he said, chuckling. "Wakefield clearly didn't teach you the most important thing about decisions."

"And what is that?"

"That once you decide to do a thing, you should do it at once."

And with that sage advice, the viscount swept her into his arms again, whereupon it was rapidly borne in upon Lady Philippa as she responded uninhibitedly to his passions that if she did not marry him soon, she stood in grave danger of acquiring a reputation for being fast that would have nothing whatever to do with whether or not she rode with the Melton men.